portraits *of* Celina

SUE WHITING

Portraits of Celina
is first published in the United States in 2015
by Switch Press
A Capstone Imprint
1710 Roe Crest Drive
North Mankato, Minnesota 56003
www.switchpress.com

Published by arrangement with Walker Books Australia Pty. Ltd.,
Sydney.

Library of Congress Cataloging-in-Publication Data is available on
the Library of Congress website.

ISBN: 978-1-63079-024-0 (jacketed hardcover)
ISBN: 978-1-63079-030-1 (eBook)

Summary:
Celina O'Malley was sixteen years old when she disappeared. Now,
almost forty years later, Bayley is sleeping in Celina's room, wearing
her clothes, hearing her voice. What does Celina want? And who
will suffer because of it?

Photo credits: Cover Image © Lee Avison / Millenium Images, UK
Designed by Kay Fraser

Printed in China.
092014   008476RRDS15

for Lizzie
my sunshine girl

prologue

The day I turned sixteen, we buried my father.

No one realized what day it was. Not even me. We were too stunned. How could someone you love die — just like that?

Memories of the day he died are muddled. Some are so sharp and focused, they almost hurt. Others are so foggy and distorted, it's as if I am viewing them through the thick end of a bottle.

I remember the sky, dark and brooding.

I remember Amelia going out, and Loni coming over.

I remember the sound of the downpour.

Seth wailing about his Batman toy.

The sweet smell of rain.

Then comes the full-focus part — the part I long to erase, for fear of reliving it forevermore.

But it refuses to go away, and I can still see every detail. I can still hear that thud as Dad falls and cracks his skull on the stone bench. See the angle of his head to the rest of his body, the thin stream of blood trickling from the corner of his mouth.

Feel the stillness of him, the rain pelting his face.

Did I scream? Cry out? I don't know.

I can only remember standing in the soaking rain, water dripping from my chin, not knowing what to do. How could he be laughing, breathing, living one minute, and then gone forever the next?

Looking back, I realize it was the first time I experienced how cruel life can be. How swiftly a simple act can change it.

It wouldn't be the last.

one

The following January

It's a simple act, the pulling on of jeans. But for me, the snug fit of Celina O'Malley's jeans is uplifting — exhilarating almost. Every nerve ending tingles. I swirl in front of the mirror, admiring the way the faded denim hugs.

I am wearing Celina O'Malley's jeans. Celina O'Malley. A name I have, my whole life, associated with family legend and secrets, with tragedy and loss. With death. Is Celina dead? Murdered? Am I wearing a dead girl's jeans? I am at once thrilled and appalled.

I pull off my pajama tank top and slip on a tie-dyed T-shirt. Again, it fits as if it were made for me. I almost yelp, catching myself in time as I remember that everyone else is asleep.

There's no reasonable explanation for the odd cocktail of emotions racing through me, and what is especially weird is the feeling of connection. *What is going on?* How can I feel connected to some distant relative who vanished from the face of the earth almost forty years ago? But it feels good, and it's the first time I've felt any kind of happiness for a very long time. It's as welcome as a sun-filled sky.

I slide onto the floor on my stomach and prop myself up on my elbows. I stare at the wooden chest with its contents — the possessions of another life — spilling onto the floorboards, filling the spaces between the packing boxes and plastic bags that are jammed with the remnants of my own life.

My old life.

A stale smell fills the room. Camphor wood. Cheap perfume. Age.

I reach out and caress the items lying nearest to me: a peasant blouse, a white knitted bikini, and a striped poncho.

Inside the chest, I find an ugly belt made from knotted rope and wooden beads. Next, a fistful of multicolored scarves and a pair of silver hoop earrings stuck into cardboard. I tie a scarf covered with bursts of bright purple around my head, slip the earrings on, and find myself giggling. If only Loni was here — she'd love this.

How old was Celina when she disappeared? I wonder, fingering the silver hoops absently. Fourteen? Fifteen? Sixteen — like me? I've heard whisperings of Celina's story many times, but it's a topic that only the brave members of the family bring up — and I am not one of them.

I empty the chest, inspecting each item. I'm conscious that my behavior is kind of odd, manic even, but I am gloriously driven. And with each new piece, I am tickled by the thought that I'm somehow getting to know this Celina O'Malley. Strings of beads; a stack of old vinyl albums still in their plastic covers that includes Neil Young, Cat Stevens, *20 Explosive Hits '71*; brown woven leather sandals and a clunky pair of cork platforms; a ragged old photo album.

I am pulling open the sticky cover of the photo album, when my door groans open. It's Mom. A thin cotton nightgown hangs from her bony frame like a sack, and her hair is frizzy from restlessness. She looks much older than her forty-nine years, as if every one of those years has been intent on wearing her out.

"What are you doing?" she whispers. "For God's sake, Bayley, it's almost three."

It's as though I'm five again, with my hand in the cookie

jar — or worse, as if I've been caught robbing a grave. What *am* I doing? How can I even touch this stuff, let alone wear it?

Mom's eyes lock on the open chest and its contents. I watch as my mother tries to make sense of what she's seeing, and worry about how she's going to react.

She slides onto her knees beside me. In the mellow one-lightbulb glow, carved tigers and elephants parade across the sides of the wooden chest. Grime fills the cracks, and varnish sticks up in sharp peeling daggers. Mom reaches out and traces her finger over the crude peace sign painted on the inside of the lid, then the rainbow and butterflies surrounding it.

"Christ," she says and frowns at me. "I don't understand. Gran said the place was emptied years ago. Emptied and boarded up . . ." She picks up a red polka-dot dress and holds it to her cheek. "Oh, Bayley. Look at me; I'm being silly. This must be *Celina's*. But I don't understand how it's still here — after all this time."

I nudge closer to her. "Did you know her? Celina?"

Mom nods. "Of course. She was my cousin. Your gran's favorite niece. We used to come out here for holidays — Easter, Christmas. We stayed for the whole summer one year, when I was about nine or ten." She peers into the chest, hugging herself tight, as though suddenly cold.

"What happened to her?" I dare to ask. "Really."

Mom eyes the floor as if the answer is contained in the grains and knots of the floorboards. "No one knows for sure," she says after a while. "Set off to school one day and was never seen again." She pushes herself clumsily to her feet, the memory of it seeming to weigh her down. "It's ancient history, Bails. Best put this stuff back, and I'll let Gran know it's here. It'll throw her — but she needs to know."

Mom pauses at the door, staring back into the room. "Jeez, it's drafty in here." She rubs her arms. "I'll have to get the builders to take a look. Now, get some sleep. There'll be lots of unpacking tomorrow." The door closes, and I am left sitting in the midst of all this *stuff*, feeling like I've woken from some bizarre and slightly disturbing dream.

I climb onto my bed, part the stiff new curtains, and press my forehead against the coolness of the window. Even in the murky darkness, peering through the shadowy fingers of a Norfolk pine, it is beautiful here. There is no denying it. The lake, surrounded by silhouetted hills and untamed land, glistens in the moonlight. It's still. Quiet. Alone.

Why on earth are we here? I ask the lake. What was Mom thinking, uprooting us and moving us away from everything and everyone we love, right when we need them most? I can't understand the logic of it.

A sad family moving into a sad house.

I curl up under my fuzzy blanket. Behind my closed eye-lids, I try to imagine my life here, in this broken-down house set on the shores of such a lonely, lonely lake. But it's futile; I can't even begin to imagine a life here. Not for any of us.

Instead, I imagine Celina O'Malley.

Celina in her tiny bikini, tanned and lithe, diving off the dock into the lake.

Celina, long dark curls tumbling over her shoulders, strumming a guitar and singing. Her face made golden by a small campfire.

Celina in jeans and a T-shirt, purple scarf around her head, weaving through the field beside the lake — laughing, squealing, deliriously happy . . .

I allow these visions to reel through my head, trying to bring Celina's face into focus — but she remains slightly fuzzy and out of reach. Despite this, in some peculiar way, these glimpses are a comfort to me, and I wonder if there *is* actually a chance at happiness for us here.

As I feel myself drifting off, a strange uneasiness wafts through the dreamy darkness, and I burrow deeper under my blanket.

Finally, sleep takes me.

I sleep like a lamb.

two

It's the alarm in the voice, rather than the loudness, that snaps me awake.

"Bayley! Wake up! Wake up!" Seth leaps onto my bed and shakes my shoulders. "Wake up. It's Mom — she's gone."

I sit upright, see the terror in my brother's eyes and jump out of bed. "What do you mean?"

Seth wipes the snotty stream under his nose with his Batman cape and gulps down a sob. "Bayley, she's gone. Gone." He grabs hold of my hand and drags me out of the room. We thump down the stairs, barely missing the holey third step, into the front room, and out the open door.

I am momentarily blinded by the harsh glare of sunlight on the lake. I shield my eyes and take a step backward.

But Seth is frantic and won't allow me the time to adjust. "See!" he says, pointing. "The car's gone, and she's not inside anywhere. And her phone's still on her bed." Seth crumples onto the steps, pulls his cape around him, and gives in to his tears. The sight tugs at my heart. How many times has he cried into that cape these last eight months? Sometimes I feel like ripping it off him and tossing it away. How are we ever going to be able to forget if we constantly wrap ourselves in the past?

I sit beside him, rest my arm over his shoulders, and do my best to cheer him up.

"She'll be back. You'll see," I say, hoping that I'm right. With Mom being so unpredictable these days, I can't be sure of anything anymore. "She's probably gone into town — to the shops."

I help Seth up and guide him inside and through to the kitchen.

"But why didn't she tell us or leave a note? She always leaves a note."

"She probably couldn't find a pen." I wave my hand at the towers of unpacked boxes.

I open the fridge, pull out the small carton of orange

juice, and pour some into a glass. There's barely enough to fill a couple inches of the glass. "Here, have a drink, and we'll make some breakfast. She'll be back before you know it."

Seemingly unconvinced, Seth takes the glass. Just then, Amelia appears at the kitchen doorway in her pink robe and fluffy slippers. "Okay, Mom, tell me I'm dreaming. This is some freakish nightmare, right? We haven't really moved to this dump in the middle of nowhere, have we?"

"Mom's not here," Seth says.

Amelia flops into a chair. "Great. Bet there's no food either."

"OJ's gone," I say, pleased that Seth had the last of the juice before Amelia got her hands on it. "There's some bread on the counter."

"Bleh," says Amelia. "I'm so sick of toast." She gazes around. "Besides, who could find the toaster in this mess? Where is Mom, anyway?"

Seth pulls at his ears — the other habit he's come to rely on more and more these past months.

"Leave your ears alone," snaps Amelia. "They'll end up dangling below your knees if you're not careful."

"Shut up, Amelia," I say. "He's worried about Mom."

"She didn't leave a note," adds Seth.

A shadow of worry momentarily darkens Amelia's face

but quickly morphs into annoyance. "That'd be right — she brings us out to the sticks and then abandons us without any food. Hansel and Gretel revisited."

Seth leaps up, his chair thudding backward onto the floor. He glares at Amelia then runs off, black cape flapping.

"Way to go, Amelia," I say and storm out to find Seth. I find him in the Norfolk pine that stands outside my bedroom window, steadily climbing up through the branches.

"Come down, Seth!" I yell up at him. "Don't listen to Amelia. Come on, buddy. You're making me nervous."

Seth settles on a branch level with my window. It rocks under his weight. The screen door slams shut, and Amelia bustles out onto the porch, her robe flying open to reveal two large black-and-white eyes staring out from her stomach — black-and-white eyes that belong to *my* T-shirt!

"That's mine!" I snarl. "It better not be ruined. Loni gave it to me."

"*Loni gave it to me,*" Amelia mimics with a scowl. "Get over yourself." She leans across the porch railing and twists her head upward. "Seth, come down before you break that scrawny neck of yours and I get the blame."

"You could try apologizing," I say.

Amelia scrunches up her nose and looks at me with contempt. "What are you wearing, anyway?"

I glance down at my clothes and am immediately aware of their musty, locked-in-a-chest-for-forty-years smell. I had forgotten that I put on Celina's jeans and T-shirt. Blood rises to my face, and I turn to Seth, my neck craning. I raise a hand to shade my eyes from the sun's glare.

"Come down, Seth. Please."

"This is ridiculous," Amelia snorts, then heads back inside, robe fluttering.

Seth wraps the tattered cape around his knees and nestles against the trunk. The poor kid seems to have settled in for the long haul.

I bite at my lip and peer out toward the lake. Something catches my eye. Something is moving in the shimmer of the water on the far side. I strain to bring it into focus. Too big to be a waterbird, it moves smoothly, parting the lake before it.

A boat? Mom?

Mom in a boat?

I spy the old rowboat still marooned beside the dock, as it was yesterday, and discount the notion.

My eyes latch back onto the approaching vessel. Its rhythmic glide draws me toward it. Who could it be? Why is it coming here? I stumble forward, barefoot, vaguely aware of spiky tufts of grass scratching the soles of my feet. I gather momentum until I'm almost running.

"Where're you goin'?" Seth yells from his perch.

"Stay there," I call back. "Wait."

I stop at the edge of the lake. Mud oozes between my toes and stains the bottom of the jeans. "Hey!" I call out. "What are you doing?" It sounds lame, but I don't know what else to say. The boat, white and slender like an arrow, doesn't break a beat. "Hey! You in the boat!" I try again, realizing — worrying — that a stranger is approaching and we are stuck here, alone.

"Who is it?" Seth appears beside me.

"Don't know."

"Hello, boat!" Seth shouts, cupping his hands around his mouth. For a little guy, he has a loud voice. His words echo across the lake.

The boat stops abruptly. An oar flails in the air, then is dipped back in the water. A figure — male — breaks into a wide smile and waves.

"Hey!" he calls. "Hi." He gets to his feet, and the boat rocks beneath him. He holds out his arms to balance himself, and the boat steadies.

Even from this distance, I see he is about my age, maybe a little older. He is shirtless and only wearing a pair of dark shorts. Tanned and athletic, his shoulders are broad, his thighs strong and muscled. I blush — embarrassed at the way my eyes linger, appraising this stranger. I don't know what to do.

Where is Mom?

"Wha—what do you want?" I manage to stammer.

"Hang on," he calls back. "Can't hear you." He slides back down into the boat and maneuvers it expertly in our direction. In seconds he is walking through the shallows in front of us. In one hand he holds an oar, and with the other he guides the boat toward the shore.

Protectively, I take hold of Seth's hand, but he pulls free. "Cool boat," he says.

"Thanks, Batman," says the boy. He slaps Seth's hand in a high five.

I raise my chin. "What are you doing here?" It's an attempt at assertiveness, but my voice squeaks, mouse-like.

He places the oar onto the muddy shore and flicks his bangs out of his eyes. He smiles up at me. His eyes are the same blue-green as the lake, and his smile is wide and open. For a brief moment, I am hypnotized.

"Just training," he says, breaking the spell. "I live across the lake. We're neighbors, I guess." He points to the willow-lined far bank.

Neighbors? This is something I never considered, and the reality of it stings. One of the few good things about moving here was the inherent isolation: the chance to be away from the sympathetic faces and the claustrophobic surround of well-wishers.

"Sorry. I'm . . ." He seems far less sure of himself now that he is on dry land. He rubs his scalp, then holds his hair back off his face with both hands. "I'm Oliver. I knew someone was moving in — saw the builders working like crazy to fix the place up, but I didn't think it was ready yet."

It's not, I want to say, *obviously*. But all I manage is, "We moved in yesterday." Then I spy Seth splashing around the kayak, one leg over the side, trying to get in. "Seth, get out of there."

"He's okay," says Oliver. "Do you want to give it a try, little guy?"

"No!" My voice is fierce. I grab Seth by the arm and pull him out, my jeans now soaked to the knees. "Come on," I say. "We have to go and get breakfast."

"But there's no food," says Seth. "And Mom's not—"

"Shh," I warn. I can barely breathe, filled with the overwhelming need to get back inside.

"Sorry. I didn't mean . . ." Oliver starts. "I guess . . . I better get back to it." He picks up his oar, pushes his kayak off the shore, and slips into it with ease. "See you later," he calls and rows away.

Seth watches him go, shoulders slumped.

My heart thumps in my chest. I feel exposed. Vulnerable.

Seth turns to face me. "What's wrong with your face?" he asks.

I touch my cheek. "What?"

"It's all red and blotchy."

"It's hot, okay? Come on, let's go find something to eat."

"And find Mom?"

"Yep. And find Mom."

I stride off, not daring to look back.

three

It is almost lunchtime, and Mom still hasn't made an appearance. My emotions swing like a giant pendulum from worrying to seething and back again. Sad thing is, this is nothing new: same old, same old. So much for our fresh start.

A gust of hot wind rushes into the house. The back door slams shut, and specks of plaster and muck rain down onto the kitchen floor. The ceiling has water stains and bulges, with an ugly split right above me. I can't imagine what the place was like before the builders invaded more than a month ago. It is barely habitable now.

"Hey, you in the Batcave," I call to Seth, who has spent

hours inside an empty packing box. "One box to go. What do you think is in this one? Maybe the Riddler's hiding out. Or the Penguin. Want to come see?"

Seth doesn't answer. He's gloomy and whiny, and his ears are red and swollen from constant tugging. I know that with every passing minute, he is becoming increasingly anxious.

Finally, tires crunch on the gravel. *Mom. At last.* The Batcave is flung to the ground, and Seth shoots out the door.

I plop onto a kitchen chair, arms folded. I hear the thud of the car door and Seth's voice demanding: "Where have you been?" I don't hear Mom's answer. I don't want to.

Mom walks in laden with plastic shopping bags. I turn my back to her in a rare act of defiance.

"Wow, you've been busy. Thanks, sweetie," Mom says. She hauls the bags onto the bench. "There's more in the car, Bails."

I don't move.

"Come on! The quicker we get it in, the quicker we can organize some lunch," Mom says encouragingly. "Seth tells me you've all been starving to death."

I get to my feet and shove the chair back under the table. My body is rigid with hostility.

Mom rubs my stiff shoulders. "What's wrong with you?" Her voice is unusually light, laced with laughter.

"What do you think?" I say and shrug out of her grip.

"My," says Mom, her tone sarcastic, "have you been bitten by the Amelia bug?"

"Where *were* you?" I say. "You disappear at the crack of dawn without leaving a note. The phones aren't working, we have no way to contact you, and you're gone for half the day. What do you *think* is wrong, Mom? Seth was so worried that he hid in an empty box all morning, pulling his earlobes off. We've been here less than a day!" I stomp out to the car, wondering why I seem to be the only one acting like a parent.

I grab a bag stuffed with fruit and veggies out of the trunk. Mom is suddenly behind me. She's so close that I struggle to turn round. "Sorry, Bails," Mom says. Her voice is shaky. "I didn't think I'd be this long. I was just going to go out quick while everyone was asleep to get a few things and . . ."

I pick up another bag, wiggle past her, and head to the front steps. I press my lips together — I don't trust myself to say anything right now. I might even speak the truth for once.

Mom runs alongside me. "Come on, Bayley. Don't be like that. I need your support, sweetheart. You know that."

Don't I ever? Good old, dependable Bayley. Always there for everyone else. I lug the bags up the stairs, push open the door with my foot, and tramp inside.

Mom isn't finished. "I'm sorry, okay? I lost track of the time. What do you want from me? A written apology? Hey, don't you want to hear my news?"

Exasperated, I drop the bags and rub my eyes with both hands. I hear the fragility in my mother's voice, and it frustrates me. I turn to face her. "What, Mom? What news?"

"I got a job, Bails!"

"Job? What job?"

"There was a sign in a Chinese restaurant for waitstaff. Only casual. But it's a start. I didn't think I'd have a hope —"

"Waitstaff?" I interrupt. "What do you know about being a waitress?"

"Obviously enough, otherwise they wouldn't have hired me. I'm not useless, you know." Mom shifts to the defensive.

"That's not what I meant," I lie, pulling cans of tomatoes and beans out of one of the bags and sliding them onto the near-empty pantry shelves. "You've never worked in a restaurant before. Will you know what to do?"

And how long will it last before it all gets too much for you? Like everything else?

"Well, actually, I have. Admittedly, it was a long time ago —"

"What? When you were in college?"

"Yes. Does it matter? It didn't seem to worry the people at the Wok and Roll who have just hired me."

"What about *designing*, Mom? I thought you said you would be able to do some freelancing. Get back into it — the things you love doing. The things you're good at."

"And I will." Mom feigns determination.

"Mom! You promised. The whole move was our new start — to get back on track and everything."

"Don't lecture me, Bayley. Besides, you're one to talk — what about you?"

"Me?"

"When was the last time you went running?"

"That's different—"

"No. It's the same. Talk to me when you're back training again. In the meantime, let's drop it, okay? I *will* get back to design, but right now we need some steady cash — we do have to eat. Speaking of which, if you finish putting all this away, I'll get cracking on some lunch. Where's Amelia?" Mom swivels around. "And where did Seth go?"

"I'm right here." Seth is back in his Batcave, munching on a banana.

"Hello, sassy monkey," says Mom, peering into the box. "Why aren't you helping?"

Seth takes a chomp out of the banana, bares banana-coated

teeth, and says, "Has Bayley told you about her boyfriend yet?"

Mom pulls a surprised face at me. "Boyfriend?"

"Her? A boyfriend?" Amelia materializes in the doorway, still in my T-shirt. Her hair is snarled, and her eyes blink from the midday light. "Yeah right. Hey, do we have actual real food?"

Mom raises one eyebrow and looks from Amelia to me, but her gaze lingers on me. She grimaces. "You still have those clothes on."

"Yeah, and she stinks like some old bum," adds Amelia. "Thrift store chic is so yesterday, Bayley. But you'd have no idea, would you?"

I rub my hands down the sides of the jeans, searching for some kind of smart comeback, some witty remark to explain myself. But all I can manage to do is sound pathetic when I say, "Well, why are you wearing my new shirt, then, if I'm so lame?"

Amelia counters perfectly. "Yeah. Wearing it to *bed*," she says to prove how pathetic I am.

"Amelia, please," says Mom, and then turns back to me. "Go upstairs and get changed, Bayley. It doesn't seem right."

"Right? What do you mean?" says Amelia.

Mom takes a tomato and starts cutting thick slices. "Bayley

found some clothes and things in her room. We think they might be Celina's — my cousin."

"The dead chick? The one that got murdered? And you're wearing her clothes? You're seriously weird, Bayley."

My stomach clenches, and all I can think to do is flee. I take the stairs two at a time to my bedroom and fling the door closed behind me.

I yank off the jeans. Throw off the T-shirt. Ram them into the chest and pull down the lid.

I rummage through the plastic garbage bags littering my floor until I find my favorite shorts and tank top. Once I'm dressed, I flop onto the tangle of sheets on my bed, my cheeks burning with humiliation.

I know I shouldn't let Amelia get to me like this. But her words ring in my head — *The dead chick? You're wearing her clothes? You are seriously weird, Bayley.* — and they sting more than they should. She always makes me feel like such a baby.

My eyes are drawn back to the chest, and I'm filled with a furious urge to flip open the lid and wear whatever I choose. *To hell with them all.*

"Bails!" Mom's voice drifts up from the kitchen. "Lunch."

With a sigh, I push myself up off my bed and head downstairs.

"The whole country retreat thingy might be fine for you,

Mom." Amelia's never-ending argument meets me before I get to the bottom stair. "But I need *people* — a social life. Not endless fields of colorless grass and a weedy lake. I mean, how can we even live here? There is rubble — actual rubble! — piled up at the end of the hallway. The place ought to be condemned. Not to mention that overgrown garbage heap out in the back — there could be anything in there."

"Put these on the table," Mom says in response. "Seth, pour some milk for everyone, will you?" As I enter, Mom hands me a bowl filled with fresh green grapes. "Here, have a grape."

"Mom!" Amelia, holding a plate of sandwiches, stamps her foot in frustration. "Stop ignoring me."

"What do you want me to say, Amelia? 'Oh dear, what a big mistake! Let's pack up everything and go back to our old house and kick out the new tenants because, gee, Amelia refuses to give this a try!' Really, Amelia, you are nearly eighteen — try acting like it for once."

Amelia fixes Mom with a hate-filled glare. "Try treating me like it," she says through clenched teeth. She slams the plate on the table and walks out.

Mom collapses into a chair, rests her elbows on the table, and holds her head with her hands. I ache for her and feel guilty about my own outburst only minutes before.

She raises her head and runs shaky hands through her messy curls. Dark circles shadow her eyes — she looks fragile, as if sculpted from tissue paper.

Just as she slides the plate over to Seth, Amelia rushes back in, grabs two sandwiches then rushes back out.

"Here, have a sandwich," Mom says to Seth. "And tell me about Bayley's boyfriend. Not like her to be such a fast worker."

"Haha," I say, and bite into a cheese and tomato sandwich.

"Ol-i-ver," says Seth in a singsong voice.

Mom hoists up her eyebrows and pretends surprise. "Oliver, is it? And where did he come from?"

"From across the lake," I say. "He says he's our neighbor. You didn't say anything about neighbors."

"Well, this isn't exactly the Outback, Bails. Of course there are people on the surrounding properties. I think a kid from across the lake somewhere used to hang out with Celina . . ."

At the mention of Celina's name, sharp pins prick my arms. A lump of sandwich wedges in my throat. I swallow hard and try not to let my face betray my unease.

Pressing a finger to her lips, Mom squints, as if trying to remember something. "Now, what was the property called? Lakeview or Lakeside? Or was it Lakelight?"

"Do you think it would be the same family?" I ask.

"We're talking forty-plus years here. I doubt it — farming families don't seem to do that old generational thing much these days. Anyway, how did you get to meet this Oliver?"

Mom's question floats past me. Inexplicably, I am lost in a dense jungle of thoughts and questions about Celina.

"Bails?" Mom says. "Hell-oo? Anyone in there?"

"He was in a boat," I hear Seth answering for me. "A rowing one. Bayley wouldn't let me go in it, and her face went all red."

"Shut up, you," I say, and elbow him playfully in the ribs. "Actually, Mom, it was scary. We're pretty alone out here. I didn't know who he was, you weren't around, the phone isn't working yet, and we had no car or anything if we needed to escape. We really need another car . . ."

"Letting that imagination run wild again, Bayley?" says Mom. "We'll have the phones fixed by the end of the week. And, yes, once you get your license, we'll talk about a car for you and Amelia. But in the meantime, I think you'll find you're perfectly safe here. Country people tend to look out for each other and—"

"Then who was looking out for Celina?" The words slip out before I can call them back.

four

The moon glows faintly through wispy lines of cloud. Its rays tracing a silvery path across the lake — across to Oliver and Lakeview or Lakeside or whatever it's called.

I turn away from the window and rest up against the wall, listening to the irregular beat of frogs croaking in the distance.

Everything seems so odd here, and I can't seem to settle down. I'd give anything to be able to send a message to Loni, to tell her how much I miss her already.

I let out a small sigh. Second night blues, I guess.

My thoughts turn to the chest, and I flick on my bed-side lamp. The chest sits against the wall and beckons to be opened. *Why not?* I think.

I grab my blanket and stuff it into the gap between my door and the floor to prevent light from spilling into the hallway, then go over to the chest and open the lid. The hairs on the back of my neck bristle. It's kind of eerie, peering into the life of a dead girl, but also strangely thrilling.

"Peace, sister," I say to the painted peace sign on the inside of the lid, holding up my fingers the way I have seen people in movies do. I stifle a giggle. I really am crazy, aren't I? What would Loni think if she could see me now?

I pull out the piles of clothes, examining them, holding them up to the light. I finally decide on the peasant blouse and denim shorts.

I tie the purple scarf around my head like a headband, knotting it above my ear, and examine my reflection in the mirror. Not bad, I decide. The scarf sort of suits me. It keeps my curls at bay and accentuates my eyes. I make a Loni-style Sexy Pout at the '70s me in the mirror, followed by Uber-Cool Supermodel pose. Ha! I am such an idiot. Grinning, I run my fingers over the embroidered yoke of the blouse. It is pretty gorgeous and reminds me of pure happiness — a daisy-filled field on a perfect day — and its puffiness suggests that I actually have boobs worth noticing.

I complete the outfit with a couple of strings of beads and the cork platforms. The buckles are tarnished with age, and they take some convincing before I can clip them in place and take off on a practice walk. I wobble across the room; heels are not something I am used to wearing. Guilt stabs at me. Dad always threw a huge fit at the mere mention of me wearing anything other than sneakers or sensible, grandma-style sandals. He wouldn't let me risk twisting an ankle. That would have spelled disaster — it's hard to win with a bad ankle. "Sorry, Dad," I whisper — and then nearly trip over myself.

To regain my balance, I prop myself up against the end of my bed, and stare out of the window. I take in the shadowy view through the branches of the pine tree and wonder if Celina would have looked at this exact same view. Maybe she stood in this exact spot, wearing these exact clothes. A shiver runs through me, and I have that unsettling sensation of déjà vu.

How tall would the tree have been forty years ago? Would the lake have changed much? What would Celina have thought about as she stood and took in the view? My stomach tightens. These are very strange thoughts, and I know I am obsessing.

I cast my eye across to the far side of the lake and think about Oliver, unsure if I am pleased or annoyed by the presence of such a good-looking neighbor. Loni would have labeled him a hottie and been hooking up with him behind the barn by now.

If only I had Loni's spark — her talent for making the world fizz and bubble around her, her gift of putting boys under her spell without even trying.

But I'm no fool. I know I'm not the type who would ever be able to weave magic over anyone, much less someone like Oliver. Besides, once Amelia has him in her sights, I won't stand a chance.

Still, I can't help wondering if he goes to Tallowood High. If he will catch the same bus as me. If he will be in some of the same classes. It might be good if there's at least one familiar face when I start school at Tallowood in a few weeks . . .

Jeez, be honest with yourself, Bayley! You'd give anything to be hooking up with Oliver behind the barn right now.

Loni may lament that she's already seventeen and still a virgin, but I lament that at almost seventeen, the sum of my experience with the opposite sex is playing spin the bottle at Eleni Christofi's thirteenth birthday, and I am pretty sure that doesn't count. But what can you do when every boy you're interested in doesn't seem to know you exist, and all the boys who seem interested in you, *you* don't want to know *they* exist?

Suddenly, the stillness of the lake is broken. My breath catches in my throat. Something is moving on the water again. *No way!*

Gliding across the glowing track of moonlight is a boat. I grab my phone from my bedside table. It's 1:13 in the morning. Why would anyone be out in a boat at 1:13? Training? Yeah right! What is this Oliver guy up to?

Without pausing to think, I flick off the platforms, pull my blanket out from under the door, and tear down the stairs. I carefully pick my way through the living room, my hands leading me through the darkness to the front door. The stubborn old beast lurches open with a screech, and in the still night air, it sounds as loud as a scream. Heart thudding, I pause, waiting for some kind of response from the rooms above. When there's none, I scoot into the darkness, sprinting across the gravel drive. As the stones dig into the soles of my feet, I question the wisdom of dashing out like this without shoes. In fact, as I am swallowed up by the night, I question the wisdom of the whole escapade.

What am I doing?

But still I run, run like I haven't for months and months. I go into the field that fronts the lake, the grass rustling and scratching as I mow through it. Then I'm shooting across the lake edge, gritty sand flicking behind me. I don't stop until I'm ankle deep in water.

Feeling suddenly exposed — a lone figure on the empty shore — I search for some kind of cover. I edge to the dock, slip behind one of its hefty wooden support beams, and lean heavily against it. Gone are the days when I could run five miles without raising a sweat.

I stay there for a few moments, long enough to summon the nerve to take another glimpse at the lake. I lean out from behind the beam and scan the expanse of water before me. It is still. And empty. Not even a ripple marks the surface. I stand upright, out of the cover of the dock. Had I imagined it? A boat couldn't disappear into thin air, could it? *Only if it didn't exist at all, you knucklehead!*

I check the lake one final time before turning to head home.

Then I hear it. The crunch of sand to my right, as if something is being dragged through it. A night bird is startled into flight, and I duck behind the support beam, my heartbeat like a drum in my ears.

SUE WHITING

I peer into the darkness in the direction of the noise. Clouds now totally obscure the light of the moon, and night has closed in on me. Is there something on the shore? I can't be sure, but I can't stay here. What was I thinking? Why am I out here alone?

I worry that the dash back across the field will leave me too exposed. Exposed to what? To Oliver? And if so, why am I this afraid? He seemed harmless enough. But something — call it instinct, intuition, whatever — tells me that I have every reason to be afraid and that I have to find a way to get back to the safety of the house, unseen.

I remember the scraggly bushes in one corner of the field and the row of poplars hugging the fence line to the south. If I could make it to the bushes, I would have a better chance of being concealed. I don't pause to think about it. On hands and knees, I slip out onto the sandy shoreline and edge toward where I hope to find some cover. I can make out some bushes to my left and dart toward them.

I only take a few steps.

"Holy mother of God!" A face materializes right in front of me. I reel backward. The face, veiled in shadows, contorts and seems as shocked as I feel. It repeats its horrible cry: "Holy mother of God! No! Nooo!" and a wrinkled hand reaches out for me.

I scream and bolt, dumping the plan to stay concealed and replacing it with the plan to *get the HELL out of here.* I don't look back. I don't want to know if the face is following. The face — a man's face — wrinkly and saggy and snarling at me, with a sour chemical aroma wafting from it, seemingly suspended in the darkness. But I know this is only a trick of the night. The face must have a body attached. It has to.

I run and run. My breath is ragged and my head pounds. I fly up the porch stairs, heave open the door, and slam it behind me. I lock the deadbolt, willing it to be strong enough to hold out whatever danger lies outside. I push my back against the door and slide down to sit on the floor. I am shaking.

It's then, as I hit the floor, that my chest heaves and I start to cry. The lights flick on and Mom tears down the stairs, face stricken. She falls to her knees and gathers me in her arms, asking, "What is it, Bails? What happened, baby?" But I am sobbing so hard, I can't speak.

* * *

In the darkened kitchen I sit at the table, exhausted and jumpy. Mom stands to the side of the window, raises the curtain slightly, and peers out. One hand holds her robe together at her throat, a slight tremble in her fingers. It's a timid pose that reminds me of those nightmare days after Dad's accident.

"Can't see a thing, Bails," Mom whispers. "Nothing on the lake as far as I can tell. No movement along the shore."

"Maybe he's hiding somewhere," I offer. It's not an encouraging thought.

"Perhaps. But why would anyone do that? It's all very strange." Mom sighs and moves away from the window. She sits opposite me and places her hands over mine. "I'm sure it'll end up being something totally innocent. I guess, when you think about it, this place has been deserted for decades — it could have been someone who has camped or fished here for years, not realizing that people have moved in. You probably scared him half to death too."

It sounds logical enough, but regardless, I am not convinced. The vile chemical smell of the stranger has stuck with me, making me feel sick to my stomach, and my instincts scream that there was something not right about what happened.

"But his face . . . I couldn't really see much of it, but it was sinister, Mom. Scary and . . . ugly," I say, struggling to conjure a clear image in my mind.

Mom gives a small grin. "Ugly doesn't equal axe murderer.

And anyone would look scary if you've frightened him." She rubs my hands gently. "Now, Bails, how about you tell me what you were doing out there in the middle of the night — and why you're dressed in those clothes from the chest again. Huh?"

I hang my head and shrug.

"Come on, Bails — what's going on?" Mom leans toward me and searches for my eyes. "This isn't like you at all."

I keep my gaze on the table, slipping my hands out of Mom's. How can I explain what I don't understand myself? "I don't know, Mom," I say. "I was messing around with the clothes, and then I saw something on the lake and I started running. I didn't think about it. I just ran down to the lake."

Mom sighs. "Come on," she says. "Let's get to bed and try to get a few hours of shut-eye, okay?"

I shake my head. I couldn't possibly sleep.

"I've locked all the doors and windows. He's probably long gone by now," she assures me. "If it makes you feel better, we'll report it to the police in the morning, okay?"

"How about reporting it now?"

"No phones yet, remember? Besides, I don't think country police stations are manned at night."

"We were safer in the city," I say. "I don't know if I can get used to this wholesome country life."

Mom draws her collar together at her throat again, her eyes troubled. She hesitates.

I feel as if she is about to dissolve, to admit what a useless situation she has gotten us into.

But instead she says, "You will in time. Now, how about a quick shower to get that sand and mud off, and then why don't you come sleep with me? Like when you were little?" Mom smoothes my hair out of my eyes, tucking it under Celina's scarf, and her lips wobble into a tentative smile.

I give a weak smile back. It's been a long time since Mom has comforted me like this, and it feels good, but I shake my head. I think I'd rather be alone and scared than beside my sad mother all night.

"And Bails?" Mom says as we leave the kitchen. "Let's keep this to ourselves for the time being, okay? I don't need to give Amelia any more ammunition to hate me for bringing her here, and Seth, well, you know how panicky he gets these days."

I nod. I understand completely.

five

It takes forty-five minutes to drive into Tallowood. The trip is slowed by a long stretch of narrow, unsealed road that winds out of the valley and up to the highway. It's our first trip into the new town, and the car feels charged with energy — though the energy is somewhat polarized. At one end of the spectrum is Amelia, sitting in the front, sour-faced and silent, her iPod earbuds jammed into her ears, wearing her disdain like a fashion accessory. And then there's Seth. He's so bouncy that he tangles himself in his seatbelt twice and squeezes his juice box so fiercely that it sprays the back of Amelia's hair.

Mom and I sit somewhere in between, our enthusiasm dulled by our shared secret and also by Mom's obvious annoyance with me when I came down for breakfast wearing Celina's clothes again: flared jeans, a T-shirt, and a purple scarf. I don't have a clue why I am wearing them — but I simply couldn't resist. To Mom's credit, she didn't say anything. She didn't need to.

Sitting in the backseat with Seth, I can't get last night from my mind. I play the scene over and over. I can hear the raspy voice: *Holy mother of God! Holy mother of God!* I can almost feel that sour breath in my face. I fiddle with the scarf tied around my forehead and tell myself to forget it, to think of something else.

The road rises up and over a bumpy mound, and a gully appears ahead. Thick rods of morning sunshine angle through the canopy above, lighting the lacy fern fronds below, and once again I have that strong sensation of déjà vu, as if I have taken this drive before. Many times. But not in Mom's car, in an old van of some sort with a rumbly engine and a stick shift.

Images crowd my head. I can see myself in the van, riding up front, and I can feel the vibrations as it bumps over the grooves in the dirt road, the tires losing traction on the loose stones. I can see the way the road twists up and then down the mountain, the forest thickening, rocky cliffs rising up from the road on one side, tiny plants dangling out of cracks in the wall. I can feel my excitement. An almost uncontainable excitement. I am going to town to meet Suzie and Deb, and I can't wait to tell them my news. They're not going to believe me when I tell them what I've planned. They will be so shocked.

Hang on! I don't know anyone in town. I don't know any Suzies or Debs. I don't have any plans.

And I'm flung back to reality, to the back seat of Mom's car, my stomach turning over. Where did that come from? It can't be a memory. Did I invent it? But it felt so real. So intense.

Then a chilling realization strikes me: I wasn't seeing myself at all; I was seeing Celina.

Celina in the front seat of her parents' Volkswagen van.

But how? Did they even have a Volkswagen?

This is stupid. I have Celina on the brain. I'm nuts to even consider that I know anything about Celina or her life.

I think back to the "visions" of Celina I had on the first night, when I discovered the chest. How real they felt. Same as the vision I just had. I play with a loose thread on the pocket of my jeans — Celina's jeans — mulling these images over. By the time Mom pulls into one of the many empty parking spots angled along the wide main street, I have broken into a cold sweat. Something seriously creepy is going on here.

* * *

Tallowood is so vintage country, it's almost a cliché.

Mom and I scuttle down the main street to the police station like a pair of criminals. Mom had bribed Amelia into taking Seth up the hill to look at his new school.

A female officer greets us with an open smile. "Hot one, eh?" she says, then folds her arms onto the counter. "What can I do for you today?"

Mom fidgets and stumbles over her words as she tries to explain last night's incident. Now, in the light of day and the harsh glare of the fluorescent lighting of Tallowood police station, it sounds lame, even to me.

The police officer takes down a few notes. "Did this man harm you in any way, Bayley?"

I shake my head.

"Did he say anything that was offensive or that would give you reason to be concerned about your safety?"

She is making me uneasy. "No, not really. He just said, 'Holy mother of God,' and then he yelled, 'No!' But he was really creepy. Besides, what was he doing out there, anyway?"

"Good question — but one could also ask what you were doing out there in the middle of the night."

"I saw the boat and went to investigate."

"By yourself? Was that wise? Why didn't you wake your parents?"

The word "parents" is like a slap across my face. It stings.

"Bayley isn't on trial here," Mom says. "The point is, some strange man was lurking about on our property in the middle of the night. We're new here. My hus—" Mom falters. "My husband passed away last year, and that's left us feeling a little vulnerable."

"I'm very sorry to hear that, Mrs. Anderson." The response is automatic and insincere. "Look, I'll call around and talk to your neighbors, see what I can find out. Your property has been vacant and unused for a long while — boundaries blur over time, if you know what I mean."

"Yes. Thanks," mumbles Mom, smoothing her hair nervously behind her ears.

"In the meantime, I suggest you take a drive over to the neighboring properties and introduce yourselves — let them know you've moved in. That's how we do things here in the country."

The officer sounds friendly, but I don't miss the barbs in her words. Numbly, I follow Mom out of the station and into the oppressive heat of main street Tallowood.

* * *

We meet Amelia and Seth in the only café in town. It's all metal chairs and square tables, and a dirty fan whirs ineffectively from the ceiling in the middle of the room. I am so twitchy that it takes all my resolve not to yell at it to shut the hell up.

"The menu is decent enough," says Mom, over-brightly. A blast of heat surges inside as a bell dings and the door opens. I am surprised that the laminated menu doesn't melt in my hands. "As good as any café along the mall in Cronulla," she adds.

Amelia rolls her eyes and slides down in her seat.

"Well, what does your new school look like, Seth?" Mom says, still trying to brighten the mood.

"It's old," says Seth.

"Ancient," adds Amelia.

"And small," continues Seth. His eyes flit around and he pulls at his ear.

"It'll be great," says Mom, guiding Seth's hand away.

Seth reaches for the saltshaker and fiddles with the peeling "salt" sticker on the side.

"After lunch, we'll hike up to the high school on the hill and check it out. We'll need to organize school uniforms—"

"Don't bother," Amelia snarls.

"What?" Mom seems wary.

"Don't bother," Amelia repeats. "I won't need any uniforms because I'm not going. Simple."

I've been dreading this. Amelia had confided as much to me, but I had held on to the dim hope that it was an empty threat.

"What do you mean, 'not going'?" Mom says, her voice climbing to match the temperature outside. "You're a senior — of course you're going. You're so close to being done."

"Exactly," says Amelia. "I'm not changing schools halfway through my senior year. End. Of. Story." Amelia crosses her arms and glares at Mom, both defiant and triumphant.

"Yes, you will, young lady. You are not throwing away your future out of stubbornness. End. Of. Story."

"You should have thought of that before you dragged us out here. What kind of mother makes her daughter leave school in the middle of her senior year?"

Mom is dumbstruck.

"A real shitty one," hisses Amelia. She stands up from the table and saunters out of the café. The door closes with a ding behind her, bringing another wave of heat to slap us in our faces.

Seth slips off his seat and onto Mom's lap. She puts her arm around his shoulders and says, "Go see which way she went, Bails."

My stomach feels as if it is filled with cement. I hate the way Amelia does this — always making a scene and wrecking things. I bash through the doors, my temper swelling. The door flies open and straight into someone who is about to step inside. He moves back quickly, but not before the door bops him on the nose.

"Hey! Watch it!" he shouts, covering his nose with one hand.

"Sorry!" I say, embarrassed.

The guy uncovers his face, and the cement in my belly flips over and liquefies as I realize that I'm staring into the blue-green eyes of Oliver.

"Hey, you're the girl from the lake." His face lights up with recognition.

"Yeah. Uh . . . Bayley," I say.

"Uh Bayley . . ." He grins and rubs his nose.

"I'm so sorry."

"No worries, Uh Bayley. In a hurry?"

"Oh . . . I was . . . you didn't see a girl walking down the street, did you?"

"Lots of girls out there," he says, amused. "What does she look like?"

Warmth creeps up my neck. "A little taller than me. Curly dark hair. Kinda like me, really, only . . . uh . . . different and . . . you know . . . better." I am rambling, trying to push fantasies of hooking up behind the barn as far as possible from my mind.

"Better, huh?" says Oliver. "No kidding."

I don't know what to say. *Loni, where are you when I need you?*

"Oliver!" shouts Seth, and jumps off Mom's lap.

"Hey, Batman," says Oliver, then strolls toward our table.

My cheeks are radiating more heat than the air outside. "Gotta go," I breathe.

Oliver turns back to me. "Yeah. Bye."

I flee.

Once I'm out on the scorching pavement, I glance up and down the street and try to still my beating heart.

Amelia is nowhere to be seen.

six

I wait across the road until Oliver leaves, sipping on his to-go coffee and carrying a white paper bag, before heading back inside the café.

Mom orders some sandwiches for all of us, which we devour quickly, then we split up to search for Amelia. Mom takes off up the street, carrying Seth piggyback; I take the main street.

It's not the first time I have had to help find Amelia. The last time, when she was finally found passed out on Wanda Beach at about four in the morning, lying in a puddle of her own puke, was the reason Mom moved us out here.

Amelia had been trouble for a while, but since Dad's accident, she had ramped it up a few gazillion notches, and it had been scary to witness. This particular night though, it was Mom who was scary. Her fury was raw. And there seemed to be no end to it.

She cleared the kitchen counter of all dishes in one fell swoop. She even threw her favorite crystal vase against the wall with such force that the family photo collage jumped off its hook and smashed to the ground.

It wasn't until Seth appeared in the doorway, rubbing his eyes and wondering what was going on, that she seemed to snap out of it. She dropped to her knees, wailing, and I ushered Seth back to bed with some bullshit story that I can't even really remember.

When I returned, I felt as though I was in the eye of the storm. An unnerving calm had descended. Amelia was nowhere to be seen, and Mom was bent over, plucking tiny pieces of blue patterned china off the tiles and tossing them into a box.

"Leave this to me," she said reasonably, as if talking about cleaning up spilled milk. "Go get some sleep."

The calm lasted for weeks, but it made me feel far from calm. It rattled me. When Gran arrived with pizza on a Friday night, I knew something was up. Friday is Gran's busiest night with the Soup Van she drives around the inner city, feeding the poor and homeless. Gran missing a Friday night is serious business.

So during a commercial break in a rerun of *The Big Bang Theory*, with us holding pizza boxes on our laps, Mom announced her plan for saving the family. She got it out in a rush, told us we were leaving straight after New Year's and that it was what Dad would have wanted for us. Then she grabbed her car keys and headed off to buy celebratory cookies-and-cream ice cream before the first commercial even finished. She left the three of us on the couch, thunderstruck.

I was aware that we were in some kind of family crisis and that Mom wasn't coping; that much was obvious. The pressure had been building for months — I simply didn't expect this particular escape valve. None of us did.

And Amelia's role in it all infuriates me still, my anger festering with each step I take down the street. *She's just selfish.* It's fine to throw a tantrum. It's fine to be shitty with Mom. It's fine to quit school if that's what she wants. But why take off? Especially when she knows what a state it will put Seth in. It would serve her right if we left her behind.

My T-shirt sticks to my back, and I regret my decision to wear Celina's jeans. I feel like a furnace on legs. I poke my nose inside each of the shops lining the main street. The buildings look tired, and many are more or less empty and easy to eliminate with a glance through the window. They make me wonder what kind of town Mom has brought us to. It's as if the heat has sucked all the life out of the place, and it occurs to me that the chances of getting any kind of part-time work is about zilch — in fact, it's probably a bit of a miracle Mom got that job at the Wok and Roll. What are we doing here? Thanks a lot, Amelia!

There's a decent-sized newsstand with a couple of aisles filled with magazines and cards and a separate post office booth. I wander down the aisles of magazines and peer into the back section, which is full of dusty stationery.

No sign of Amelia, but there is a large basket filled to the brim with slim notebooks with swirling silver patterns on the covers. "One dollar each," a sign above the stack says. I find myself leaning over the display, leafing through the pages of one of the books, smiling as I remember the journals I used to keep. Before Dad. Before it became too painful to write.

I go to walk away, but for some reason I can't. The empty pages seem to call me, and my heart thumps against my ribs. Before I realize what I am doing, I have grabbed a bundle and am handing over my money to the cheery man at the register.

"A real bargain, isn't it?" he says.

"Yeah," I agree, though I am unsure what is driving me to buy them. Beside the register is a display of magazines: *The Year in Design.* "I'll have one of these too, thanks."

I slip out onto the street, conscious that I'm really not myself today. I scan left and right for Amelia. Still no sign of her.

The final corner of the main shopping mall is home to some kind of New Age-y craft, gift, and crystal store. I step inside. A heady mix of pan flute music and the aroma of scented candles assaults me. This place seems very un-Tallowood like.

A tall woman with wild orange hair sits behind a high front counter. Reading glasses on the end of her nose, she is absorbed in some kind of crafty project, wielding a glue stick over a double page of a book. She looks up and smiles — though the smile doesn't quite reach her eyes before her mouth flops open. She drops the glue stick, and it clatters onto the tile floor.

"Damn," she says, sounding flustered. She swoops down to pick up the glue and knocks a couple of small bottles off the counter in the process. One smashes into tiny pieces. "Oh Lord, now I'm in for it. Break a bottle — misfortune's your new best friend." She flounces about, picking up the shattered glass, all the while taking every opportunity to steal glances at me.

I give the woman a nervous grin and edge toward the nearest aisle, certain of a growing desire to escape.

"Go ahead, dear," says the woman whose eyes are now openly scanning me from head to toe. "Don't mind me."

My insides squirm. Something feels wrong. I head off down an aisle stacked high with sparkly beads and candles and knickknacks, intent on getting out of this shop as swiftly as possible. But when I reach the end of the row, the woman reappears, blocking my way. Her hair streams behind her like a fiery mane.

She is flushed and breathless. "Sorry for staring, dear," she says. "You must think I'm rude. It's just that scarf . . ." Her hand reaches out toward my head. I jerk away. "That scarf, it . . . it . . . it reminds me of something, someone . . . Actually, you remind me of —"

I don't give the woman a chance to finish. I take a few faltering steps backward, then hurry away.

"Sorry, dear!" calls the woman. "I didn't mean . . ."

I reach for the door and tug it open. But something makes me stop. I turn back to face the woman. "Celina," I say, not knowing why. "I remind you of Celina O'Malley, right?"

The woman approaches. Her eyes are glassy with emotion.

She stops a few feet in front of me and touches the scarf with shaky fingers.

"Yes." Her voice is soft. "Celina. I tie-dyed and embroidered that scarf for Celina O'Malley for her fifteenth birthday."

I pull the scarf from my head and pass it to the woman. She takes it with trembling hands and holds it to her nose. "Celina," she says. Tears smear mascara down her face. She smoothes out the scarf along the countertop and points to a tiny painted message along one edge.

Happy birthday, Celina. Friends forever. XOXOXO. Love, Deb.

Deb. Meeting Suzie and *Deb* in town.

I go wobbly at the knees. The woman catches me before I flop to the floor in a faint.

* * *

I sit on a stool in the tiny crammed storeroom in the back of the shop and sip at the spicy herbal tea Deb has made me.

"Drink that up. It should do the trick." Deb is so anxious, she doesn't seem to know whether to laugh or cry. "When you walked into the shop, I swear, I thought I was seeing an apparition — a freaking ghost. Do you have any idea how much you look like her?"

I shake my head. "She was Mom's cousin. Both my sister and I have the O'Malley hair and skin and —"

"No, dear. It's more than the hair. You are a dead ringer. Celina's double. Why, these clothes — they're exactly what Celina would have worn. Miss Hippie Chick through and through. Oh, how I miss her. Even after all these years."

Deb blows her nose and wipes the mascara from under her eyes. I am too embarrassed to confess the fact that these are indeed clothes that Celina would have worn.

"Where did you find this scarf? It's so weird. What were the chances of it still being around? Lord, I must have made that nearly forty years ago. Maybe more."

"It was in a wooden chest in Celina's old room."

"Not the peace chest!"

"Maybe . . ."

"I can't believe it. I felt some strange energy in the air today, the moment I got up. But this, this is too much."

Tell me about it.

With one eye trained on the shop front, Deb quizzes me about my family and the house, the chest, and the lake. She seems to absorb everything I say, and despite a fair amount of mumbo jumbo about vibrations and omens and energy, I can't help but warm up to her.

"Oh lordy," says Deb. "Sorry about the language — you're not religious or anything, are you? Sorry if you are — I can't help myself. I just can't believe all this. It takes me back." She draws in a deep breath. "It was so sad — so terribly, terribly sad . . ." Deb fans her face with both hands. "Sorry, dear. You don't need this."

But oddly enough, I *do* need this — all of it: Deb's emotion and memories and stories. They breathe oxygen into the enigma that is Celina O'Malley and send blood coursing through her shadowy veins. And I tingle with a growing new awareness: maybe I am here in Tallowood for a reason.

* * *

It is well over an hour before I leave Deb's shop. It isn't until my phone rings with a call from Mom that I'm vaulted back to the present and back to the search for Amelia.

Amelia, however, doesn't want to be found. I am not sure who is more frantic — Mom or Seth.

Around four o'clock, Mom is contemplating visiting the police station again, when Amelia moseys up, silent and sullen, to where the car is parked. She slips into the backseat without even a word of apology.

The car is filled with unvoiced anger. It is a long trip home.

seven

Celina O'Malley was sixteen years old when she disappeared in 1975, presumed murdered. She was a hippie chick: flower power and peace and all that; a free spirit with a heart bigger than most, who brought a little sunshine into the lives of those who knew her. When she vanished, the world was left less shiny because of it.

I stop writing and ponder for a bit, trying to recall the other snippets of information I gleaned from Deb. It feels good, writing it down, as if I am getting acquainted with Celina. And as crazy as it sounds, I like the feeling. I smooth out the pages of the notebook, pressing my palm firmly down the gutter, flattening it open.

Celina's best friends were Deb and Suzie.

Writing this sentence makes me jittery. How did I know about Deb and Suzie before I met Deb? With a shiver, I continue.

Deb was the crazy one who saw life as one huge opportunity for mischief and adventure. Suzie was more sensible. The one who kept them all in check. But the three were inseparable — a sister-hood of sorts: the Peace Sisters.

It was Celina who decided upon their name and persuaded them that the Age of Aquarius was still alive and well, even in the '70s. She inspired them; she was infectious. And you couldn't help but follow her and get caught up in her plans.

As soon as they finished school, the Peace Sisters were going to travel the globe— singing folksy ballads about peace and love, trekking through forgotten lands, and saving the planet.

I laugh, remembering how excited and gushy Deb was as she told me about the Peace Sisters' grand plans. It all sounded like something from some old movie.

But of course, that changed on that awful morning when Celina O'Malley walked out her front door, across the pebbly driveway, along the dirt road, and down to the main gate to catch the school bus and was never seen again . . .

I shudder.

I recall Deb's shock when I walked into her shop. Do I really look that much like Celina?

The photo album! I almost forgot about it. I leap off my bed and rummage through the peace chest to find it.

But my fingers strike a hard edge below the album. I put the album on my bed and then dig out the object lying flat on the bottom of the chest. It takes a bit of effort, but when it lifts up, I am astonished to find a framed artwork — a collage made of bits and pieces.

As I hold it with outstretched arms, I see it is a face. The tufts of long dark curly hair seem to be made from short snips of real hair, the eyes shaped from dozens of tiny pieces of icy blue crystals, and the skin made from an odd mix of translucent insect wings and the fluffy bits of dandelion heads. I wonder if it's a portrait of Celina.

Whatever it is, it's beautifully strange but also strangely spooky. I put the picture facedown, back into the bottom of the chest, and turn my attention to the album.

The pages are so brown they look tea-stained, and they're stuck together at the edges. They make a ripping *squelch* as I pull them apart.

The first photo is a small black-and-white of a baby in a long, white, frilly dress and knitted bonnet, smiling out of a wicker baby carriage with gigantic wheels. A scrawling, handwritten label underneath says: *Celina, six months and three days.* There are several baby shots, some with her parents, I guess — Uncle Pat and Aunty Mary? — holding her with obvious love and pride. Small tears form at the corner of my eyes. This is too sad. All of them gone. How could such happiness end in such tragedy?

I work through the album, scanning the school pictures of unruly kids outside a small schoolhouse. I spot a girl with wild hair, who I imagine is Deb. I wonder which one is Celina and which is Suzie.

By sixth grade, the photos are in color, and I almost whoop when I see the wild hair is flaming red. Yes! It's Deb, for sure. Beside Deb stands a girl with a wide grin and a devilish sparkle in her eyes. Her hair is dark and curly, pulled back from her face with a white headband. Celina? I flip through to a color snapshot of a girl about thirteen in a crisp new school uniform standing on the front porch of this house. The caption reads: *First Day at Tallowood High, 1971.*

The resemblance is uncanny. I have a photo of me on my first day of high school that is just like this. I flip through the next pages, my heart thudding harder and harder with each page as I witness Celina growing up before my eyes.

The last photo is of three beaming girls, standing on the end of the dock, which is painted a glaring lime green. They're gleefully holding their fingers up to the camera in peace signs. *The Peace Sisters: January 1975.* The tallest wears a striped bikini with a white shirt thrown over it. Her orange hair is twirled on top of her head, and I identify her easily as Deb. Beside her is a girl with a shy smile, large floppy hat, and huge sunglasses. She is shorter than the other two and needs to stretch to sling her arms around the others' shoulders. Suzie, maybe?

Then my eyes lock on to the image of the girl on the right — Celina — and study the long, wavy hair, the round face and dark, almond eyes, the smattering of freckles across the nose, the slim shoulders and long, skinny limbs, the way she tilts her head to one side and tucks her thumb into the belt tab on her shorts. No wonder Deb got such a shock. I stare into Celina's eyes and feel as if I am gazing into my own.

With a sick feeling, I realize that there is no denying it: I *am* Celina's double.

As I let this sink in, the photo seems to come to life in my mind. I see the three friends jostling for space, wiggling and giggling, screeching when they nearly step off the back of the dock.

"Ow, that was my toe!" says Suzie with a laugh.

"What's your toe doing under my foot?" Deb shoots back, sticking out her tongue.

"Hurry up, Robbie!" cries Celina. "Take it, for God's sake, before these two drag me into the lake."

"Say cheese, girls." Robbie holds the camera to his eye and squints. "Come on, stop moving. It'll come out blurry."

"Cheese!" the girls all yell out.

The camera clicks, and the three friends fall into the water, creating a splash that swamps Robbie and his camera.

Celina climbs up the ladder and peeks her head over the edge of the dock. "Whoopsie," she says. "Hope the camera's all right, Robbie."

Robbie dries his camera on his T-shirt. "Me too," he says, frowning.

Suzie and Deb climb back up onto the dock. There's a lot of laughter, even from Robbie, who doesn't seem too concerned about the camera.

The group walks up a track worn through the front field. Robbie reaches for Celina's hand and she smiles up at him. The sun is shining and a soft breeze mutters through the poplars. The easy sound of someone playing guitar wafts down from the house.

"Dad," calls Celina, once they've reached the top of the

driveway, "can you get us some towels? Robbie pushed us off the dock." The girls roar with laughter.

"You mean, you fell in and the splash was so big that you wrecked my camera," counters Robbie, with a smile.

There is a feeling of enterprise about the house. A large vegetable garden takes up the space to the side of the barn, planks of wood stretch across trestles, pots of paint sit open on the garden table, and the smells of sawdust and fresh bread scent the air. The Norfolk pine doesn't yet reach the roofline.

Pat pushes himself out of the hammock strung from the porch rafters, puts down his guitar, and holds the stepladder steady beside the front door. "I bet you're all capable of getting towels yourselves," he says. His manner is relaxed and there is a calmness in the way he moves.

Mary climbs the stepladder, a thick blond braid snaking down her back. She carries a short length of decorated timber.

"What's that?" asks Deb, shaking the water free from her orange mane of hair.

Mary holds it up with pride. "Like it?" she asks. "I made it this morning."

"Karinya," Suzie reads the word that sits amid a wreath of painted flowers. "What does it mean?"

"Place of peace," says Mary. "Now that the house is finally finished, it's time it had a name, don't you think?" Mary places the sign above the door. "Is it centered?"

"Good enough," says Robbie. "But shouldn't it be next to the door?"

"Don't go there," says Pat. "My good woman here tells me we must walk under it, so that peace will pass over us each time we enter the house. And who am I to argue with such wonderful logic?"

Robbie? Karinya? Where did all this come from? I shake my head to free it from my overactive imagination and draw my knees up to my chest, my eyes darting around the room in search of answers. Why do I know these things? How do I know these things? I think back through the bits of information Deb told me. She didn't mention any Robbie or anything about the house being called Karinya. It's the same with how I knew about Deb and Suzie — I shouldn't have known.

"Why? How?" I ask the ceiling. But I close my mind to any answers. I push them away. I don't want to know. I slap the album closed and slide it and the notebook under my mattress.

An uncomfortable feeling invades me, and I recognize it for what it is.

Fear.

eight

It's overcast. The lake is as colorless as the sky.

At the breakfast table, Amelia attacks a piece of toast with a butter knife. Seth has his nose buried deep in a comic. Mom, hollow eyes downcast, stares into her mug of black coffee as if it contains some weary secret. Her toast lies untouched on the plate before her.

I slip *The Year in Design* magazine onto the table. "Thought you might be interested in this, Mom," I say, wondering if anyone will notice the quiver in my voice. My emotions are so jumbled. The visions, the things I shouldn't know, the unnerving connection to someone long dead are all tumbling around inside me.

Mom glances at the magazine and nods. "Oh, thanks." She doesn't even open it.

I feel like screaming. I can't bear the familiarity of this morning scene. So much for Mom's plan that a new life in a new house would help us heal. I am beyond disappointed.

"I bet the lake would be good for swimming," I say, desperate to distract myself from my own agitation. "Maybe we should go for a swim later?"

Amelia shovels sugar into her tea. "Have you *seen* the weather?" she says. Her spoon spins in violent circles around the teacup. "It's horrible. Oh, what a joy my life is."

I could joyfully strangle her.

I grab a banana and head back upstairs. I don't have the energy for this today; I can't cope with tiptoeing around my brittle family. I throw Celina's striped poncho over my head for warmth, fish the notebook out from under my mattress, and slip down the stairs and out the front door.

I need air, space around me, some time to think. I need to sort out what is going on and rid myself of this fluttery tension, the growing sensation of unease trapped inside my chest.

The morning sky hangs heavy with the threat of rain. It

matches my mood. I slide the notebook down inside the poncho and head north to a rocky outcrop, the beginning of the rugged cliffs that plummet into the water on this side of the lake. For the first time since we arrived, the lake is choppy, as if the breeze is giving it goose bumps. The whole place feels wild and alive.

I climb up a jagged mound of rocks and sit behind a small bush that has sprung up in a split in the stone. I pull out the notebook, the pages fluttering in the wind, and I read over what I wrote the night before. With each word, the swirling anxiety inside me only intensifies, so much so that when my phone beeps in my pocket, I almost jump out of my skin.

It's a message from Loni. There's been no signal back at the house, and I'm surprised to discover that I have full reception from this part of the lake.

Hey, Bails! What's happening? Miss you.

I have to reply. My fingers hover over the keys, wondering what I should say.

Hey, Loni. Guess what? Made a new friend. Too bad she's been dead for nearly forty years.

Or maybe something more to the point.

Hey, Lons. It's official: I've turned into a psycho.

Or the not so original:

I see dead people.

Instead, I settle for:

Miss you too. Service is sketchy. Will Skype as soon as we have internet set up. <3

Her reply is almost instant. *Make sure you do. A lot has happened in the 75 hours and 22 minutes since you left me. Have news. Big news. HUGE!*

I grin. That is so Loni. I do a mental countdown, knowing that Loni won't make it past five before she spills with the news. Ten, nine, eight, seven . . . *Beep.* Impressive — even for Loni.

Yolanda dumped Johno! YAAAAY!!!!! Happy dancing. He's gonna be mine. We must make plans.

I would love to be making plans with Loni right now.

Yay, you! Go Loni! I reply, and put my phone down, my heart aching.

A gust of wind makes the pages in the notebook flap so much, it looks poised to take flight. I get it under control and try to think back to my conversations with Deb, but my brain isn't interested. It veers off, and an unexpected image fills my mind.

Celina. She's sitting on the porch steps eating water-melon. It is sweet and juicy. Pink streams run through her fingers and down her arms. She is laughing hysterically . . .

Stop! I tell myself. Enough already.

I pick up my pencil and force myself to concentrate on the things *I* know, the things Deb told me. Maybe if I get it all down, I can be done with it. Then I can move on, forget about Celina O'Malley and forget the visions and the things I shouldn't know. Put a lid on my fear.

I start to write.

From a very early age, Celina had a great sense of herself: who she was and where she fitted in the world. Born to subsistence farming, green, hippie parents, she embraced the whole hippie scene. It suited her perfectly. And as best friends who adored her, Deb and Suzie couldn't help but be swept along by her enthusiasm and passion for peace and love and changing the world.

While most kids their age were embracing discos and mirror balls, the Peace Sisters gave up meat, became tree huggers, and sang Bob Dylan songs around a campfire by the lake.

Celina treasured life. That's why it's such a tragedy, such a waste, that her life was cut short, and why there is no way in the world that she would have taken her own life, no matter what anyone says. Deb was adamant about this.

Celina bubbled with love. She loved her family. She loved her friends. She even loved cockroaches and venomous spiders.

But most of all, I loved Robbie.

I? Robbie? Where did that come from?

I don't have time to think about how strange this is, and I stiffen my body to ready myself for another vision. But no vision this time — my pencil zeroes in back on the paper like a dart to a bull's-eye. The paper tears slightly, but I keep writing, my pencil scarily taking on a life of its own.

Robbie and I grew up together. He was born two months and three days before me, and our mothers became real close friends because of it. Apparently, we spent our first year lying side by side on a variety of rugs while our mothers worked together on a devious plan to try to inject some life into the boring old Country Women's Association. I can't remember any of this, of course. But all my earliest memories have him there somewhere. Mud pies and bee stings. Pillow forts and crayon coloring. Tea parties and tire swings. Endless swimming lessons and bike rides. It was always Robbie and me. Always.

That was until we were about nine years old and we were playing school in the barn, and for some reason, we decided to practice every swear word we could think of.

I don't know how it started, but once it did, we couldn't stop. and soon we were cracking up and yelling profanities at the top of our lungs. It didn't take long before Mom was standing at the barn door, hands on her hips.

Robbie skittered off home, and I got a bar of soap stuck in my mouth, which was pretty harsh punishment from my liberal-minded parents. For some reason, the whole escapade drove a wedge between us, and we barely spoke to each other for about six years. Silly, I know, but that's how it was.

Until the school picnic at the swimming pool at the end of tenth grade.

Robbie came and sat beside me on the edge of my towel. I had on my white knitted bikini and an orange shirt. My hair was tied back by the purple headscarf Deb gave me for my birthday.

"Hi," he said, and I noted that his voice had become deep and raspy.

I said hi back, and there was something in his eyes that changed everything . . .

I stop writing. I feel like I've had my breath knocked clean out of me. Damp with sweat, I've been clutching the pencil with such ferocity that my fingers are aching.

Where did that come from? Why am I writing in first person? As though I am Celina. As though I know what happened nearly four decades ago. Is this my wild imagination again?

Yes, yes! That has to be it, I tell myself. That *must* be it.

Must be.

Has to be.

Please let it be. Please.

But I know it's not.

I cast my eyes over the frantic scrawl filling the double page of my notebook. It's not even my handwriting.

nine

I'm standing on top of the rock, twitching, rocking from one foot to the other, not knowing what to do. A terrifying white noise rings in my ears. I can't think straight. I must be going psycho. Crazy. I have to be.

"It's that way," comes a voice from behind me. I jolt to a stop, my limbs prickling, too afraid to turn around.

"Take the path to your left." The voice again. Male. Vaguely familiar. I slowly swivel on the spot.

Bobbing in his kayak on the choppy water below me is Oliver, his oar resting across his lap. "Hi!" he says, grinning. His unexpected presence angers me.

"Stalker," I snap.

"Whoa, easy," says Oliver and holds up both hands in surrender.

"You've got no right to sneak up on me like that."

"Sorry. Thought you must be looking for the Circle, that's all."

I close my eyes and clutch the notebook against my stomach. I'm making an idiot of myself.

I attempt a smile. "Circle?" I say, but my voice is off.

Oliver looks bewildered. I can't blame him — my moods are as choppy as the lake.

"It's over there." He points toward the rocky cliffs a little farther along, then dips his oar in the water and starts to paddle off.

"Wait!" I yell out.

He stops, his boat pointing away from me. He doesn't bother to turn around.

I bite my lip. "Where is it exactly? This Circle?"

"There should be a path to your left; it will lead you straight there. You can't miss it." He looks over his shoulder, and his eyes are sharp like blades. "I'll meet you there, if you want. Unless that's too stalker-ish for you."

Too flustered to think straight, I find myself nodding. "Thanks."

I climb down from my perch on shaky legs. The path is narrow. Spiky branches reach out from either side, touching each other, and I can't be sure that I haven't strayed off into the bush somewhere. I feel so raw, so confused. I strike out at the branches that block my way and flick me in the face as I stomp through. What am I doing?

The air becomes thick with the smell of damp earth, when finally, the vegetation thins and the path leads into a narrow chasm, a rocky passageway of sorts. Shadowy and dank, the rock walls are mildewy and stained with lichen. They soar up to the gray sky above. It is just wide enough to walk through, and at one point I need to turn sideways to fit. I dip under overhanging rocks, shrug off some hanging vines, and then step onto a stone platform — and out into another world.

Before me lies a tranquil lagoon, cut off almost completely from the rest of the lake by towering cliffs, streaked orange and yellow. I stop for a moment, too stunned by the unexpected beauty of it to move.

"Wow," I manage as Oliver negotiates the narrow opening to the lagoon from the lake.

"Told you it was awesome." Oliver's voice echoes off the cliffs and whirls around me. He paddles across to where I stand and jumps out of the kayak. He splashes through knee-deep water, then clambers up the rocks. I can't help but notice the confident, fluid way he moves.

"What is this place?" I ask.

"Some kind of ancient geological fault — a sink hole, or something like that."

"Wow," I say again.

"I don't have a clue, to be honest. But it's pretty cool, huh?"

"I didn't know it was even here."

"Not many people do."

Oliver sits on the ledge. I join him, sitting awkwardly with my legs crossed. I'm still holding the notebook tight against me.

"Sorry about before," I say. "You scared the crap out of me."

"You were pretty scary yourself."

I hang my head, embarrassed.

"Forget it." He slides off the rock into the water, and gazes up at the cliffs around him. "You do a mean crazy eyes, though." He opens his eyes wide and pulls a freaky sort of face at me that makes me laugh.

He cups his hands over his mouth and yells: "Watch out for crazy eyes." The words bounce around the cliff walls and come echoing back to us: *Watch out for crazy eyes . . . crazy eyes . . . crazy eyes.*

Now I'm giggling.

"Try it," says Oliver.

I shake my head.

"Come on. It's a rule."

"A rule?"

"Yep. You have to make a noise. Anything. Burp "Twinkle Twinkle Little Star," if you have to. Fart. I don't care. Just make a goddamn noise." Oliver whistles, claps his hands, and shouts a loud, "Yahoo!"

I slide the notebook under my backside and cup my hands. "Canoeing stalker," I call.

"It's a kayak. Get it right, crazy eyes."

"Kayaking stalker," I try to shout it. But I am so full of nerves, it comes out crackly.

"Is that the best you can do? Maybe it's that blanket thing you're wearing. It's probably sapping all your energy or something. Take it off and try again."

I narrow my eyes at him. "It's a poncho, for your information, and I'm not falling for that one." And before he can reply, I let loose an enormous, "KAYAKING STALKER!" It's so loud that even the echo shouts back at us, and we both burst out laughing.

"STALKER."

"CRAZY EYES."

Our words ricochet from cliff to cliff and ping around us until we are enclosed in a pinball game of rebounding "crazy eyes" and "kayaks" and "stalkers" and our own sidesplitting laughter.

Oliver stops abruptly. "That is very uncool."

"What?"

"Laughing at my laugh."

"I am not," I say. A small chuckle escapes from the side of my mouth, because his laugh is pretty funny — high-pitched and jerky and almost girlish. "Really."

Oliver raises his eyebrows at me. "Lying is also very uncool, crazy eyes." And we both melt with laughter again. "And so is wearing a blanket."

"Poncho," I counter.

A silence settles over us, but inside I am buzzing. I'm hanging out with Oliver — messing around, having fun.

"What were you doing up there on that rock?" Oliver asks after a while.

"Uh . . . nothing." Tension creeps back into my chest. "What are you training for?" I say to avoid giving a real answer. "The King of the Kayak cup, or something?"

Oliver gets a steely look in his eyes. His jaw juts out with determination. "The Sydney University row team next year.

The Olympics, eventually." He says it as if he is already on the team, that there is no doubt he'll make it. It reminds me of my own similar ambitions — ambitions that were left behind at the starting line the day Dad smashed his head and died. I'm surprised at the bitterness I feel. Or is it envy of Oliver who still has everything?

"You're sure of yourself," I say.

"Hey, if I don't believe I can do it, who will? And then why bother? It's those other doubters who need convincing — and you can't listen to them. Otherwise, when you're racing, all you can hear is them squawking in your ear. You know, telling you you're a loser. Then you're done, and you *are* a loser. Literally. Don't you think?"

"Yep. Good to aim high, I guess."

"Shoot for the moon, and if you miss, you'll end up in the stars." Oliver springs to his feet. "That's what Mom always says, anyway."

"Deep. I like it."

Another silence envelops us, and I try to summon the courage to broach the subject of my brush with that man the other night. "You get out on the lake a lot," I say lightly. "Anyone else use it much?"

"Nah. There's no public access."

This shocks me. "Really? No one?"

"Yeah. That's why hardly anyone knows about The Circle. Why?"

I hesitate. I don't want to sound like an idiot again. "I saw a man the other night — late. He rowed right over to our property."

Oliver shrugs his shoulders. "I guess it could have been Grandpa. Or Dad. How late was it?"

"Very. About one in the morning."

"One? Definitely wouldn't be Dad. Grandpa's a bit eccentric, but I doubt even he would be out at that hour. You sure you weren't dreaming?"

"I'm sure. What do you mean by eccentric?"

"He's an artist. They're all a little wacky, aren't they?"

"I guess."

"Well then I suppose it must have been Grandpa," Oliver says. "He's a harmless old guy, though. Don't let it worry you. It's pretty safe around here."

I resist the urge to bring up Celina. Why is it that everyone feels so safe in a place where something so terrible happened? I can't work it out, but at least there is some reassurance in my sinister stranger probably being Oliver's wacky grandfather. But oddly, I don't feel reassured at all. I feel tense.

"I better start heading back home." I push myself to my

feet. As I do, my foot kicks the notebook and sends it flying across the rocks toward the water. I yelp and give chase.

Oliver lunges for it and grabs it just before it plops into the lagoon. He raises it in the air with both hands. "How's that?" he shouts, and his words come echoing back.

"Give it to me!" I yell frantically.

Give it to me . . . give it to me . . . to me, the echo bobbles around me, mocking me. Tears fill my eyes.

Oliver mumbles something under his breath.

"Give it to me. Please. Now."

Now . . . now . . . now.

"Keep your pants on."

Pants on . . . Pants on . . . Pants on . . .

I snatch the book out of his hands, aware how strange my actions must seem. "Thanks," I hiss. "I've got to go."

To go . . . to go . . . to go . . . The words chase after me as I make my escape.

I truly am an idiot.

ten

The last things to go back into the peace chest are the silver hoop earrings. I hate taking them off, but they have to go. Things are getting way out of hand; I can't go on like this. Up on that rock, writing as though I was channeling the ghost of Celina O'Malley was unnerving, and I am acting like a crazy person.

I give the chest a long hard look. "You!" I whisper at it. "It all started with you. Damn you." *Incredible.* I am talking to a wooden box. It's time to end all this nonsense, once and for all. Sever ties with the long dead.

I close the lid and secure the clasp, and I am overcome with sheer and absolute relief. Phew. Now I can forget about Celina O'Malley, can regain my sanity.

But what to do with the silver notebook? I look at it for a moment, then I slip it under my mattress. I'll deal with it later. Perhaps a ceremonial burning might be in order. The thought brings a grin to my face.

In one of the still unpacked plastic bags full of clothes, I find my swimsuit. The wind and gray skies have vanished, and the afternoon has become steamy. I really need a swim after all this; it's the perfect way to cleanse myself of Celina.

Celina . . .

My eyes lock on the chest; my mind conjures up the photo of Celina on the dock. Was the knitted bikini in the photo the same as the one in the chest? I wonder. The thought intrigues me — I should check it out. Maybe try it on . . .

I take a step toward the chest and reach for the bronze clasp.

No! I tell myself. *Stop this.* But like an addict, I'm drawn and consumed with a deep, almost tortured, longing that is overriding any kind of rational thought.

It's as if the wooden chest is luring me, urging me to open it — daring me, almost. *Open me up. Look inside. Come on, just for a second. It won't hurt.*

I press my fingernails into my scalp to stop the turmoil inside — to stop these stupid, stupid thoughts. I really am going crazy.

The chest has to go. That's all there is to it. I grab one end before I can change my mind and drag it out into the hall.

"Hey, what are you doing?" Mom is hopping down the hallway, buttoning up her blouse and pulling on a black shoe at the same time. Seth is following, right on her heels.

"Putting this in the barn or somewhere."

"Oh no you don't. The barn is full of trash, and the builders will be here tomorrow. They don't need to be tripping over something else. Back to your room with it, thank you very much." The words come out at a hundred miles per hour. Mom jams her blouse into her pants with frantic fingers and then twirls on the spot. "What do you think? The Wok and Roll called. They want me to do a shift tonight."

The pants are way too big. Scarcely gripping her hips, they sag around her backside, and I'm reminded once again of how much weight Mom has lost.

"You look great," I lie, and continue dragging the chest down the hall. I am determined to get it as far away from my bedroom as possible. Now. This minute.

"Bayley, what part of 'take the chest back into your room' didn't you understand?" Mom turns to follow me and almost trips over Seth. "Watch out, Seth. Please, give me some room, for goodness sake."

"I'll put it out in the back somewhere. Out of the way, don't worry."

"No. Not outside in this weather. Gran needs to see it first. Leave it in your room for now. I don't have time for this, Bayley. Here, take Seth down to the lake or something, will you? I need to get organized."

"No," says Seth and clutches Mom's leg like a two year old. "I don't want to."

"Go on, buddy. It's a beautiful afternoon." Mom tries to pry open Seth's grip. "Please let go. I have a lot to do."

"What time are you leaving?" he asks.

"Around four." Mom lumbers back toward her room, Seth still attached.

"What time will you be home?"

"I'm not sure. When you're asleep . . ."

Their voices fade as I heave the chest back into my room.

I stand hunched over it, wiping the moisture from under my nose. Frustration and anger and confusion run like molten lava through my veins, and I kick at the stinking thing, stubbing my big toe.

The pain is welcome.

* * *

Sitting at the end of the dock, my bare feet dangling over the edge, I tune into the lapping of the water, the buzz of a dragonfly skimming the surface beneath my feet, the crackle of a breeze through the reeds jutting into the middle of the lake. Even with Amelia flapping around, pretending she's an Olympic swimmer, the lake is wonderfully peaceful. I will my mind to rest, to mirror the lake's tranquility. But it refuses. It churns with thoughts of Celina.

Where did you disappear to, Celina? Is your body out there somewhere, rotting in the bush? At the bottom of the lake? What would a body look like after forty years of decomposition? A skull? A few bare bones? I give a shudder.

I scan the cliffs to the north of the lake. The gully beyond the cliffs is thick with wild scrub and leads off to nowhere. I try to distinguish where the entrance to The Circle is, and my cheeks flush as I'm reminded of how much of a fool I made of myself there. All because of Celina — the presence that won't leave me. She may have been a peace-loving hippie chick, but she doesn't seem to want to give *me* any peace.

I slap at a fly that is intent on resting on my lips and flop onto my back. It's too hot! How could the weather change so radically in one day? It's almost eight and nearly dark, but the air is still thick and burning.

Amelia splashes her way to the dock and climbs up the rickety steel ladder on the side. "Not quite as good as back home, but better than a cold shower, I guess." Wrapping her towel around her, she lies on her back beside me as she takes heaving breaths. "Whoa, that was exhausting."

"You were only in there for a few minutes."

"We're not all fitness freaks like you, ya know. Most of the world doesn't just go running for hundreds of bloody miles every week for fun."

I feel like I've been stung by a scorpion. Could Amelia really be that wrapped up in herself that she hasn't noticed I haven't even put on my running shoes, let alone run anywhere, since Dad died? I slide my hand across my stomach. It is soft and squishy and I silently mourn the loss of my six-pack, that hard ripple of strong stomach muscles. I probably couldn't run more than ten steps without wheezing.

Amelia throws her arms onto the dock and stretches out like a star. "Mom thinks she's so smart," she says, "thinks this place is going to make a difference. Well, it's not. It's gonna kill me — even with this lake."

"We know," I say.

Amelia ignores me. "God, I need a drink."

"Go get one. And see if you can drag Seth away from the TV while you're there."

"I'm not talking about lemonade, idiot." She lets out an exasperated sigh. "You're so immature, Bayley."

"Yeah, and getting smashed every Saturday night is real mature."

"What would you know?"

I give up. "Whatever."

Amelia's phone lights up on the pile of clothes beside her. She sits up and grins as she reads the message, holding the screen well away from my line of vision. She taps in a reply and then rolls onto her back. "What?" she says to me, her tone accusatory.

"I just didn't know there's coverage out here," I say.

"I only found out yesterday."

I roll my eyes. "There's coverage farther around the lake too. It's annoying how sketchy it is."

Amelia looks up quickly from her phone. "Don't tell Mom."

"Why not?"

"There's no need, is there? Besides, I'd rather she didn't know."

Yeah, that's not suspicious.

"You're up to something."

"Get over yourself. What could I possibly be up to? I may as well be locked up in prison. I only want to text my friends without Mom's suspicious eyes always following me, that's all."

Sure, Amelia. I don't trust my sister one bit.

"Hey, look. First star," Amelia says, pointing to the sky above. "See it?"

"No," I say, my eyes searching, aware of Amelia distracting me.

"Right there, pinhead. Right in front. The wish star. Quick, make a wish! Before others appear."

The wish star. What to wish for? For Dad never to have run out onto the back patio in the rain to get Seth's dumb Batman toy? For the last eight months to never have happened? For the disturbing visions in my head to vanish like Celina? For Oliver to think that acting like an idiot is sexy and cool?

Amelia cups her hands over her mouth and yells to the sky, "I wish I could get out of this hole!" She flips onto her stomach. "No wonder that Celina chick disappeared. Who wouldn't want to get away from this place? I mean, it's *so* boring. Dead boring. I bet Celina felt it too — bet she ran away to the Cross or something, and the family was so filled with O'Malley shame that they made it sound like some big tragic mystery."

Something about what Amelia says sends needles up my arms. I run her words back through my head. Did Celina hate this place, like Amelia? I haven't considered this; my visions have always shown Celina living a charmed hippie-chick life. I cast my mind back to the things Deb told me. No — there was no mention of anything but Celina loving her life, loving the lake, the house, and her family. But what if Deb isn't remembering it right? What if she's making Celina's life seem wonderful, when really it was far from it? What if there are things that Deb never knew about?

I contemplate this, staring up into the darkening sky, watching as more and more little stars pierce through.

Amelia's phone beeps again and this time the message makes her hiss with an excited "Yes!" She jumps to her feet, gathers up her things, and starts charging down the dock.

"Hey, where are you going?" I yell.

"I've got stuff to do," Amelia replies. "Besides, it's getting dark, and someone should be inside keeping an eye on Seth, shouldn't they?"

A knot tightens in my stomach. When has Amelia ever thought about anyone but herself? Whatever she's up to, it can't be good.

eleven

I can't sleep. Even with three heavy packing boxes filled with books and trophies and school stuff stacked on top of the chest, the pull of what's inside it is so strong. The temptation to open it still burns fierce within me.

I fling a large old blanket I found in the laundry over the towering heap.

There, that should do it. Out of sight, out of mind.

But I'm fooling myself in more ways than one, because I'm the one who is out of their mind. That's a certainty. Even with the chest closed, I know Celina hasn't gone away.

I lie in bed, restless and tormented, the insistent croaks of the frogs in the lake driving me insane — a loud reminder of how strange and unfamiliar this place is.

I long for the sounds of my old life: the swish of passing traffic, Mrs. Jolson's squealing opera singing next door, the thump and roar of the distant surf, even Amelia's breathy snore. Anything to block out the frogs and fill my mind with something other than Celina O'Malley. I got it so wrong this morning at the lake; Oliver isn't the stalker, Celina is.

I thrust a pillow over my head, just as a sharp creak sounds from downstairs. I sit upright. What was that? Is Mom home already? I glance at my phone — it's not even ten. Way too early. Mom had said she wouldn't be home until midnight at the earliest. Regardless, I strain to hear Mom's footsteps. But there are no footsteps, only the front door groaning followed by the click of it shutting. Then nothing.

My thoughts fly back to the night of the stranger. I catapult out of bed, dragging my blanket onto the floor behind me, and scamper to Amelia's room. I pull open the door.

"Amel—" Her bed is empty. I rush to the window, just in time to catch sight of her jogging down the driveway and around the corner toward the gate.

Great. Just great.

I tiptoe down the hall. I don't want to disturb Seth; it took me almost an hour and a dozen stories before he settled down enough to sleep. But once I'm past his room, I speed down the stairs and out the door in pursuit of my sister.

Amelia is already out of sight. The sky is clear, the moon one slice off full, and I am surprised at how well I can see. I make my way down the driveway, through the open gate, and onto the dirt road. I can hear soft voices. Several. And laughter. A car door is clicked shut. I race down the road. Up ahead, a white sedan is parked at the edge of the road, partly obscured by scrubby bushes. A group of four or five people is huddled around it.

"Amelia!" I shout.

"It's my sister." I can hear Amelia's rough whisper. A cigarette is flung to the road and ground out. A door is opened and something thrown onto the seat. There is a lot of giggling.

Amelia breaks from the group and charges up to me. She stinks of cigarette smoke, and the lousy thief is wearing a row of my red bangles up her arm. "You following me now?" she demands.

"What are you doing with my bracelets?" I snarl.

"You followed me out here to ask me that?"

"Where are you going?" I say, the words an accusation. "Who are they?"

"Friends. We're hanging out for a bit. Nothing to get so upset about."

I tug at the edges of my thin tank top, dragging it down as low as possible. I'm suddenly aware that I am almost naked, dressed only in the tank top and undies.

"Don't run away." I say the words before I've even realized I've thought them, and the fear of the possibility rises up my throat. "It will kill Mom. Don't do it."

Amelia rolls her eyes. "I'm not running away, moron. Just having some fun. Now go home."

"Don't do this to Mom." I'm pleading.

"I'm not doing anything to Mom. She's the one who's doing all this to me. Besides, she'll only know if you tell. It's all up to you, Bayley." She takes a few steps toward the car, before turning and adding in a softer voice, "I'll be home before Mom gets back. I promise. They're passing through on their way up the coast to a music festival. They've only come to say hi."

"Promise you'll come back."

"Promise — as long as you don't tell."

I hesitate and chew at my lip.

"Tell Mom and *I'll* tell her about the sick story you're writing in that book under your mattress. You are seriously deranged, Bayley." Amelia's smile is nothing short of cruel.

Confident she has secured my silence, she races down to the car and slides onto the backseat.

The car makes a quick U-turn and disappears down the road in an explosion of dust.

I'm hit by a hefty dose of reality. Nothing has changed. Nothing is going to change. We are stuck on the same path as we were before, and there's no way off it.

I walk back down the road. I don't know if I have ever felt so alone.

twelve

Over the whine of electric saws and the relentless punch of nail guns, there's a crunch of gravel under tires, a honk of a horn, and a "Where is everyone?"

"Gran!" I cry, bolting from the barn to the car. I throw my arms around my grandmother's neck before she is even out of her seat. "Mom didn't tell us you were coming."

"Your mother is full of surprises, isn't she?" She locks eyes on Mom, who is hovering alongside me.

Gran embraces Mom. Mom clutches onto Gran fiercely

and buries her head in Gran's neck and shoulder, choking up. Some tears well up in my own eyes.

Gran breaks free and rubs Mom's back. "Now, what does someone have to do to get a cup of tea around here?" Mom relaxes, and she and Gran walk arm in arm up to the front steps. "Look at this place, will you?" Gran says and waves her free arm around. "It's been a while, I tell you. But that lake — it never stops being special, does it?"

"Gran!" Seth bursts out the front door, his cape flying. He launches himself at our grandmother.

"Hey, careful," warns Mom. "You'll knock poor Gran over."

"He's fine, Kath," says Gran. She grabs Seth and carries him under her arm like a roll of carpet. "I'm not as frail as you say I am. Besides, this scrawny runt is lighter than old Tinky." She tickles Seth's feet. "Hey, don't they feed you around here?"

"Only scraps," Seth yells, giggling and kicking his legs about wildly. "And birdseed."

"How long are you staying?" I ask.

"Not sure. Till you lot drive me crazy, I suppose."

"Really?" I say. I'm very suspicious. Not because Gran isn't a big part of our family, but because she is so devoted to the

Soup Van and her "regular suspects," as she likes to call them, that she can rarely get away for more than a couple of hours at a time. "What about Arnold and Missy Moo and the others you take care of? How are they are going to cope?"

Gran doesn't answer, she just winks and continues lugging Seth under her arm. "You've got quite a crowd working here, Kath. The place is scrubbing up well."

"Hi, Gran." Amelia stands meekly on the porch. I'm astounded that she's up and dressed already — and not appearing even remotely hungover.

"Hi, sweetheart," says Gran, her voice soft. She puts the squealing Seth down and pecks Amelia on the cheek. "This country air must be agreeing with you. You're prettier than ever."

I wait for the usual thorny reply, but when all I hear is a soft, "Thanks, Gran," followed by an over-excited Seth dragging Gran inside, I feel relieved and grateful that the Soup Van can do without her for a while. Gran is exactly what we need.

I take a step to follow the others inside. But there is a hand on my shoulder and a voice right behind me saying, "Uh . . . Bayley . . ."

Whirling around, I discover Oliver standing right behind me.

"Whoa, sorry," says Oliver. "I didn't mean to scare you again. I yelled your name, but with the saws and Batman squealing and . . ."

I gulp and steady myself, straining not to think about my stupid behavior yesterday, and I caution myself to steer clear of making eye contact with those greenish-blue pools.

"My grandma's here," I explain.

"Oh, I . . . is your mom around?"

"Oh, yeah. Um, come inside." I rush up the steps and into the house, as if fleeing from a grizzly bear. I am a lunatic.

Oliver follows.

"Oliver!" Seth jumps off Gran's knee to circle around and around him. "This is my grandma."

"Hey." Oliver gives a small wave.

"Call me Maree, dear," says Gran.

Mom is filling the kettle. "Hi there, Oliver. Would you like some tea?"

"Have one," says Seth. "Pleeeease."

Oliver seems uncertain. His eyes flit around the room until they rest on Amelia.

"Hi, Oliver," says Amelia, smoothly. She reaches into the cupboard and pulls out some cups.

"Hey," says Oliver. "How's it going, Amelia?"

My face burns. When did these two meet?

Mom is similarly puzzled. "Oh, I didn't know you two knew each other."

Oliver holds his hair back off his face with both hands. It's clear he's uncomfortable. "Yeah . . . uh . . . we met —"

"In town," Amelia finishes for him.

In town? When? The other day when Amelia went missing for hours? Something's obviously going on here. I think back to last night — to the white car and the group huddled outside. Amelia said it was her friends from Cronulla on the way to a festival, but why would they come out this way? It didn't sound convincing last night and it seems even less so now. Was Oliver in that car? With me in my underwear on the road, acting like a moron? The thought makes my heart plummet.

Has Amelia hooked up with him already? I turn to leave.

"Where are you off to?" asks Gran.

"Oh, you know, better get back to it. There're boxes to move and stuff. The builders need the barn cleared." I swing my arms like the village fool and take a few faltering steps backward as I speak. *Get back to it? Boxes to move?* I sound like such an idiot.

"Yeah," says Oliver, and for a moment I worry that I've broadcast my thoughts somehow and that Oliver is agreeing with me. "Yeah, I have to go too," he continues, to my enormous relief. "Thanks, anyway. But Mom asked me to row across and see if you guys would like to come over this weekend for a barbecue. She's going to ask the Ralphs as well. She would have called, but she doesn't know your name . . ." He reaches into his pocket and pulls out an envelope. "Anyway, she said to give you this. It has our phone number and everything."

Mom takes the envelope. She pushes her hair behind her ears. "Why, thanks . . . Oliver. That is . . . so . . . kind. But . . ." Her voice is shaky.

"Tell your mom that we'd love to come," says Gran. "Kath will give her a call later. Won't you, Kath?"

Mom stares at the envelope and eases herself onto one of the kitchen chairs.

"Kath?"

"Huh? Oh, yes, yes — I'll call as soon as the phone's working. It's not connected yet, and we don't have any cell phone coverage . . . hopefully we will by this afternoon."

"Great. Okay, thanks." Oliver backs away, and we clatter out and down the front steps together.

Stop being an idiot, I tell myself, all too late as I stumble on the last step and do an embarrassing trying-to-keep-your-balance dance involving flailing arms and bendy legs.

"Whoa." Oliver reaches out to catch me.

I manage to dodge his grasp, regain my footing, and walk on like nothing happened. I slip into the barn, saying, "Gotta start moving those boxes. See you."

Oliver pauses outside the barn, then nods and says, "Yeah, okay. See you Saturday, I guess." He heads off to the lake.

I prop myself up against the barn wall, sure my unsteady legs will give out at any moment.

thirteen

Now pretty much empty, the barn is a great hollow space — almost cathedral-like with its high ceiling and strips of afternoon sun slicing in through the gaps in the boards. Sitting cross-legged in the middle of the dirt floor, I am overwhelmed by it.

I'm beat. Grimy. Gross. Stinky. My body aches from hours of hard work, and I crave a shower. If only I had the energy to get up.

I flop back and gaze at the patches of blue peeping at me through the roof, too tired to care that my hair is resting in a pile of swept-up crap.

Exhaustion: I know you well. There's nothing like throwing yourself into work to keep your mind off your troubles. That's something I've learned over the past months. *Bayley Anderson, Family Workhorse and Resident Maid.* Though in all honesty, I know that I've pursued the role — it's been my survival tactic.

But now, stretched out here, dead tired, my worries come rushing back in: looping, rotating, and flicking from one worry to the other inside my head.

Celina. Dad. Mom. Oliver. Oliver and Amelia.

Oliver and Amelia. Was it jealousy that made me work like a demon? What's there to be jealous about? Every time I've seen Oliver, I've either acted like a complete jerk or a total idiot. If Oliver is interested in Amelia, who could blame him? Besides, who would want to hang out with some crazy girl who believes the ghost of Celina O'Malley is communicating with her?

For God's sake, brain, shut up! Give me a rest.

I close my eyes and command my mind to be still, but a new thought nudges its way in. My eyes shoot open.

Mom. The barn. Mom and the barn.

And it seems so obvious.

This place oozes with possibility, begs for creativity. I sit up and look around. On my feet now, I walk to the far end, lean up against the wall, and take it all in. Yes. It's perfect. Fix the barn up and make it into a studio, and Mom won't have any excuses. She will have to start designing again, start playing around with the things she loves the most: color and light and beauty. How could she not be inspired here? She thrived on it before, and she can again. I know it. And as soon as she starts to be her old self again, everything will settle down. Order will be restored, and maybe I might be a little less insane.

It all seems so simple, and a tiny seed of hope wedges into my heart, giving me renewed energy. I drag a box of garbage into one corner and pick up the broom. I kick a few rotting boards out of my way. One flips over. It's a wooden sign of some sort, covered in thick grime. I use the end of my T-shirt to wipe it clean.

Karinya.

The sign tumbles out of my hands and clatters to the ground. *Karinya. Karinya.* The word ricochets around in my head, and then I see it. That vision. Robbie and Mary talking. Mary hanging a sign above the door. Karinya. Peaceful place.

I am feeling anything but peaceful. I pick up the sign, and the whole scene replays for me. I hear Pat strumming his guitar and giving Mary instructions. I see Celina, Deb, and Suzie, all dripping wet, begging Pat to get towels for them.

Robbie wipes his camera and worries about his lens getting damaged by the splash of water.

"Bayley! Come here for a moment!" Mom's voice drifts across the yard, pulling me back to the barn. "Bails!"

With unsteady hands, I turn the sign over, wondering what to do with it.

"Bails!"

"Okay! I'm coming." I dash off across the driveway, leave the sign by the front door, and make it up the stairs in four huge bounds. My head is swirling.

There is a commotion coming from my bedroom: loud cursing mixed with shrieking laughter and a sound like air whooshing out of a giant balloon.

Mystified, I slowly open my door. Mom and Gran are both on the floor giggling like school kids, a large inflatable air mattress bucking on the floor between them.

"Wretched thing!" wheezes Gran, giving the mattress a kick.

"Careful. Don't put a hole in it," Mom says. She slaps down Gran's foot. "Or you'll be sleeping on the floor, and we'll have to listen to you complain about your poor old joints."

"Careful, you," warns Gran.

The sight before me is unexpected. I can't remember

when I last heard Mom actually laugh. I smile — perhaps Gran's presence is already having an impact. I hang back, not wanting to intrude.

"Bails!" Gran calls out.

I step into the doorway. "What's going on?"

Gran leans on her knees and pulls herself up with a sigh. "This stupid self-pumping mattress isn't behaving. Can you give us a hand?"

My eyes move around the room. There's Gran's suitcase and purse, a basket full of her odds and ends, her pillow, a toiletry bag, and car keys.

"Gran's going to bunk with you for a couple of days," says Mom. "But I can't believe your room is such a mess. You spent all day in that old barn, yet you haven't unpacked a thing here."

There's gratitude for you.

"What on earth have you been doing up here?"

Believe me, Mom, you don't want to know.

"Could you move some of this stuff off the floor? Give Gran a bit of room?" Mom points to the mound of boxes on top of the chest. "And what is going on here?" She whips off the blanket and frowns at me, waiting for an answer. "It's like the Leaning Tower of Pisa, Bails. You're lucky it hasn't come tumbling down on you, or that Seth hasn't knocked it over."

I tense up. My eyes latch onto the peace chest.

Gran follows my gaze. She stares at the chest, a quizzical expression on her face. Then she pales and grabs the side of my bed to steady herself. "Oh, my," she says. "Is that what I think it is?" She takes a hesitant step toward the chest. It's strange to see my always-in-control Gran appear this intimidated. This is the woman who drives around the inner city in the middle of the night feeding the homeless.

"Yes, I think it is," says Mom. "It's full of Celina's things."

"Celina's? The peace chest? It can't be — we took that with us when we cleaned the place out. I remember packing it up with some of Celina's things — keepsakes, you know. I can't believe we left it behind." Gran looks me squarely in the eyes. "Have you opened it, Bayley?"

My nod is barely perceivable, and I wonder how Gran will react when she hears that I've been wearing Celina's clothes.

"What are these boxes doing piled on top?" asks Mom. "Really, Bayley. It's ridiculous."

Gran sighs. "Suppose I should peek inside."

I shiver.

"Come on, Bayley. Move those boxes for me, will you? They look pretty heavy." When I don't move, Mom adds, "What's up, Bails?"

"It creeps me out."

"Really? It creeps you out?" says Mom. "You've been wearing Celina's clothes since we got here. Didn't seem to bother you then. Come on. Give me a hand."

"You've been wearing her clothes?" Gran's tone is spiky. "I hope you've been treating Celina's things with respect, Bayley. They hold a lot of memories. They're not playthings."

I feel humiliated. "I wasn't playing. I . . . I . . . like them. They fit me perfectly. I —" I stop, not trusting myself to go on without revealing too much. The discovery of that sign is still making me reel.

I shrug and then lug the boxes onto the floor in the hall. The peace chest stands uncovered and alone against my wall, and I feel equally exposed. I flip open the lid. The colorful contents blaze at me as if seizing the moment of escape. A shiver runs up my spine, and the room feels charged with a strange electricity.

"Wow, I can't believe it," says Gran. She reaches out and runs her fingers across the pool of fabrics. "And you've been wearing these?"

I nod.

"Sorry, Bayley, but I don't think that's right."

I bristle. "There's a whole lot that isn't right about Celina," I say, feeling trapped and foolish and unexpectedly angry. "Like, why is this chest even here? How could you leave it behind and not realize it? Especially if Celina meant so much to you."

"Bayley, watch your tone," cautions Mom. "Don't talk about things you don't understand."

"That's just it," I say. "I don't understand." I shove my hand into the chest and rummage around until my fingers find the photo album. I flick through the pages then thrust the album at Gran.

"Hey, be careful with that," says Gran.

"Why didn't you tell me?"

"Tell you? Tell you what? What are you talking about?" Gran takes a step back, slips her glasses on, and peers down at the photo. "What's this about, Bails?"

I stab at the photo of Celina on her first day at high school. "I look exactly like her. Exactly." I flip the page over, and the next and the next. "Why didn't you ever say anything?"

Gran sinks onto my bed. She studies the photos, then looks up at me with glassy eyes. "I didn't realize," she says. "Both you and Amelia have always been more O'Malley than Anderson, but I hadn't realized that the resemblance with Celina was this strong."

Mom drifts across to peer over Gran's shoulder. "Whoa. That's amazing."

I am close to tears. "How could you not know, not realize? I'm like her twin or something, and I never knew." My voice rises, packed with emotion. "It's all such a big horrible secret. No one ever talks about what happened. Not really anyway. All anyone will say is that she disappeared and that she was never found, and then her parents were killed in a car accident a few years after. No details. Only the O'Malley death stare if you dare to bring it up. The house gets cleared out and boarded up for almost forty years, and no one in the family seems to think any of this is strange. No one. There's not even any photos of them anywhere, Gran. You have photos of the whole family on that wall of yours at home, but none of Celina and her parents. Why?"

I drop to the floor, draw my legs up to my chest, and wrap my arms around them. I know I've been ranting and that I've lost my temper for no good reason.

Gran and Mom seem too shocked to answer. They examine the photo album in silence.

Finally, Gran shuts the album with purpose. "You have no idea what it was like, young lady." Her mouth is tight, her shoulders tense. "It was a very dark time for the whole family. It nearly killed your grandfather. And it was in our faces all the time — everywhere we went: in the papers, on the

TV, the radio, in the sympathetic expressions of our friends and neighbors. There was no relief, not for a minute. After a while, it gets to you, Bayley. It really gets to you."

Gran's agitation vibrates through me. She gets up and walks to the window, parts the curtains, and peers out. "I don't know if you realize," she says more to the lake than to me, the tiny crystals dangling from her ears glinting in the mellow light, "but Celina was more than a niece to us. We were close — she was almost like another daughter. And when Pat and Mary died, it was the last straw. It had been heartbreaking enough for your grandpa to watch his favorite little brother and his beautiful wife suffer so much, trying to come to terms with something too terrible even to contemplate . . . then for them to die in such tragic circumstances, well, it was more than we could bear. Grandpa collected up the photos and articles and other little keepsakes and put them all in a special box in the trophy cabinet. He couldn't stand having them stare at him all the time. We came up here and sent everything off to a charity — it's what Pat and Mary would have wanted. But the house was loaded with too many painful memories, and that's why we boarded it up and abandoned it. I wanted to sell it — but your grandfather couldn't. Is that enough information for you?"

Gran turns to face me. "I know you've had your fair share

of tragedy, Bayley, but that doesn't give you the excuse to take it out on me like that."

I hold back my tears. I want to say that it has nothing to do with Dad, nothing to do with what we have been through. That it has everything to do with the hammering in my head that's telling me that for some reason, Celina is communicating with me. And I don't know why, or what to do. But I clamp my lips and hug my legs tighter.

"I think I'll go for a walk," says Gran. "Check out that lake." She leaves the album on my bed, steps over the air mattress, and pushes past me. She is close to tears, and I feel like a bitch.

Mom slips past me without a saying a word. She's also ready to bawl.

Well done, Bayley. Proud of yourself? I kick out at the chest and the lid slams shut with a resounding thud.

fourteen

I have to face it. Celina O'Malley has become an obsession.

It's middle-of-the-night still, and I close the kitchen door behind me, turn on the light, place my laptop on the table, and boot it up. The curtains puff in the wind, making me jump. I yank down the window. I am so edgy these days.

I type "Celina O'Malley" and "missing persons" into Google, partly amazed that we actually have an internet connection. Numerous hits come up.

I click on the first link. It's the local police website. I scroll down the page until there, right before me, in stark black-and-white, is a photo of a serious-looking Celina with the caption: *Celina O'Malley, missing since April 7, 1975. Age 16.*

Seeing this documented in such an official way makes it much more real. I click out of the site and out of Google. I can't bear to see Celina's face like this — in a police file, among the countless other missing persons. Empathy for Gran and Grandpa and Aunty Mary and Uncle Pat and what they must have gone through, followed by disgust at my own outburst, swamps me.

But with a ghoulish fascination, I reopen the link.

Celina was last seen as she left for school at around 7:30 a.m. She had arranged to meet a friend at the bus stop on Greenhill Road, but never arrived. Despite an extensive search of the area, she has not been seen or heard from since. Police hold grave concerns for her safety.

Reported to Tallowood Police Station.

Was she meeting Deb? Or Suzie? Or this Robbie — if he's real and not someone I've dreamed up. Did they think something was wrong, or did they get on the bus, thinking Celina was sick or late? How did they feel when they realized something terrible had happened? I can't imagine how I would cope if Loni disappeared like that.

I skim through the other links and crawl through the information. The other sites say much the same thing, but with each site and each listing, my insides tighten and twist. I feel as if Celina is standing behind me, peering over my shoulder. I snap my head around. There's no one there. Of course. But I have come to realize that just because you can't see something, it doesn't mean it's not there.

I keep searching. I note the repeated mention of the "extensive search" and "thorough investigation" and how they had "exhausted all leads." I find an article about how a group of about ninety volunteers from the surrounding areas, led by the mayor himself, searched for more than six weeks after the police search was called off.

I lean back in my chair. My brain checks through all the things that have happened since I got here, the information that I've gathered. Celina wants me to do something — I'm sure of it. It's as though she has been waiting all these years for me to open the peace chest and put on those jeans.

But what is it? And why doesn't she simply tell me, instead of giving me tiny glimpses of her life? Does she want me to find her remains? Uncover the truth? Find her killer? I get all goose bumpy. And for some reason, the image of that stranger and his haunting words, *"Holy mother of God! Holy mother of God!"* come back to me. Instinctively, my eyes lift to gaze out through the window toward the lake, and my nostrils fill with that sickening smell. That snarling face looms large in my mind's eye. But why? Wasn't that Oliver's grandfather?

This is crazy!

I turn my thoughts to the phantom Robbie and whether he existed or not, and whether the other things I've "seen" actually happened. The best person to help me here is Deb. I search for a website for Deb's store and find a rudimentary homepage with contact details.

I start typing out an email.

Subject: Celina O'Malley

Hey Deb,

This is Bayley. The girl you met the other day, the one living in Celina O'Malley's old house at the lake. Sorry for giving you such a fright. I didn't realize that I looked like Celina. No one had ever told me before. No one. Ever. Not even Gran O'Malley — which is actually weird. I found Celina's old album, and it was spooky. There are some photos of you and Suzie too.

I can't stop wondering about Celina and what happened to her. Why was everyone so sure she vanished? Was there any evidence that she was kidnapped or hurt? Did anyone think that she might have just run away? Was she unhappy at the time? Did anyone go searching for her in Sydney or somewhere else?

Or maybe she fell off a cliff or something? Did they ever find any of her stuff — like her school bag or anything? I read online that a friend was waiting for her at the bus stop. Was that you? That must have been so horrible. Also, did you guys know someone called Robbie?

Sorry for all the questions, but I can't stop thinking about her.

Thanks for taking care of me when I fainted.

Bayley

I press send before I can change my mind.

I know the questions about Celina running away are stupid though. I know Celina is dead. I know that a dead girl is communicating with me.

fifteen

I step into the stillness of the early morning. The air is crisp, and as I set out toward the lake, I am transported back to happier times — to those mornings a lifetime ago when the world was barely awake and I would slip on my running shoes and head to the beach with Dad before even the streetlights had turned off. The sun's first rays would burst from the horizon, the surf fresh and silvery blue. Sand squeaking beneath my shoes. The wind in my hair.

This morning, the lake is smooth and shiny, but to the south, banks of towering dark clouds loom, threatening to ruin the early brilliance.

I take what seems like a path leading from the dock to the southern edge. The track follows the shoreline for as far as I can see. I am almost tempted to run. Here. Right now. To pound my way along the path. But I don't. Running was part of my life before. It has no place in my life now.

I round a bend. The landscape here is very different from the rocky northern side. Here it is open fields, fences, and a few horses grazing in the distance. This land can't belong to us, and I wonder if I'm trespassing. The hills roll into the darkening horizon, leading, I suppose, to Oliver's house somewhere.

Oliver. My attention turns to the lake.

I'm not disappointed. In the radiance of the low sun on the lake, I see that I am not alone. A single kayak is making a path from south to north.

Oliver. Training.

Oliver. Determined. Disciplined.

Working hard to achieve his goals. I envy him. I wish I had the guts to be following my dreams, to be training again.

I stop and watch — the strength of each stroke, the smooth efficient pull through the water — and wonder what is going on between him and Amelia. Where and when did they meet? I feel a stab of jealousy. *Jeez, Bayley, get over yourself.*

I shrink back into some bushes before he spots me, just as the first drops of rain wet my face. Crap! I hadn't noticed how swiftly the dark clouds had taken over the blue sky. I turn up the collar of my jacket, say a silent farewell to Oliver, and charge off — aware of the maddening nervous flutter in my chest that seems to erupt whenever I set eyes on him.

* * *

I scoot around to the back of the house and slip inside through the laundry room. It's about half past six, and I am soaked to the skin. The damp drizzle had given way to a heavy downpour with little warning. What is it with the weather around here?

I yank off my jacket, toss it on the floor, and grab a towel from one of the shelves. I dry off my face and then tip my head over to towel my hair dry.

There are voices in the kitchen. I wind my hair into a towel turban on top of my head, then lean my ear to the door. Who could be up this early?

"Now, don't be getting yourself so worked up, Kath," I hear Gran say.

I wait for Mom to respond, but all I hear is what sounds like crying. "I'm just hopeless," is my mother's eventual reply. "I'm here, what — three days — and I have to call you to come to my rescue. Again."

"That's what mothers are for, Kath, you know that. Don't beat yourself up — you've been through a heck of a lot, what with David, and then Amelia acting up . . ."

"I don't know if I'm strong enough to face this out here, alone. What was I thinking?"

"You're only trying to do what's best."

"But my best isn't even close to being good enough, is it? I thought this was going to be perfect. That it would be what David would do. We were planning to come out here anyway, once the girls were off at college or whatever. It seemed like the most logical solution. But it's stupid, so incredibly stupid! It's been a struggle just to get the power and water working, let alone anything else — I didn't think it through."

"Hey, Kath. Shush. You had to do something. You had no choice. Amelia's one angry young woman with her finger planted firmly on the self-destruct button. You had to get her away. It's brave, what you've done. And David *would* be proud of you."

At this, Mom dissolves. "I can't do it," she sobs. "I don't have a clue on how to handle her. I can't seem to handle anything or anyone."

"Yes, you can. You're made of stronger stuff than you realize."

"Don't patronize me. I'm not one of your clients at the Soup Van who needs a sad little pep talk —"

"Kath, stop it. I don't give 'sad little pep talks' — to you or to the people at the van. Far from it. I tell it how it is. And you *are* strong. You *can* do this. Many of the people I deal with can't. But *you* can."

Mom blows her nose. "Can you call and cancel Saturday for me? I can't handle meeting new people right now. I feel too raw."

I hear tap water swirling into the kettle. "I'll do no such thing. You need people, Kath. You can't hide yourself out here. It'll do none of you any good. Part of the reason Tallowood was your solution was the community, remember? Have a cup of tea, you'll fee—"

"The community — ha! If the other night is any indication, the community is not going to help one bit. Busybodies — the whole bunch of them — throwing so many questions at me. I felt like I was under interrogation. They may as well have sat me down in the middle of the restaurant and shone a light in my eyes. *Are you really related to the O'Malleys? Has the family recovered yet? Why have you moved way out here? Did you know that house is cursed?* I really don't know if I can take it, Mom."

"Give it some time, Kath. Or better yet, why don't you forget about the whole waitressing thing and call some of your old clients. Get back into what you're best at. You'll feel so much better once you do. It will be good for your soul. Truly, it will make all the difference."

Yay, Gran! I'm glad that I am not the only one who sees how simple it is.

"It's not that easy, Mom. I'm not the same person I was be—"

Seth's voice bursts into the gloom. "It's raining," he declares. "Can we still swim in the lake, Mom? Hey, why are you crying?"

"Your mother just tripped and hurt her ankle." I am shocked at the slippery ease of Gran's lie.

"Come here and give me a hug, little man," says Mom.

"Where does it hurt? Hey, Gran, can you sleep with me tonight?"

"Maybe, we'll see."

"You might be more comfortable," Mom tells her. "I was surprised at the state of Bayley's room — nothing unpacked and stuff everywhere. It's odd, especially for Miss Neat Freak. She's been acting kind of strange since we got here, that's for sure." Mom sighs. "I guess it will take us all a while to adjust."

I hold my breath as I wait for Gran to tell Mom that I wasn't even in bed when she got up.

"Exactly," says Gran. "Time. Time and a bit of effort takes care of everything. Now, Batman, tell me, do you still snore like a freight train?"

"No way! You do," Seth answers.

I tiptoe out onto the back landing.

I've heard enough.

sixteen

It's the pale blue eyes in the portrait that frighten me the most. Those luminous orbs hold me captive and seem to peer right into my soul. I admire the clever way the dark curls make the round shape of Celina's face and how bizarrely the portrait seems to capture the spirit of Celina, just as Deb had described her — the energy, the enthusiasm for life — but at the same time there's something in her expression, something in those eyes that leaves me cold. Whatever it is, there's certainly something eerie about this picture. I fumble with the string across the back of the frame and peg it over a nail in the picture rail above the chest, right next to the Karinya sign. If only that sign would bring me peace.

I step away and take in the rest of the room. At last I have been motivated to get it organized. Everything is unpacked and in its place. I feel lighter, energized. Almost settled. And not even Gran giving me the O'Malley Silent Treatment and moving into Seth's room can dampen my mood. Besides, let's face it — I deserve Gran's wrath.

Stacked on one side of my desk are my pile of notebooks, a jar of sharpened pencils, my laptop, and, dangling from my desk lamp, my running shoes. I've only ever worn them once. Dad bought them for me a few days before he died. They were an early birthday present and a reward for the effort I had put into training. Now they've been relegated to the world of mementos.

I fiddle with the laces, my mind full of memories, when suddenly the lid to the chest slams down. I jump back and knock the pencil jar, scattering pencils across my desk and onto the floor.

As I reach down to pick them up, my skin prickles. The silvery notebook I had stashed under my mattress is also on the floor — lying open at the page about Celina and Robbie.

"Honestly, Bayley, do you have to slam everything all the time?" Amelia pokes her head through the doorway and pulls her earbuds from her ears. "I spilled my coffee, thanks to you."

I don't respond. I grab the book and slip it onto my desk behind me.

"You still writing that creepy story?" Amelia's lips curl into a sneer and she cups both hands around her coffee mug.

"Where did you go the other night?" I say, my voice as shaky as my insides.

"Why does it matter? I got home before Mom, like I said."

"And my bracelets, where are they?"

"What do you care? You never wear them."

"That doesn't matter. I want them back. Now."

"You'll get them back, don't worry your pathetic little self about it."

What did I do to deserve Amelia for a sister?

"And what about Oliver?" I hear myself saying. "Where'd you meet him?"

Amelia gives a sly smile. I can hear Seth running down the hall, calling out to Gran. Amelia slides into the room and closes the door behind her. "Oh, you have the hots for our athletic neighbor?"

"No, I only want to know when you met him."

"Yeah right. You're jealous! This is hilarious."

Amelia's words set a fiery heat rushing up my neck. "I'm

not jealous, you idiot," I snarl. "It's just . . . just that this is a small town, and Mom will catch you if you're sneaking into town with one of the locals."

Amelia bends over laughing. "Jealousy doesn't suit you one bit, Bayley. But don't worry. He's too Mr. Serious Sports Star for me. God, give me a break! Have you heard his laugh? Could it be any more ridiculous? But it doesn't matter anyway. He's way out of your league, little sister. I reckon he's a bit of a god to the girls around town — from what I've heard."

"From what you've heard? Where? When?" My cheeks are burning bright now, and I feel like a big baby.

"Forget him is all I'm saying. God, it's freaking freezing in here." Amelia pops her earbuds back in, takes a sip of her coffee, and slips out.

I sink down onto my desk chair. Amelia is so infuriating! *He's out of your league.* I picture Oliver this morning on the lake. Remember the bewilderment on his face when I yelled at him on the rocks the other day. Remember how I threw my little fit and ran off. She's so right.

My stomach lurching, I flip open the silver notebook. Was it just a spooky coincidence that the book was on the floor, opened to the page about Celina and Robbie? I look at the scrawling handwriting and shiver. My attention shifts from the notebook to Celina's portrait, with those cold, cold eyes that pierce deep into me and chill the blood in my veins. Swarms of words and sentences and images cram into my head until it's fit to burst.

I'm compelled to write. I have no choice in the matter.

It got serious with Robbie and me almost immediately. One minute we were barely talking to each other, bearing that childhood grudge with a vengeance, the next minute we couldn't keep our hands off each other. It was intense. Marvelously, giddily, amazingly amazing. Quite simply, we were in love.

We loved each other all summer long and then into the autumn. Robbie met me on the school bus each morning, and we rode it to school sitting side by side, tingling at being so close. Some days he had a wildflower for me.

Robbie consumed me. Totally. I opened my heart to him, and he filled it until it was about to burst. He gave his own heart to me in return. I knew how lucky we were to have found each other so young. Some people wait their whole lives and never experience what we had.

He is so great, Bayley. Wait until you meet him. You'll love him to pieces.

seventeen

"Hurry up, Amelia!" Mom calls from the bottom of the stairs. "I don't know how long it's going to take to get there, and I don't want to be late." Mom thumps off to the kitchen.

I scrutinize myself in the hall mirror. I smooth back an errant curl and adjust my scarf. Ridiculously, it has taken me all afternoon to decide what to wear. Everything I tried on made me look pathetic. It wasn't until I slipped on the red polka dot dress from the peace chest that I felt satisfied. The skirt is made from a floaty material that flares out from the waist in a way that makes you want to twirl. I finished it off with a chunky silver medallion.

Gran comes up behind me, looks over my shoulder into the mirror. "That suits you," she says, appraising me. "Is it Celina's?"

I nod, wondering how Gran is going to react. "Do you mind?" Our reflected eyes meet.

"Mind? No, not really. I guess it's good that they're being put to use." Gran runs the back of her hand affectionately across my cheek. "You're a beautiful young woman, Bayley. Don't ever forget that." She picks up her purse off the hall seat and shakes her head. "That chest! I still can't quite fathom how we left it behind. And for everything to be in such good condition after all these years — says a lot for camphor wood."

I turn away from the mirror. "Gran, I'm sorry about before . . . those things I said . . ."

"No need for apologies. I'm sorry too. I shouldn't have let it get to me like that. That chest — well, seeing all those things of Celina's — it threw me." She pushes another stray curl out of my eye. "And you're right, you're just like Celina. The resemblance is uncanny, actually, and I can't explain why I didn't notice it before. Forgive me?"

"Sure, but it . . . it all makes me feel a little weird."

"There's nothing weird about it. It's called genetics. Celina was your mom's cousin, and that's all there is to it. Now, what I should've been telling you, Bayley, is how proud I am of you. The way you have been holding your family together, it's been extraordinary, and it hasn't gone unnoticed."

I shake my head. "But Gran, how can you say that? Everything is such a mess. I've done nothing but —"

"You have shown great gumption. And I've been feeling more than a little guilty about not doing my fair share — always being tied up with the Soup Van and everything. I should have been there for you more. Anyhow, I'm making up for that now."

"You don't have anything to make up for," I say and mean it. "Besides, what are Missy Moo and Arnold doing without you?"

"Ha! They're doing fine. Missy Moo even has a job. Casual, and not enough for her to make rent, but she's excited about it." I watch Gran's face, shining like a Christmas tree, as she talks about the Soup Van, and it strikes me that that's where she should be. I am sad and guilty and grateful all at once.

Mom rushes past Gran and passes me a basket. "Here, take this to the car, will you? And make sure Seth's gone to the bathroom." She tears up the stairs. "Come *on*, Amelia. Everyone is waiting."

The basket is heavy, filled with the spoils of Mom and Gran's baking extravaganza that afternoon: blueberry muffins, chocolate chip cookies, and an apple pie. The way the items are arranged has all the signs of Mom's flair, and I feel encouraged. I hope the Mitchells aren't into really healthy foods, though. A whiff of the sugary contents would be enough to snap a diabetic out of a coma.

Just as I go to step outside, I am stopped by the sound of Mom yelling at the top of her voice. "What do you mean, you're not going? Of course you're going! Now get out of those sweatpants, put on something nice, and hurry yourself up, young lady."

Gran and I exchange worried glances.

"Sounds like World War Three has erupted," says Gran. "Wait here, Bails. I'll go and see if the combatants are open to peace talks."

Amelia's voice rockets down the stairwell. "I'll be eighteen in a couple of months, and you can't make me go!"

Seth appears in the doorway next to me, pulling on his ears. I set the basket on the porch and sit down on the steps.

"Yes, I can," says Mom. "And I will."

"Yeah, you and what army?"

"Wow, that's really original, Amelia. Where did you learn that one? From your underage drinking buddies at The Pint?"

"I don't give a rat's ass about you or anyone else in this stinking hellhole. You might've been able to drag me here, Mom, but you can't make me like it. So shut up!"

"Don't you dare talk to me like that; you have no right."

"Don't you even start talking about rights. What gave you the right to wreck my life?"

"You were doing a pretty good job of wrecking it by yourself, missy!"

"What would you know? You haven't even been on the same planet as everyone else, let alone the same town, Mom. You've been absent to the extreme."

Ouch. That had to have hurt.

There's a pause, and I wonder if I should go upstairs and check everything is okay. Then Amelia's yelling tumbles down the stairwell again.

"Look — I don't care what you think or what you say; I have no intention — *repeat, no intention* — of spending Saturday night meeting some dumb country hillbillies. So just leave me alone!"

Amelia's door slams, and a thick silence fills the house. It's as if Amelia's anger has sucked out all the air, leaving the rest of the household holding their breath in the vacuum.

"What are hillbillies?" Seth whispers. He pulls his cape around his legs and rests his chin against his knees.

"Nothing," I answer lamely, worrying what is going to happen next.

"Why is Amelia angry all the time?" he asks.

"That's a good question, buddy. Maybe you should ask her. Not now, though," I add.

"I don't like it when she yells."

"Neither do I. But we've always got each other, right?"

"Are we still going to Oliver's?"

I open my mouth to reply as Mom and Gran come trudging down the stairs. Mom's face is flushed, and her eyes are red.

"Come on, you two," says Gran. "In the car. We don't want to be late."

"Is Amelia coming?" Seth asks.

"No. She's too much of a grouch tonight, don't you think?" Gran takes Seth's hand.

Mom picks up the basket and closes the door behind her. She is totally worn out and exhausted. I wonder if I'm ever going to be able to forgive my sister for what she is putting our mother through.

eighteen

It's quite a hike to get around to Lakeside. It requires driving all the way out to the main highway, then another five miles down it, before finally turning off and driving in toward the lake.

I'm surprised by the drive back in. From my glimpses across the lake to the imposing trees and orderly fields of Oliver's property, I had been expecting rolling hills of grazing sheep and patchwork fields of grain. Instead, the terrain is rugged, the road cutting through steep gullies thick with vegetation.

Despite this, I'm enjoying the drive. A stiff south wind has swatted away the miserable weather of the morning, leaving behind another breathtaking afternoon. Everything is brighter, greener, and crisper, as if it was all scrubbed clean. Seth is engrossed in his comic book — how he doesn't get carsick is beyond me — and Mom and Gran are locked within their private thoughts.

This leaves me alone with mine as well.

I'm so nervous. Except for the time I had a crush on Bede Walters in seventh grade, I've never felt this rush of anticipation about meeting someone. Maybe I've experienced it vicariously, through Loni — Loni is always jumping about like an idiot at the prospect of her latest love. But this is new territory for me. I think back to when Oliver and I were hanging at The Circle together and how fun it was — us yelling out and laughing till our sides ached. I remember his strange, high-pitched laugh and smile. It may irritate Amelia, but I like it. It's unique, distinct. Then I remember what Amelia said about Oliver being some sort of god to the local girls, and I wonder if she was making it up to upset me or whether it's really true. *He's way out of your league.* I sigh. I'm kidding myself to think that he would be interested in me.

I pick up my phone to check the time and notice that I have signal. Even with the new carrier, the signal around here is as unpredictable as the weather. I type a quick message to Loni before I lose it again.

On my way to barbecue with HOT neighbor. XOXOXO Bails.

The reply from Loni is almost instant.

No way. Tell me more!!!!! Details. Now.

I smile at Loni's response. I can hear the passion in her message. Will I ever make a friend like Loni here? I start to reply, but I notice that I've lost the signal again. I think this country life may do me in.

We climb up a steep incline. Once over the crest, the landscape flattens out and opens into the farm-style fields I had been expecting.

"Down here, on the right," says Gran, pointing. "That gate there."

Mom puts on her blinker, turns into the dirt path, and stops outside of a wire gate with a large sign beside it announcing: *Lakeside — Olive Grove and Family Farm.*

Seth leaps out to open the gate.

My stomach does a double backward somersault.

* * *

It's funny looking at the lake from the opposite side. It challenges my perspective and flips everything over. The sun is low in the sky, resting just above the hill behind our house and casting a golden glow to the water. I'm amazed to see how much the Norfolk pine towers above the roof, how unruly and kind of wild our side of the lake appears. Although, it *has* been deserted for nearly four decades.

Mom pulls into a circular driveway, outside of what seems to be the main building — all glass and steel — nestled in a cluster of older cottages, barns, and sheds.

As I step out of the car, my stomach goes from having tickly nerves to being plain nauseous. Not a great start.

A soaring glass door slides open and loud music surges out, followed by a tiny woman dressed in denim shorts and a tank top, carrying a ginger cat. She sets the cat down and dazzles everyone with a wide grin.

I blink. *Does that woman have pink streaks in her hair, or am I seeing things?*

The woman approaches. "Hi! So glad you made it," she says. Her face is elfish and pretty and seems to suit her startling crop of spiky pink hair. Her nose scrunches up as she smiles. This couldn't be Oliver's mother, could it? She seems far too young. The woman shakes Mom's hand and then Gran's. "I'm Annie Mitchell. Sorry Bob and Oliver aren't here — some problem with a fence or a tractor or manure or something . . ." She screws up her nose and giggles. "They'll be back soon," she adds. "It's not much of a welcome, I know. And the Ralphs send their apologies too. Timmy, their youngest, is sick with the flu or some sort of bug. Anyway, it's better if they stay at home — wouldn't want to be spreading those nasty bugs about."

Annie babbles away as introductions are made and we're ushered inside. The house is cavernous: all hard surfaces, starkly white, and filled with light. Not exactly your typical country homestead, I suspect, though Annie isn't exactly your typical farmer's wife either. Seth sidles up beside me, his eyes wide.

"It's a bit big for the three of us," says Annie. Her voice echoes as she turns down the music and guides us through the large tiled living room and to the kitchen area at the far end. "But it's our dream house. Bob had it built when we moved back here from Sydney. He couldn't bear living in the old farmhouse again, and I wanted something that reminded me of our Sydney house. Now, Seth, how about a Coke? Or some juice? What would you like?"

"Coke, thanks," whispers Seth, winding his arm around my leg.

"Okeydokey. And what about you, Bayley? I've got a bottle of bubbly cooling in the fridge. I thought *finally* having some neighbors across the lake was reason enough to celebrate, don't you think? Just name your poison" — she glances over at Mom and grins — "if it's okay with you, Kath."

"Coke's fine," I say before Mom has a chance to answer on my behalf.

Mom hauls the basket of baked goods up onto the shiny stone countertop. "Just a few goodies," she says.

"Holy moly, it's a feast," Annie says, peering into the basket. "You didn't need to bring anything, but I'm sure glad you did." Annie chuckles and pops a cookie into her mouth. "Oh my God, who cooked this and where have you been all my life? You can't get things like this in Tallowood, as I'm sure you've discovered already."

Annie pops the champagne cork and pours drinks for everyone. Already there's a feeling of ease in the room, though my stomach refuses to stop gurgling. Seth lets go of my leg and starts exploring.

My eyes sweep around. I have never seen windows this huge in a house before. They soar right to the top of the barn-like ceiling, bringing the stunning view of the lawn and lake and countryside up close and personal. A sidewall is home to several artworks. Drink in hand, I wander over for a closer look.

They're incredible. The pieces are abstract, but totally captivating, collages of some sort. They're made out of

thousands of small pieces of different kinds of materials —
stone, twigs, leaves, bark — all stuck closely together.

"Not bad, are they?" Annie falls in beside me. "But you
need to stand back a bit to really appreciate them."

I take a couple of steps back, and the sea of specks in the
painting transform almost magically into a dramatic gorge
towering above a still waterhole. "Wow," I say, aware that my
legs have become weak and my hands are trembling, sloshing
the Coke inside my glass. I have a strong feeling that I've seen
this art before. Another vision? I wonder. "That's amazing."

"Bud — Oliver's grandfather — did them." That must be
the wacky, artistic grandpa. Wacky and talented. "He's a bit
of a genius, the old Bud. It's all made out of found objects
that have been crushed or chopped up, stuff he collects
mainly off of Lakeside. It's made him a fortune, not that he
spends any of it," Annie whispers conspiratorially. "He didn't
go into art until he was well in his forties — surprised the
whole family and the county. He was a farmer turned shire
mayor, then he gave it all up and started slapping little pieces
of stuff on a canvas and became some kind of legend in the
art world."

Gran and Mom join us, gazing up at the art with obvious
admiration.

"This is very much like a piece I have hanging in my

sunroom," says Gran. She leans forward and peers at the signature scrawled across the bottom corner. "Bud — yes, that's it."

"Oliver's grandpa," I say, curiously disappointed that my déjà vu has been explained so readily this time. I *have* seen this art before. I loved that collage, especially when I was younger. I used to marvel at how the pieces of rocks, leaves, sand, and twigs came together to make a landscape, how it glinted in the sunshine.

"Okay, that makes sense," Gran says. "It was one of the few things I kept when we cleared out the house. Couldn't bear to give it away for some reason."

"Well, it's a good thing you didn't," says Annie. She sweeps her arm around the room. "These are all Bud's experiments with pointillism, but instead of using tiny splotches of paint to create a scene, he has applied the same principle to environmental collage. Splotches of nature, I suppose. That's how he made his mark. The ones down the hall are much more minimalist and mostly figures and portraits, but they work in a similar way. You can't really see their form until you step back."

I'm no art expert, but it's easy to see that Bud's art is special. But still, looking at them is making me anxious. I wipe my palms on the side of the red dress; they're hot and sweaty.

"So, Maree," continues Annie, "depending on the size and style of your piece, it could possibly send you on a first class trip around the world. Maybe twice!"

Gran's face lights up. "Well, I never — and I was so close to putting it out at your garage sale, Kath. It was only the other week," she adds for Annie's benefit. "But I couldn't, for some reason. Sentimentality, superstition — who knows?" She turns to face Annie. "To be honest, Annie, it's not my style. But I think I may have changed my mind."

We're all laughing when we hear loud footsteps racing across the tiles and Seth yelling, "Holy guacamole, it's Oliver!"

Warmth sweeps up my neck and washes across my face. I feel myself turning an attractive shade of tomato as I watch Seth drag Oliver by the hand into the kitchen area.

"Yo, Batman. How goes it?" Oliver is grinning, his hair falling untidily across his face. My heart seems to take on a life of its own. *Calm yourself, you idiot. He's out of your league, remember?*

A stocky, weather-beaten man with a shiny bald head follows Oliver into the kitchen. He has an amused expression on his face as he watches Seth tug Oliver around.

"Bob," says Annie, and she rushes over to take the man's arm. "At last. I'd just about given up on you two. Here, come meet the new neighbors." She beams at everyone. "I never thought I'd ever be able to say that. New neighbors! Yay!"

Bob steps toward us, a beer in one hand. His face lights up with a warm smile, his eyes sparkling with mischief. He twists the lid of the bottle with ease, then looks up at me.

Our eyes lock. His eyes are the same greenish-blue as Oliver's, and I am shocked by the way his gaze makes my heart almost leap from my chest. It seems as if the world falters for a moment, forgets to keep turning or something, and I have the sudden need to sit down. But I can't tear my eyes away from this man, Oliver's father. I have to press my arms against my sides to stop them from reaching out and hugging him.

Bob seems equally transfixed. But his tanned face drains of color, and the bottle he's holding slips from his grip. The sound of glass smashing on tile reverberates around the hollow room and stuns everyone into sudden silence. The ginger cat scurries off down the hall.

Laughing, Annie steps out of the way of the spray of beer and glass, breaking the moment. "Drunk already?" she quips. "And I thought you and Oliver had been attending to very important farm-type business. Foiled — again!"

But Bob doesn't respond to Annie's cheerful gibe. He is clearly rattled. Then, finally, with a, "God, sorry, Annie," he snaps into action. "Step back and I'll get the mop and bucket."

"Broken bottle, misfortune's your new friend," I say robotically, remembering Deb's words.

"It smells like a brewery in here," Annie says. "Oliver, why don't you take Kath and Maree and everyone for the grand Lakeside tour while we clean this up."

"Yeah, thanks, buddy," adds Bob, on his hands and knees, collecting bits of shattered glass.

Before Oliver can answer, I slip out the sliding door, escaping with the ginger cat.

nineteen

Oliver's father's staring face won't leave my mind. I push my hair back behind my ears and am shocked at the tremble in my fingers.

He must be at least fifty — probably more. He's Oliver's dad. And married. To the gorgeous Annie. Yet I'm acutely aware that despite these realities, all I can think about is being held by him, kissing those sun-dried lips, and running my fingers through his hair. God! He doesn't even have any hair! What is wrong with me? What kind of a sicko am I? It's gross. Disgusting. But real.

I follow a few steps behind the rest of the family. I am conscious of Oliver up ahead as he points out various buildings and goes on about barns and studios. But I can't take anything in.

"Bayley? Yoo-hoo? Anyone home?" I snap out of my trance to find Mom holding onto my arm and Gran, Seth, and Oliver gathered in a semicircle around me.

"Are you okay, sweetheart?" Gran's voice soft with concern. "You seem kind of shaky."

"Ah . . . I'm not sure," I say, my mouth dry. "I feel a bit weird."

"You better sit down." It's Oliver. "Over here, on the step." He takes me by the elbow.

His touch sends a jolt right through me. I yank my elbow free and swat him away furiously. "Let *go* of me. I'm fine." I hear the touchiness in my voice, but I am too filled with anxiety to care.

"Hey, Bayley," says Gran. "Take it easy. He was just trying to help."

I am desperate for some space. The worried faces around me are making me worse. "Sorry," I say. "I feel a little queasy. I'll sit here for a sec and get some air. You go on."

"You sure?" Mom says.

I attempt a smile. "Yep. Please. I'll catch up in a minute."

"Can you show us your boats?" Seth asks Oliver.

Oliver hovers near me, hesitating.

"Yes, I'd like to see them," says Gran, who is staring intently at me. "Lead the way, Oliver." And thankfully the group heads for the boatshed.

Once they disappear from view, I hang my head between my knees and suck in heavy gulps of air.

That moment — that long, breathless moment I locked eyes with Oliver's father — replays in my head. And I am sickened and shamed to the very center of my being.

* * *

A splash of cold water on my face does little to restore my composure. I look at my reflection in the bathroom mirror. I am pale and wild-eyed — as if I had just seen a ghost. The thought sends a shiver surging through me. There's no ghost to be seen, but somehow I feel a ghost is almost certainly involved. It's how and why that's the puzzling part. I swirl a gulp of water around my mouth, spit it into the sink, and ready myself. *Smile*, I tell myself. *Walk confidently*, I urge. *Don't wobble.*

The chatter of dinner conversation and laughter wallops me as soon as I open the bathroom door, and my knees threaten to buckle. *You can do this. You have to do this.* Swallowing down some rising bile, I head down the long hallway, through the sliding doors, and out to the front patio. I walk as though I'm drunk.

The night is closing in, and I welcome the shadowy ambience. Lighted orbs like pale moons wash the table of expectant faces in a dusky otherworldly glow.

"There she is!" says Annie. "Perfect timing. Bob's getting the steaks. We've left you a seat next to Oliver."

Gran slides her chair back and catches me by my arm as I pass. "You sure you're okay, sweetheart?"

Not trusting myself to speak, I nod, give a rubbery smile, and slip into my seat.

"Dig in, everyone," calls Annie as she and Bob bring plates of barbecued meat and bowls of salads and bread to the table.

Oliver passes me a bowl of green salad. My hands shake as I take it from him, and I curse them for betraying me. I pass it quickly on to Seth.

"Not hungry?" says Oliver, startling me.

"What? No . . . yes . . . um . . ." Here I go. The blathering idiot strikes again.

"Just serving Seth first," I say and pluck out a lettuce leaf with the tongs and pop it onto Seth's plate.

Seth scowls. "I don't want that. Let me get my own." He tosses the leaf onto my plate. I raise my eyebrows at Oliver as if to say, "Kids!" and then fix my concentration on filling my plate with salad that my swirling stomach has no interest in receiving.

I push some carrots around my plate, letting the babble of voices flow over me as I try to collect myself. I'm sitting so close to Oliver that I can feel the heat of his arm next to mine, yet it's the man at the head of the table, the man whose twinkling eyes keep sneaking glances at me, who is causing me so much anxiety that I feel it as physical pain. And each time I catch his eye, it's as though I've woken up from a dream, the kind of dream that only moments ago was vivid and real, but in the light of day is vague and dangling out of reach.

A loud shriek of laughter startles me, and I look up to see everyone roaring. Oliver's laugh is the loudest and rises above the others.

"And now they call it the Undies Tree," Gran is saying between wheezes. "There are dozens of pairs hanging up there above the van. It's like a colony of rainbow bats."

"It sounds so colorful and exciting!" says Annie.

"Colorful, maybe. Exciting, no. These people are pretty sad cases, actually. Breaks your heart sometimes."

The conversation turns serious and I fake interest, but it's only a cover to watch Bob. I scrutinize the way he sits upright in his chair, how he's left his steak for last, and the way he seems to cock one ear toward whomever is speaking. I am bizarrely fascinated.

Then Mom asks about people using the lake.

"Just us," says Bob in a croaky voice, and I so want to stroke that face. "Oliver mainly, for training. There's no other access. That's why the National Parks has been trying to get its hands on the gorge and the land around it — to give the lake public access. But somehow Bud keeps dodging them."

"They've been after me to sell too," adds Gran.

"No public access?" says Mom, her eyebrows knitting together. "Well, that's strange, isn't it, Bails?" My nerve endings prickle as Mom brings me into the conversation. "The other night — late — Bayley saw someone on the lake. When she went to investigate, she bumped into a man near our dock."

"Perhaps it was Bud," suggests Gran.

Annie screws her nose. "Possibly. He does go out on the lake occasionally. But at night?" She looks at Bob.

"Doubt it. It wasn't you, was it Oliver?"

"No. Bayley told me about it the other day. I think it must have been Grandpa."

"Yeah, the man was old, I think, and wrinkly," I say, the words catching on my dry throat. "He grabbed my arm. His hands were thick and scratchy, and he had a scary, kind of raspy voice."

Bob and Annie chuckle. "Certainly wasn't Bud, then," says Annie.

Their laughter makes me feel silly. "Why?"

"Bud is mute," says Bob. "Hasn't uttered a word in, what" — he turns to Annie — "ten years?"

Annie nods. "Yep, it must be. He hasn't spoken since, Hetty — Bob's mom — passed away," she explains, lacing her fingers through Bob's and smiling up at him with empathy. "Poor Bud hasn't been quite right since Hetty passed. That's why we came back — to help out."

"What man?" Seth kneels up on his chair and tugs at his earlobe. "You didn't tell me."

"Oh, it's nothing, Seth," says Mom. "Bails and I forgot about it until now. Didn't we, Bails?"

"What about Amelia? Did you tell Amelia?" he asks nervously.

"Amelia," says Annie brightly, obvious in her attempt to steer the conversation in a different direction. "She's your oldest, isn't she, Kath? Where's she tonight?"

Seth plops back down on his chair. "She's at home. She didn't want to meet any dumb country hillbillies."

"Seth!" Mom and Gran say at once.

Bob, Annie, and Oliver all laugh out loud.

But I am reliving that night by the lake. *Holy mother of God. Holy mother of God. No!* If no one has access, and it wasn't Bud, the wacky grandfather, or anyone else from Lakeside, then who was it?

twenty

Seth is asleep, his head resting heavily on my shoulder. I heave him off and open the car door. My shoulder kills.

The house is in total darkness.

"Carry Seth in for me, will you, Bails?" says Mom, and she hurries up the front steps.

"Come on, Batman," I say. "Time for bed." Without opening his eyes, Seth climbs into my arms. I groan under his weight as I swing him out of the car.

"The front door's been left wide open," Mom calls.

"Amelia would forget her head if it wasn't screwed on,"

says Gran with fake levity, breaking into a slow run to join Mom who is hesitating at the front door. Gran pushes past Mom and flicks on the light switch. "Amelia, are you up?" she calls.

I lug Seth up the porch steps and follow Mom and Gran inside. Asleep, the kid's a dead weight. I'm just delivering him into bed when I hear Mom's panicked voice. "She's not in her room." Followed by the rush of footsteps thudding back downstairs. "Amelia! Where are you? Amelia!"

I close Seth's door behind me and join Gran and Mom as they flick on light switches and tear around the house in search of Amelia.

We find her in the kitchen. The stench of alcohol announces her presence well before we spot her. She's slumped in a chair, with her face planted in a bowl of noodles on the table and her fingers wrapped around a near-empty bottle of vodka.

Mom shakes her shoulders roughly. "Amelia! Wake up! Amelia! For God's sake, wake up."

Amelia turns her head to one side, opens an eye, and squints at Mom. "Heys, Mom . . . shor home," she slurs.

"You're drunk!" Mom accuses.

"No duuuh," says Amelia, bringing her head out of the bowl, strands of noodles hitching a ride on her curls. "Geshh ya can get hammered in the counshry, ash shwell as the sheety." She lifts up the vodka bottle and stares at it.

Mom draws in a deep breath, her eyes blazing. For a brief moment, I think she's about to lash out at Amelia — to slap her drunken face. Instead, she turns and walks out of the room.

Amelia tries to stand up but trips over the legs of the chair — or her own feet — and ends up sprawled out on her back on the linoleum.

Gran drops to the floor and kneels beside her. "Give us a hand, Bayley," she says.

At the sound of Gran's voice, Amelia turns on her side, curls into fetal position, and slurs, "Gooshnight, Gran."

I want to leave her there, but Gran won't have it. She flips into Soup Van mode and tends to Amelia with both tenderness and firmness.

It takes a wet washcloth to the face and much cajoling before Gran is able to coax Amelia off the floor and lead her to the sofa in the living room to sleep off her binge.

"I hope she has one hell of a headache tomorrow," I say as Gran and I plod upstairs.

"There are few sure things in life, Bayley," says Gran. "But a headache tomorrow for Amelia is most definitely one of them."

"Good," I spit out. "She deserves it."

* * *

Once again, I am too rattled to sleep. I sit cross-legged on top of my blanket, desperate to sort out the stuff racing around inside my head.

He's old enough to be my father. He *is* Oliver's father. Where do my supposed feelings for Oliver fit into this?

I get up and start to pace.

His eyes held me like freaking magnets. My heart leaped out of my chest, and all I wanted to do was rush into his arms and hold him to me. Why?

And what about *him*? He was acting weird too. Like Deb, he had that same shocked, I-think-I'm-seeing-a-ghost-so-let's-smash-a-bottle-on-the-floor reaction. But why didn't he say anything? He must have known Celina. They would've been around the same age, probably went to the same school. A "Gee, you look familiar" or "You remind me of someone — sorry for staring" or a straight "You're the spitting image of Celina O'Malley" would have sufficed. But no, he said nothing. The whole evening, in fact, was plain disturbing.

I stop pacing and stand in front of Celina's portrait. Just like Bob's, her eyes draw me to her. They're mesmerizing, and I feel as if each tiny piece of crushed bluish crystal is trying to tell me something.

The blood drains from my face. *A collage, made from bits and pieces.* Did Oliver's grandfather make this? And if he did, when did he make it? Before she died or after? I suppose it doesn't matter much, but it sure shows the talent of "old Bud." This portrait seems to capture more of Celina than any of her photographs.

Sheesh! Can my life in this house by the lake get any more baffling? It's all freaking me out, and I'm tired of pretending that nothing is happening.

Maybe I'm having some kind of breakdown. Maybe it's the stress of the past year. Mom has crumbled, Amelia's out of control, and Seth has withdrawn behind his Batman cape. Maybe it's my turn.

If only it were that simple.

Still too wired to sleep, I sit at my desk and boot up my laptop. Maybe Deb has emailed back.

Automatically, I log in to Facebook and am surprised to see that Loni is also online. A message pops up.

Loni: *Hey.*

Loni! How I miss her. I'd give anything to be back in Cronulla with her now — even if my life was screwed up

there. Anything would be better than the weirdness that sur-
rounds me here.

Me: *Hey. Whatcha doing up?*

Loni: *Nothing. What about you? Don't you have to be in bed
at sundown in the country so you can get up at dawn and milk
those cows?*

Me: *LOL. That's why I'm up — putting on the milking apron
now. It's my hot new look.*

Loni: *Miss you, Bails.*

Don't say that. You're killing me. I try to compose myself
then reply: *Same. What's happening with Johno?*

Loni: *Yolanda took him back.*

Me: *Bitch.*

Loni: *Definitely. How was the hot neighbor?*

Me: *Oh, you know . . .*

Loni: *Spill.*

Me: *The usual. Wild sex in the haystacks while everyone else
was chewing tobaccy and downing whiskey.*

Loni: *Yay you. So when can I come?*

Me: *Please come soon. But I have to say, haystack sex is
overrated.*

Loni: *Good to see that you're still completely insane. Miss you.*

Me: *Yeah.*

Emotion swells into my throat. I have to log off, or I'm going to tell Loni everything. Then Loni will know for sure that I really *am* insane. And I don't want that — Loni is the one person I've been able to depend on these past few months.

With tears brimming, I write: *Gotta go — can't make those poor cows wait too long. Their udders will be scraping the dirt.*

Loni: *Poor things. Go rescue those tits. Love you. Bye.*

Me: *Bye XOXOXO*

I sign out before I change my mind and go straight to my email account.

At last there is a reply from Deb.

Hi Bayley,

Sorry it has taken so long for me to reply. I'm not real tech-savvy and always forget to check my email.

Don't worry about asking all your questions. It's actually good, because since you visited, I've been remembering a whole bunch of things that I haven't been brave enough to think about for a long time. I've even been in touch with Suzie. She's some hotshot lawyer. We don't have much in common these days. Still, it was good to make contact.

Celina was such a wonderful friend, and although the time of the Peace Sisters was cut short, we did have a fabulous life together, with many rich experiences and such a unique and special bond.

I had forgotten about that — grief for Celina swamped it and left behind a gaping hole.

Lord! Sorry for rambling. In answer to your questions, Celina disappeared without a trace. Nothing was ever found. The possibility of her running away was explored briefly, but those who knew her also knew that she loved her life here too much to run away. She simply had no reason. She had us all under her spell — we would have done anything for her. And Robbie — Robbie was the love of her life.

So Robbie does exist. I didn't make him up. I'm not sure if I'm relieved or freaked out by this revelation.

Poor, sweet, adorable Robbie. When Celina disappeared, he couldn't function. He withdrew from school, sports, everything — withdrew from life actually. In hindsight, I think he was probably suffering from depression. His family ended up taking him on a long overseas trip, and then he finished school at a boarding school in Sydney. I didn't see him again until about ten years ago when he came back to help out after his mom passed away. It was great to see him happy again. I remember thinking Celina would've been so glad to see him finally getting on with life. You may have met him — Bob Mitchell over at Lakeside.

Wow, for someone who hates email, I have been babbling on!

Positive energies to you, Bayley.

Deb

So Bob is Robbie. I let this fact sink into my brain to see where it fits with the other pieces of Celina's puzzle.

Bob is *Robbie.*

Bob!

Of course.

He is so great, Bayley. Wait until you meet him. You'll love him to pieces.

twenty-one

"Wake up, Bayley! Wake up!" I open one eye to find Seth on his knees bouncing on the bed beside me. "Why are you sleeping in your clothes?" Seth doesn't give me a chance to reply before he launches back into his plea for me to wake up — now. "Hurry! Oliver is coming over in the big rowboat to get me and take me back to Lakeside so we can go kayaking. Like he promised. He's nearly here. Hurry!"

I sit up and rub my eyes. My head feels heavy and my mouth furry. "Promised?" The word comes out as a croak.

"Last night in the boatshed. He said he might, and now he is! Come on, get ready."

"Why? Make sense, Batman."

"Grandma says I can't go by myself and Amelia's sick and I don't know where Mom is. So if you don't go, I can't. Please, come on. Hurry!"

Bob is Robbie. Last night's revelation hits me over the head, and I'm not sure I want to go anywhere near the Mitchells right now. At least until I've figured out what's going on and how I feel about it. I'm sure my reaction to Bob had everything to do with Celina. Was I seeing him as if I were Celina? Through Celina's eyes? Feeling her feelings? And what does that mean? Did Celina's spirit slip inside me somehow? Is it still there? I shudder. That is too frightening even to think about.

And then there's Oliver. I've blown it there, without a doubt. I acted like an absolute psycho. Again. I really can't face him so soon.

Seth looks at me, his eyes pleading and his fingers reaching for his ears. I want to say no, but I can't bear Seth's disappointment. I cave. "Okay! You win. I'll go."

* * *

"Here, Batman, put this on." Oliver helps Seth thread his scrawny arms into the armholes of a life vest.

Seth tries to squirm out of it. "I can swim. I don't need this on."

"Yes, you do," I say. "Gran said so."

Seth groans.

"It's one of the rules of rowing too," adds Oliver. He clicks the safety buckles into place and directs Seth to wade out to the boat.

It's already warm. The air is sticky and thousands of buzzing insects are making such a racket that I'm secretly pleased at the thought of Amelia having to cope with a hangover in this weather.

I swing my bag onto my shoulder and follow Seth, holding the long cotton overshirt from the peace chest that I'm wearing over my swimsuit out of the water. I'm hot and restless and welcome the coolness of the water washing around my legs.

Oliver holds the boat steady while we climb aboard. He takes Seth's arm and almost flings him in. I move to the opposite side, determined to be independent. *Be dignified,* I tell myself. *Act natural. Cool. In control. You can do it.* As I hoist one leg up and over, I'm grateful for my long, spidery legs. But as I launch my other leg in, the boat sways under my weight, and I plop unceremoniously onto the splintery middle bench. So much for dignified.

Oliver doesn't appear to notice, though. He bounces into the boat and plonks down beside me. He reaches for the oars and slides them into the round metal rowlocks on each side. He seems so confident and comfortable in this old rowboat. An expert.

Seth stands up. "Can I row? Can I row?" he asks, seemingly unaware of the boat swaying.

"You can when we get the kayaks," says Oliver. "Sit down at the front, Batman. You can be our navigator. Lead the way."

I grin. Oliver is so good with Seth. I start to move to the backseat, but Oliver reaches across me and places an oar in my hand. "Not so fast. You don't think *I'm* going to do all the work, do you? You guys weigh a ton."

My face flushes. "Gee, thanks!" I sit back down and take the oar with both hands, pretending to be indignant.

"Have you ever rowed before, crazy eyes?" Oliver asks.

"Oh . . . yeah," I say and flinch and smile and redden all at once as I recall the day he first called me that. "But I'm not very good," I add.

"We'll have to fix that. You can't live on the lake and not be a good rower." He says it with such certainty and enthusiasm, as if it's simply impossible to live by the lake and not be infected with his passion for the sport. He holds his oar to his chest and winks at me through his scraggly bangs. "Ready?"

I nod, dip my oar in the water, and drag it back.

"Hey, are you feeling better?" Oliver stares ahead, not breaking his rhythm as he speaks.

I manage to say, "Yeah . . . much better. Thanks . . ." and try to smile. "I felt like a such an idiot," I add.

"Nah, you were okay." He snares me with one of his killer smiles.

"Holy cow," says Seth after our first few precarious strokes take us zigzagging away from the shore. "Can't you guys row straight?"

Oliver bats his oar into the water and sprays Seth. "Watch it, Batman, or I'll call my friend the Joker."

"You're the jokers. I thought you said you were fast."

The two continue to spar, leaving me to concentrate on matching Oliver's strokes so that the boat doesn't turn in my direction constantly.

"Are you going to Tallowood High?" Oliver lobs the question in my direction.

"Yep."

"What grade?"

"Eleven."

I curse myself for my mastery of the one-word conversation stopper as Oliver focuses his attention on superhero talk with Seth. I'm mostly relieved. With each stroke, we're moving closer to Lakeside and Bob/Robbie, and I am growing increasingly uneasy.

By the time we reach the shore, the sun is scorching my back through the flimsy cotton of my shirt. My head is pounding, and I am nauseous and dizzy again.

Oliver bounds over the side of the boat, and then reaches in and grabs Seth out. "Fly, Batman!" he says as he wheels him through the air to solid ground.

He wades back in and takes my hand to help me out. My legs and hands are shaking, and I hope that Oliver won't notice. I drop my bag onto the shore, and my nausea increases. I feel as rotten as I did last night. I pull off my shirt, wade back into the water, and dive under. When I break the surface, I see that Oliver and Seth have followed me in, and the three of us lounge around in the shallows. No one seems in a hurry to move.

"Maybe it's too hot to take the kayaks out today," says Oliver.

"Awww," moans Seth as he dog paddles over to Oliver, his life jacket bobbing along the surface, making him resemble some new species of turtle. "You promised."

I float on my back and look from the cloudless sky to the nest of buildings among the trees. There's no sign of Bob or Annie, and I'm relieved. But there's something about Lakeside that makes me unsettled. As crazy as it sounds, there's something sinister about it, and I need to get away from here — soon. I pull myself to my feet and raise my eyebrows at Oliver.

"To the boatshed, Batman," he says.

twenty-two

The lake is tranquil, and the shade of the cliffs on this far side is welcome.

Oliver maneuvers his and Seth's two-man kayak to circle mine. "Crazy, huh?"

I nod in awe of the towering rocks, rippling with scars of blue and rust streaming down them.

"Wanna go to The Circle or the creek that heads up into the gorge? It should be out of the sun and pretty cool up there," says Oliver.

"Wherever is coolest." I turn my kayak to fall in behind Oliver's.

"To the gorge, Batman," says Oliver.

"To the gorge!" repeats Seth. "Stroke. Stroke."

Oliver and I join Seth's chant. "Stroke, stroke." And as we enter the gorge, our laughter bounces off the cliff walls and veers into the bush.

I tilt my head and take in the wildness of it all: the craggy steepness of the gully; the majestic stance of the rivergums, lording it over the tangle of scraggly trees and thorny blackberry bushes tumbling to the water's edge; the depth of the isolation. We could be hundreds of miles from home, rather than merely a stone's throw away.

We paddle around a small curve, and Seth yells at the top of his lungs, almost wetting himself with excitement every time his words come bouncing back. Up ahead, the gully widens, and a pebbly bank emerges on one side. We row into the shore and drag the kayaks up onto the pebbles.

"Mom packed some snacks," says Oliver, pulling out a backpack. He looks inside, then grins. "Actually, I think it's the stuff your mom and grandma made for us last night."

I do my best to ignore the reference to the previous night. I don't want anything about it slinking back into my mind.

We hunker under the shade of some boulders and devour

the warm blueberry muffins and the slightly melted chocolate chip cookies. I savor the sweet bursts of flavor across my tongue and, exhausted from rowing, I flop onto my back.

Seth wiggles out of his life jacket and lies beside me, muffin smeared from ear to ear in a large blueberry-stained smile. I reach over to wipe it off, but he rolls away, leaps to his feet, and heads off to climb the boulder behind us. His Batman cape flies behind him.

He stands at the top of the boulder with his chest puffed out. "I am the Batman," he says solemnly to the trees and sky.

"He's sure into Batman," says Oliver.

"Yeah," I say, not wanting to go into it further and reveal the sad reasons behind his fixation.

"You be careful up there," I say, then lie back down and close my eyes. I sense Oliver lying beside me. It's thrilling.

"I haven't been up here for ages," he says.

"It's great," I say, keeping my eyes closed. The sun makes oranges dance across the insides of my eyelids.

"Yeah. I used to come up here when I was about Seth's age, I guess, collecting stuff with my grandpa, you know, for his collages. Used to love it."

"It's like some kind of paradise. It's surreal."

"Yep. The city's okay for some things, but nothing beats this."

"I miss Sydney and our old place and my friend Loni."

"Same. I miss Sydney too."

"You?"

"We lived in Mosman until I was about seven. Then I went to a boarding school near there from seventh grade until a year or so ago."

I turn on my side. "Really? I didn't realize. How come you don't still go to school there?"

"Economic downturn." Oliver makes a face. "Dad lost a lot of money. His real job is in finance. The olive grove and farm and stuff are more of a hobby. He's pretty crappy at it, to be truthful. Grandpa could've helped us out — he's loaded. But he's also a bit of a tight-ass, so Mom had to start teaching music again and I came back to Tallowood High."

"Ugh, don't say those words. They give me the creeps."

A wickedness lights Oliver's eyes. "What, crazy eyes? Tallowood High? Tallowood High?"

I giggle and punch him playfully on the arm.

"Tallowood High. Tallowood High," he continues.

"I said don't say that. It's too scary."

"What — you? A scaredy cat? Don't worry. It's not such a bad place."

I grin at Oliver. "Still don't want to think about it, thanks."

Oliver turns onto his side too, props his head up with one

hand, and shakes his hair out of his eyes. He reaches out and strokes the back of his finger along the bridge of my nose. "Besides, you'll have me," he says.

I know instantly that we've just shared a moment — a moment where every possible good thing in the world has found me and is zinging through my body. My heart surges.

But the feeling is short-lived.

Suddenly, the gorge echoes with the crack of a branch snapping and falling, a panicked scream, the scuttle of rocks skittering down an embankment, more yelling, the thump of a deep splash.

And then the most terrifying sound of all.

Silence.

twenty-three

For a moment or two I'm disoriented, like I've woken up abruptly and can't quite work out where I am or even what day it is.

I become aware of Oliver, of him lying beside me. His body is rigid, alert, as he strains to hear.

But there's nothing to hear, not even the sigh of a breeze. Nothing but a silence so loud that I scream to block it out.

Oliver leaps up and plunges into the creek. And then I'm on my feet too, my heart thudding against my ribs.

"Seth!" Oliver yells, bolting through the shallows toward the overhanging boulders. "Seth!"

I thrash through the water beside him. "Seth!" I scream. "Seth!" My cries ricochet off the gully. Bounce around me — mocking me. *Why isn't he answering? Where is he?* "Seth!"

Oliver dives in. I copy, pushing my way down through the murky creek, the water stinging my eyes. I see Oliver up ahead, his strong legs kicking powerfully through waving tentacles of duckweed. I twist and turn, searching frantically for any sign of my brother, until, lungs burning, I push up to the surface to take a gulp of air.

He has to be here somewhere. He has to be all right.

This can't be happening.

Not to Seth. Not to our family. Not again.

"Bayley! Here!" It's Oliver, wading forcefully toward the bank. Seth is in his arms.

Relief then panic swamps me. I lurch after Oliver, but slow my pace as I near the bank where he kneels beside Seth.

Seth lies motionless.

I am seized with terror. I can't move, can't think. My heart pounds in my ears and every nerve ending in my body feels as if it's exploding.

My mind fills with images of Dad sprawled out on the porch, the rain assaulting his face, then mixing with the blood trickling from his mouth and washing his life away.

Oliver turns Seth onto his side. I know I should do

something, but fear has rendered me useless. I sink onto the pebbles beside them.

"There's a pulse," Oliver says. And then suddenly Seth's body convulses and he coughs and coughs. Water spews from his mouth, and he starts to cry. It's the sweetest sound I have ever heard.

"Oh my God! Oh my God!" I grab him up and wrap my arms tightly around him, my own tears dropping onto his face. "Thank God. Thank God you're all right." He vomits and spits and coughs and cries, until he pushes out of my boa constrictor embrace to sit beside me.

"Put him in the back of the two-man. You should both fit in there okay." Oliver takes control, and I'm grateful for it.

Oliver bundles Seth and me into the backseat and tosses our belongings into the front. He hauls my kayak farther up the bank, well away from the water.

"We'll come back for it later," he says as he pushes his kayak into the water and jumps in. He turns to face us. "Hold on tight, Batman. We'll get you to the doctor before you know it." Then to me he says, "Keep him awake. Okay?"

I nod and slide Seth's hair off his forehead and away from the nasty cut and egg-shaped lump protruding from between his eyes.

Please let him be okay. Please.

The trip down the creek and across the lake to Lakeside is both never-ending and over in a flash. Oliver grounds the boat, leaps out, and heaves it farther up onto the shore. In an instant, he's beside us, lifting Seth from my lap. Oliver's forehead is wet with sweat, and he's sucking in deep lungfuls of air. It's obvious he's exhausted.

I climb out and follow them. My legs are stiff from being crammed into the back of the kayak with Seth on my lap. I trudge up the grassy bank toward the nest of buildings. Once again, my stomach is turning over, and I try to reject the odd sensation that seems to accompany me every time I set foot on this side of the lake.

"Mom! Dad!" Oliver shouts as we approach his house. The massive glass doors slide open. Annie and Bob rush out.

I struggle to make my legs work.

twenty-four

"What were you thinking?" Mom flies through the hospital sliding doors and almost launches herself at me. Her cheeks are tear-streaked, her eyes wild. "How could you let this happen, Bayley?"

I take a step back, lean out of the way of my mother's fury. After spending forty minutes locked in the Mitchell's truck with the pale-faced Seth on my lap, Oliver sitting so close our thighs were touching, and Bob/Robbie at the steering wheel, sneaking glances at me in the rearview mirror, my mother's ire is the last thing I need — or expect.

"How could you?" Mom continues. "How *could* you? He's only six years old, for God's sake. He was your responsibility!"

Gran places her hand on Mom's shoulder. "Kath. Go easy on the girl."

"Go easy? When her brother almost drowned?" Mom jerks Gran's hand away. "I depend on you, Bayley. I need you — need to be able to rely on you."

"Don't I know it," I reply, and I'm almost as shocked as Mom.

"Don't you take that tone with me, young lady." It's a line usually reserved for Amelia, and it's clear that Mom is unhinged. "How dare y—"

"Where is he?" Gran interrupts.

"In the room across from the nurses' station."

Gran takes Mom by the elbow and leads her away.

"Good one, sis," Amelia mutters as she follows off after them. I'm not sure if it's a compliment or a rebuke.

Across the room, Bob and Oliver sit on hard-backed chairs. Their shock is apparent. Annie twiddles her pink streaks and pretends to be engrossed in a poster on the wall.

Great. I don't even want to think about explaining that little scene. I head in the opposite direction for the coffee machine. I need something to steady my nerves.

I get some coins from my purse, slip them into the slot,

and make my selection. There's a clunking noise and then an "out of order" message flashes red on the digital display. I curse and kick at the machine, taking out my anger.

"You know you look like her, don't you? Like Celina."

The question catches me off guard. I swing around, a chill burrowing under my skin.

Bob is standing right behind me. His hand reaches out as if to touch my hair, and I find myself tingling.

He seems to realize what he's about to do and whips his hand away.

I swallow. My mouth is dry.

"Celina O'Malley. How long has it been since I said that name out loud?"

"Thanks for driving us in," I say in an attempt to divert the conversation.

It doesn't work.

"We were together — Celina and me," Bob continues, in that raspy, gravelly voice. "We were only kids, but we loved each other. Deeply. I'm sorry I stared at you last night. You caught me by surprise."

"Really? I didn't notice." I slide my hair behind my ears. I know I sound unconvincing.

Bob grins. "I've never been back, you know. All those years with only that stretch of lake separating me from the one place on earth where I had been truly happy. Sometimes the pull was so strong, I'd swear Celina was standing there on that dock calling me back to her. But I couldn't go. I had to resist, had to be strong. Dad drilled that into me. *Be strong, son. Put the past where it belongs — in the past."*

Bob sits in the chair beside the vending machine, rests his elbows on his knees, and laces his fingers together.

"I didn't want anyone to move back into the house. Ever. I wanted it to be left alone. I was so grateful when it was boarded up and nature took it over. I fantasized that Celina was my Sleeping Beauty and that she was not dead, just sleeping behind the vines and blackberry bushes.

"And then you arrived. There you were, standing there in that red dress, staring at me with pure honesty shining out of those eyes. I never thought I'd be looking into those eyes again. Sorry . . . you must think I'm crazy."

I don't know what to say.

Bob studies his hands. It's obvious that he's trying to keep his emotions in check, and my heart aches for him. His grief is palpable.

I recall my vision of him and Celina. How easy they were in each other's company. I can see them now in the hammock, curled into each other. There's no moon or stars, and they are encased in a velvety darkness. The scent of jasmine rides on the breeze. Robbie coils a length of Celina's hair around his little finger. He leans in close, the stubble on his chin brushing her cheek. He whispers into her ear, "Together forever, sweet pea."

"What? What did you say?" Bob's brow is furrowed, deep ripples climbing up to his bald scalp.

Oh no! Did I just say that out loud? I open my mouth to explain, but I can only shake my head.

"Sweet pea. 'Together forever, sweet pea.' I heard you. How could you know that?" Bob is working himself up. "Bayley . . ."

I swallow the dry lump in my throat, turn, and walk out of the room. I'm the one that's crazy. Certifiably insane, to be exact.

I'm making my escape through the hospital doors, when Gran calls out. I swing around.

"Bayley! There you are." Gran stands with Oliver and Amelia near the nurses' desk. "I thought we'd —"

I can't do this now. Gran's puzzled voice chases me out of the doors. "Bayley! Where are you going? What's —"

I run. With my flip-flops slapping the pavement and my purse banging against my hip, I run. I go down the hill, across some kind of park, and past the rec center where the squeals of kids' swimming and playing annoy the hell out of me. I run down onto the main street and right up to the end, until breathless and bent over, I'm outside Deb's store.

Of course, it's closed. It's Sunday afternoon. I bang my fists on the doors, then lean my forehead against the glass, and try to get my breath back.

A light flicks on, and one door swings open. Deb stands in the doorway.

"No need to bang." Deb peers down at me through tiny rectangular lenses balanced on the end of her nose, spicy aromas wafting around her. "Oh, Bayley! You look awful. Come in. What's up?"

What's up? What a question. How can I even begin to tell what's up? My father is dead, and my family is deranged. My brother is in the hospital because I nearly drowned him. My emotions are a mess and my heart flips every time I see Oliver, but I have an even stronger reaction when I see his father, Bob. How sick is that? And let's not forget the real doozy: I know things I shouldn't know, remember things that happened before I was born, and write as if the long-departed, probably the murdered, Celina O'Malley is guiding my hand. Which one of those little gems should I share?

The answer is obvious: none.

"I was in town and thought I'd drop by."

Deb draws her eyebrows together. "You're standing here

wheezing and disheveled, in the main street of Tallowood, in your swimsuit and an Indian shirt, and you expect me to believe that?"

I don't reply. What could I say anyway?

Deb flicks her glasses off her nose, and they swing down across her large breasts. "Come inside, dear. Let me get some tea into you. I'm getting a truckload of negative energy here."

Deb leads me into the tiny back room. The walls are lined with messy shelves that are stacked high, right to the ceiling. I hadn't noticed them last time. I slip onto the lumpy stool in the corner. Deb fills her electric kettle at the metal sink, balances it on the one clear space on the workbench, and plugs it in. Then she settles on the director-style chair in the opposite corner. The space is cramped — almost claustrophobic — but I welcome the closeness and feel cocooned by it.

Deb doesn't try to make conversation until she's made the tea and I have it cupped in my hands. "That's Celina's shirt, isn't it?" she says.

I nod.

"And those clothes the other day — they were Celina's too?"

I nod again, then bow my head.

"A little odd, don't you think?" says Deb.

I lift my eyes and gaze through the steam rising from my cup. It makes Deb appear wavy — ghostly.

"Do you believe in ghosts?" I say.

twenty-five

"I can't go home."

"Your mom will be worried, Bayley," Deb says. "No matter what's been going on, she doesn't deserve to worry unnecessarily, now does she?"

Deb is right. I stand and stretch my neck from side to side. It creaks with stiffness.

I wish that Deb had told me that I was a nut job, that my imagination was going wild, and that I should forget it all.

Instead, she had listened keenly, her head cocked to one side, a small vertical crease between her eyes the only indication of any apprehension. Her contributions consisted of the occasional "Wow" and "Oh lordy." When I finished, Deb seemed delighted. "That sounds like Celina, all right. I wonder what it is that she wants." It was not the reaction I'd hoped for.

"I don't want to sleep in that house," I say. "Not tonight. Can't I stay here?"

"Here? But —"

"Didn't you say the other day that your place is so empty that it rattles, now that your kids have moved out? Please, Deb." I'm asking far too much. I hardly know this woman.

Deb resists and throws up every possible argument to persuade me to go home to my family. But I persist, and finally Deb rubs her face wearily and says, "At least ring your mom and talk to her."

I pull my phone from my bag and turn it on. Immediately it beeps. I have twenty-five missed calls and seven messages. I blush as I scroll down the list: Mom, Gran, Amelia, even Loni repeated over and over.

I press Grandma's number. I still can't face Mom.

"Bayley, where are you, for goodness sake? We've been worried sick."

"Sorry."

"Are you okay?"

"Yeah. I'm fine. How's Seth?"

"He's doing well. He's staying overnight — for observation. That head wound is rather nasty. Your mother is staying with him."

"But he's going to be okay, isn't he? I'm so sorry. I didn't mean for it to happen."

"Shush. No one blames you. Your mom didn't mean those things she said. It was the stress talking. She's been through a lot. You know that. Now, where are you, sweetheart?"

"I'm with a friend," I say. "I'm going to stay over. Can you tell Mom?"

"What friend?" Gran's voice instantly switches from nurturing to alarmed. "Where?"

I catch Deb mouthing: *Tell her where you are, or you can't stay.*

"I'm with Deb from the craft and gift store in town. She used to be one of Celina's friends. I'm going to stay in her daughter's old room."

"This is very odd, Bayley. Can you put this Deb on?"

I hold the phone out to Deb. She takes it and walks out of the back room and into the shop. I don't bother following. I don't really want to know what Deb is going to tell Gran.

For the most part it doesn't matter — as long as whatever she says makes it so I don't have to spend tonight in that house by the lake.

Deb returns and throws the phone onto the bench. "Lord, that was rather awkward, Bayley."

"Sorry."

"Come on, come upstairs. I'll see if Janie left anything in her closet that might fit you, and then we'll go and get some food. What do you say?"

I am too grateful for words.

* * *

There are two choices for dinner. The Wok and Roll and the Bowling Club, which Deb calls the "Bowlo."

"The Bowlo," I say with enthusiasm, and we walk along the main street and then across the road to the Bowling Club.

The place smells of stale beer and is surprisingly busy.

"Happy hour leftovers and the early starters for the Sunday night raffle," Deb says by way of explanation, and directs me through the main bar toward the bistro at the back. It seems Deb knows the entire population of Tallowood, and it takes us an inordinately long time to walk a few feet as she greets every person we pass.

I keep my eyes low, avoiding contact with these unfamiliar faces. A large group is huddled around some low tables outside the bar area. They seem to be about my age. They shout out as two more girls enter behind me and wave them over. They appear so happy and carefree. I wonder if I will ever have a life like that.

"Hungry?" says Deb when we sit down at last, opposite each other at a small table.

"Starved." My stomach growls in agreement: I haven't eaten a thing since the sugar hit on the creek bank this morning. The memory makes my face hot.

We take a quick look at the menu and both order burgers and fries.

"I know this must be rather spooky for you, Bayley, and I hope you don't take what I'm about to say the wrong way, but I'm really excited about what you told me this afternoon."

Excited is not an emotion that I equate with what has been happening to me. Creepy. Disturbing. Frightening. But exciting — not even close.

"I have this feeling that Celina wants to tell me something," I whisper across the table as our meals are placed in front of us, "that she wants me to do something."

"Thanks, Nicole," Deb says to the waitress. She nods at me. "Dig in."

There is such relief in being able to discuss this at last. Keeping it a secret had been weighing on me, and a heavy knot of tension unravels from my chest. I take a big bite of my burger and then continue. "But why doesn't she just tell me? I feel like she is playing with me — toying with me. She's telling me her story, but not what I'm meant to be doing with it. It's frustrating."

"I'm sure it will become clear in time. It's simply Celina's way. She was always like that. In fact, that's how I knew you were telling me the truth. What you were telling me was exactly how Celina was. She'd string Suzie and me along all the time — get us begging to know what she was up to. And then of course, once we found out, we couldn't wait to hop on board."

Deb fiddles around with a fry, as if remembering something. "There's one thing you should know," she says. "Celina was a beautiful, kind-hearted person. At times she was a little bossy, perhaps, and determined. We used to call her our hippie sergeant. She was a Leo, so it's to be expected, I suppose. But she won't do anything that will hurt you. You don't need to be scared of her, of what's happening. Embrace it. In the end, you will be better for knowing her, like we all were."

This is getting far too weird. Better for knowing a ghost? Maybe Deb's a little cracked too.

I'm concentrating on my dinner and reflecting on Deb's words, when a roar goes up from the group near the bar. Three more have joined the group. There are shouts of "About time" and "Hurry up. I'm starving!" The group gets up and starts walking into the bistro to the long table that stretches across the back wall.

Over the top of their voices is a hissing jerky laugh that makes me almost gag on a mouthful of hamburger.

Oliver.

twenty-six

"Hey." Oliver is beside me before I have the chance to swallow. "You okay?"

My face blazes. I cover my mouth with my hand and force down the mouthful of food. "Yeah."

I don't know what else to say. A long silence stands between us. Oliver scuffs at the patterned carpet with his battered Converse, his face unable to mask his confusion.

"How's that gorgeous mother of yours?" says Deb. I appreciate her intrusion. "Could you tell her that the art supplies she ordered for your granddad have arrived?"

"Yeah, sure."

"Are you having dinner here?" Deb continues. "Do you want to join us?"

No! Yes! My heart seesaws.

"Oh, thanks. But I'm here with the guys."

"Sunday dinner at the Bowlo — things haven't changed much since I was your age. I used to come here with Suzie and Celina and your da—" Deb stops. Her eyes swing from me to Oliver and then back to me again. "Oh, look," she says, the words coming out high and squeaky. "There's Julie. Just the person I need to catch up with about her meditation classes next week. You don't mind, do you, Bayley? Perhaps you could hang out with Oliver for a little while? Meet some of the locals?" Deb catapults out of her chair and hurries off into the bar.

Oliver slips into the seat beside me and leans his head close to mine. "Where did you go?" he whispers. "We searched everywhere."

We? Oliver was out looking for me? Maybe Annie and Bob were looking too? Bob would've been after answers, no doubt. I am beyond mortified.

"I even slipped down into the morgue," Oliver continues, his eyes twinkling, "in case you were communing with the dead. Now that's a seriously creepy place."

At first this throws me. I have a how-does-he-know-I've-been-communing-with-the-dead? moment. Then I realize that he's being funny. "You idiot," I say. "You did not."

"You calling me a liar? I'm offended. Now you *must* tell me where you went."

"Why should I?"

"To make up for hurting my feelings. Come on. Spill."

"Nowhere. I went for a walk. To Deb's. I'm staying there tonight."

"At Deb's? Really? How do you know Deb? What's going on, Bayley?" He cups his hands over mine, and the sincerity in his eyes turns me to jelly. "Come on. You can tell me — trust or bust."

"Trust or bust? What does that even mean? You are an idiot, you know that."

"You have to stop calling me that. It does nothing for my fragile self-esteem."

I giggle, but my mind is swirling. Should I tell Oliver too? Would he think I'm insane? Probably. And how could I tell him about my reaction to his father? Nope, bad idea. Very bad.

"Nothing's up. Really. It's just a lot of stuff has happened to my family in these past few months, and it's been really hard handling all of it."

"What kind of stuff?" There's a catch in Oliver's voice, and I can tell he is nervous that he's going too far.

"My dad . . ." A lump forms in my own throat. Is it always going to hurt this much just to say his name? "He died last May — suddenly."

"Crap. What happened?"

"It was stupid, really. There was this big rainstorm. Seth had left his Batman out on the patio and was wailing about it getting wet. So Dad went to the rescue, only when he went to run back inside, he slipped and hit his head on a stone bench. It was pretty horrific, and I guess we've all fallen to pieces since."

"That sucks." He squeezes my hand then swipes at the escapee tear running toward my ear. "Is that why Seth always wears that cape?"

I nod, our eyes meeting, and it feels as if we're talking to each other without saying a word.

"Hey, Oliver," yells some tall, skinny guy from the long table. "You gonna order or what?"

"Keep your pants on! I'm coming," Oliver yells, then turns back to me, his mouth curving into a smile. "Come and meet the gang. We hang out here most Sunday nights. Then sometimes we go to Marco's to play some pool or watch a movie or something. Obviously, it's pretty wild. Are you up for it?"

I look at the group — whose members have probably known each other their whole lives — and my insides squeeze together.

"Come on," says Oliver. "Katie and Tina are in your grade. They're both crazy horse nuts, but they can be okay. All you have to do is toss your head and say 'neeeeiiigh' and they'll be your friends for life."

I shake my head. "Nah."

"You mean neigh."

"No, I mean no. Pass. Not tonight. Sorry, but I'm too stressed out — what with Seth and everything."

"All the more reason. It would give you a chance to chill for a little while."

I feel everyone's eyes upon me. I take in the relaxed manner with which they huddle, how they drape themselves over one another and laugh and tease. They appear to move as one.

Oliver takes my hand and tries to drag me to my feet. He is smiling that ridiculous smile of his, the one that reaches right up to those damn greenish-blue eyes. I almost cave, but a roar of laughter from the long table brings me back to my senses. I pull out of his grip.

"Don't do this, Oliver. I can't."

I feel trapped. I don't want to go anywhere near Oliver's friends. They'll see straight through me and expose me for the crazy girl that I certainly am.

Oliver tries to coax me out of the chair again. I dig my heels into the carpet. The walls of the tiny bistro seem to press in on me, and those laughing faces become distorted, leering, raucous, swirling around me. I jump up, push past Oliver, and bolt. I rush through the crowded front bar, out the front door, and onto the street and into the absurd rosy radiance of the early evening.

I sense Oliver behind me. I can hear him calling my name, but I refuse to stop. I take a sharp turn into some shifty alley and sprint like I'm fighting for first position at the state cross-country meet. I ignore the thud of footsteps and heavy breathing behind me.

The alley is a dead end. A tall wire fence blocks off a large parking lot. I skid to a halt.

I'm considering scaling the fence, when Oliver catches me by the wrist and swings me to him.

"Man, you're fast." We are both puffing, our chests heaving. "Sorry for pushing you back there. I don't know when to stop sometimes."

I swallow the lump that has wedged itself in my throat.

"Sorry for being an idiot."

"Same." Oliver's voice is as warm and comforting as my fuzzy blanket, and I want to wrap myself in it. "Hey," he says, "just proves we have tons in common, crazy eyes."

I try to wiggle free of his hold, but he clutches me tighter and pulls me to him. He goes to say something, but instead presses his lips fiercely against mine. I'm surprised by the way my body eagerly responds. We bend into each other, heads on each other's shoulder.

My face is wet with tears. That was so good. But this is so not the right time.

twenty-seven

The river, thick with mud, slides around the edge of town like a languid brown snake. It's early in the morning, and Oliver and I stand at the top of a grassy edge, watching a pair of gray ducks ride the current around the bend and bob skillfully under a series of low overhanging branches.

Oliver cups his hands around his mouth. "Duck!" he shouts to the ducks.

"You're nuts," I say with a laugh.

"Just offering some friendly advice. Those branches pack a powerful punch." He leads me down the mushy bank to the water's edge, the earth squelching beneath our sandals.

It's already muggy, and I'm aware that I should be heading home. But I know Mom will be angry at me for staying at Deb's, so the chance to spend some time alone with Oliver first is too tempting to pass up.

"This track goes all the way to Wongawilli Bridge," Oliver says, and there is an element of pride in his voice as he shows me his town, his place.

I nod, soaking in the morning peace and enjoying the intimacy of walking hand in hand with Oliver Mitchell along the banks of the Wongawilli River. Just us and the ducks. Oliver brings my hand to his lips, and it's as if my veins have been filled with sunshine.

We walk for a bit longer until we find a grassy patch and sit down. He pulls a curl of hair from my mouth, brushes my cheek with the tips of his fingers, and sweeps his lips ever so softly across mine. It is so tender and sweet and sexy.

Oliver's cheeks are rosy and his eyes intense. It scares me a little. I am way out of my comfort zone here, but hey, bring it on.

We look out over the river. Oliver puts his arm over my shoulder and draws me in closer. "How was staying at the witch's place last night?" he says, making conversation. "Spooky?"

"Witch? You mean Deb? Don't be a jerk."

"I'm not being a jerk. She used to scare the crap out of me when I was in elementary school. She was really big . . . and that hair . . . and that white face." He contorts his face and cackles. "She scared all the kids."

"You big wuss. Deb's not scary." I could sure show him a thing or two about scary.

"Ah, but you haven't met the mysterious Madam Moon yet, have you?"

"Madam Moon? What are you talking about? You are so weird."

"I will ignore that last comment on account of you being a newbie here. But there's more to Deb than you might first realize. She used to have this fortune-telling tent at Tallowood Summer Fair. Marco and I loved it. We would wait in line for ages, just so she could give us a year's worth of nightmares."

"Okay. I'm confused."

"It was a fundraiser thing for saving the whales or something, but she was good."

"Did she use crystal balls and stuff?" I can imagine Deb doing that and see her dressed as Madam Moon.

"No crystal ball, but her tent used to stink pretty bad and she had these freaky cards and she'd gaze into her coffee mug —"

"Teacup."

"Whatever. And then she'd stare up at you and say in a spooky voice, stuff like, 'Beware the insects that follow you.'"

"Yeah, wow. Real scary."

"Do you know how many insects there are around here? I was looking over my shoulder and freaking out for months. One time she told Marco to avoid dark public places at all costs. I don't think Marco went to the bathroom at school ever again. He'd just bolt home every afternoon, about to bust."

"And you guys believed her?"

"We were kids, and she was convincing. She'd always finish with, 'Be good, study hard, listen to your parents, and good fortune will find you.'"

"I bet your parents put her up to it."

"Yeah, probably."

I reach for his hand, turn it palm up. "I can read palms, you know."

"Yeah? What does mine say?"

"It says that if you don't get me home soon, my mother is going to string you up and hang you by your toenails over the gorge."

"Well, I think you're crap at fortune-telling." He grabs my arm, bends it up to his face, squints at my elbow, and then traces his fingers around it.

"What are you doing?" I try to twist my arm free.

"Palm reading is for beginners, crazy eyes. I read elbows."

"Elbows?"

"Yes. And your elbow says that you are *very* desperate. That's desperate with a capital D."

"Must be, if I'm hanging out with you, I guess."

"Shhh. Remember, the self-esteem. And don't interrupt — you're breaking the energy flow." His finger tickles the skin around my elbow. "Let me see. Ah, yes, desperate — desperate for a handsome young rower to kiss you."

"Is that so?" I'm giggling now. He is such an idiot.

"Wait, there's more. Your elbow says that you don't just want one kiss — you want lots."

His fingers are in my hair, and he smothers kisses across my face and neck and down my arms.

I'm laughing so hard I could burst. But, hey, elbows don't lie. I desperately want Oliver to kiss me all over and never stop.

* * *

"Where the hell have you been?" Mom is on me before I even have one foot out of the car. "I've been worried sick. What's going on with you, Bayley?" Mom's hair stands out from her head like twisty gray twigs. When did she get that gray?

I step out gingerly, guilt festering. "I was at Deb's, like I said. Oliver drove me home."

Oliver stands beside me. "Hi, Kath."

"Don't you 'Hi, Kath' me. I'll deal with you later." I feel Oliver tense beside me. "I've been to the store. You were *not* there. I was standing out front, banging on that door for half an hour, and no one was there. No one. At eight o'clock in the morning. No one picked up when I called the phone number you gave Gran. And anyway, why haven't you even called me, for God's sake?"

"My phone died," I answer lamely, struggling not to give in to the tears that threaten to spill at this second unwarranted attack. "I was there. Deb does yoga in the park at dawn, so Oliver picked me up to bring me home. He was staying at a friend's place in town."

"Is that right? How long does it take to drive from Tallowood, Bayley? It's almost eleven."

She has me there.

Gran and Amelia step out onto the porch to watch the show. Then the door flings open and out flies Seth. He bounds down the stairs, and it's been a long time since the sight of his Batman cape flapping in the breeze has brought such a smile to my face. He leaps into my arms and nestles into my neck, crying, "I'm sorry, Bails. I'm sorry."

I drink in the warmth of his scrawny little body, thirsty for the solid beating of his heart. "No need to say sorry, Seth. It was an accident. I'm glad to see you're all better, though."

"Sorry," he says again.

"Hey, quit with the sorries — how about a thank you to Oliver for plucking you out of the water?"

Oliver holds up his hand for a high five. Seth slaps it. "Thanks."

"Hey," says Oliver. "It's all in a day's work for us superheroes. Kapow, pow!" Oliver lands a couple of pretend punches into Seth's side. Seth giggles and squirms and lands a volley of punches into Oliver's open hands. "Great to see you have your strength back, Batman."

"Enough," says Mom, and she pulls Seth out of my arms. "Go inside now. Doctor's orders — you have to lie low for a bit. Remember?"

"Come on, Seth," calls Gran. "Let's watch another movie. Bayley and Mom have some things to work out."

Oliver and Seth exchange a secret wink and a couple of pretend kicks, then Seth heads up the steps and inside with Gran. At Gran's insistence, Amelia follows behind them. The wire door slaps shut, and Mom gets right back to drilling me.

"Where were you last night? And don't you dare lie to me."

"I was at Deb's, at the store. I stayed upstairs in her daughter's old room."

I grab my bag out of Oliver's car. "You better go," I say to Oliver. "Thanks for the ride. Sorry about this."

He goes to protest, but I silence him with a shake of my head. Then he nods, his face like a sad puppy's, and slips into the driver's seat. I walk toward the house, deserting him, flipping between extreme embarrassment and extreme anger.

"You knew I was at the hospital," Mom shouts at my back over the hum of Oliver's car starting up. "You never thought to stop there? To see your brother? To come home with us?" She doesn't wait for me to answer. "No. You're too busy gallivanting round town with some boy you hardly know. Too selfish even to call or to see if there was anything you could do to help out. Seth has been asking for you since he woke up. I will get to the bottom of this, Bayley. Rest assured."

I glide up the stairs and inside without looking back. *Too selfish*. Yeah, that's me. The one who's been holding this family together for the past eight months. Selfish to the core.

I weave my way past Seth, Gran, and Amelia, who are all sprawled out across the floor of the living room in front of the TV. I don't dare to make eye contact with any of them for fear of losing it, and I take the stairs two at a time, reminding myself that I should know better than to think I could ever be happy.

I open the door to my room and glare at Celina's shiny blue eyes in the portrait on the wall, and I'm thrust back to my conversations with Deb. "Well," I say, full of shivers. "Are you ever going to tell me what it is you want me to do, so I can get on with my life?"

* * *

That night I sleep like the dead. But some time during the night, I become vaguely aware that the temperature has plummeted. It's freezing. Some kind of cold snap must have blown in. I gather up my blanket, pull it around my ears, snuggle into it, and slip straight back into glorious sleep.

I wake up to magnificent sunshine and a room that is already warm, and I'm frying under all the heavy bedding. I toss off the blanket and spring out of bed to open the window when I notice my notebook is tucked under my pillow, and I become chilled once more.

One page is dog-eared. Something that I never do. I open to the page, and writing is scribbled across the lined paper in messy blue pen.

And it is clear that I have been visited.

I told you that you'd love Robbie, didn't I?

And don't worry your pretty little self about it, Bayley — it was just me making you hot for him. I couldn't help myself. I needed you for a little while. It was the only way I could really experience him again. So I went along for the ride with you a couple of times.

And it was so worth it, so divine. Seeing Robbie again, really seeing him. Being that close to him, with your warm blood coursing through me. You can't begin to imagine. He might be balding, middle-aged Bob to you, but to me he is still my Robbie, my beautiful, beautiful Robbie.

Did you hear him call me his Sleeping Beauty? He still loves me, like I knew he would. A love like ours never dies. Not even that sweet-as-apple-pie Annie can steal his love away from me. So thank you, cuz; I'm still dancing from the joy of it.

Deb and Suzie were jealous of Robbie at first, you know. I guess that was to be expected. We'd been a threesome — the Peace Sisters — for as long as we could remember, and the arrival of a boyfriend ruffled their feathers some.

But I wasn't too concerned. I knew they'd come round, like they always did. Those two were as pliable as that Sculpey we used to make coiled pots out of as kids. They needed to see things from my perspective, that was all.

To be honest, I felt like I was outgrowing the Peace Sisters anyway. *Deb was a fool and Suzie a spoilsport, and I was getting tired of being the one with all the ideas all the time. They were both too needy. And the whole Peace Sister thing was feeling a little stale. Stifling, in fact.*

But I did have plans — escape plans. Tallowood and all it represented was suffocating me. I could barely breathe, and I knew there was so much more for me out there.

But sadly for Deb and Suzie, my plans didn't include them.

twenty-eight

It's taken about a week, but I now have the timing down to perfection. It's 5:25 a.m., and I'm creeping down the stairs, running shoes in hand, being careful to avoid the holey third step and intent on not waking anyone up — especially Mom. That would only ruin everything.

Once out in the fresh air of dawn, I slip on my shoes, press my iPod earbuds into my ears, and I'm off.

It feels good to be jogging again. Strange good, but good nonetheless. I love the routine of it, the way training shapes my day — and my body. I can already feel my fitness building.

By the time I pass the dock and am on the path beside the lake, I've settled into a good rhythm. I don't need to rush. I have plenty of time. Plenty of time to rack up the miles and plenty of time to be alone with my thoughts.

I've been thinking about Celina a lot on these morning runs. I keep imagining her in her school uniform, schoolbag slung over her shoulder, walking down the gravel driveway and out the gate. I hear the cry of a sole bird crack through the morning air as Celina strolls along the road, scuffing up dust. The sun slants through the trees, and her hair shines. She's smiling a contented smile, and she's thinking of Robbie, her heart light at the thought of them being together.

In the dark of the bushes to the right of her, I see a shadow lurking. Sense, rather than see, I suppose. A presence. Someone's watching her. Following her. Stalking. Waiting for the right moment.

I shudder, wondering if this scene I keep imagining is another "vision" from Celina. Regardless, these are not the best thoughts to have when you're out jogging by yourself in the middle of nowhere, and my eyes sweep across the fields to my right.

I hope it wasn't too gruesome for her. I hope that it was over quickly — one swift blow to the head or something.

One swift blow to the head. My thoughts divert to Dad. I

guess in a way he was lucky. Not lucky to have died, but lucky that his death was swift and unexpected. That he was happy at the time. That he didn't have to face the agony of saying goodbye, nor a long, painful death.

Such horribly morbid thoughts! I turn up my iPod, and I try to think of something pleasant — like Oliver.

At last, the back end of the lake opens up before me. And there he is, striking the water with his usual strength and purpose. He sees me too, waves, and rows toward the shore.

Tiny butterflies thrum their way into my heart.

* * *

We meet at a bend in the shore that's sandy and sheltered by a small grove of willows. Oliver wipes the perspiration from his face, arms, and chest with a towel, then chucks it back into his kayak and takes out a beach towel and a plastic bag of food.

"That was so good," he says. "Sprinted the last two laps. It was getting painful, but I'm so pumped."

I recognize the satisfaction on his face. Oliver gets it. It's great to be with someone who understands. Even Loni used to make fun of my obsession with training. No one except

Dad understood how intoxicating it is to work your body to the max, to push through the pain barrier, until you feel as if you can do anything. It's better than sex even — apparently. Training becomes a part of you and becomes as essential as breathing. And I am very glad to be back.

I flop onto the towel the moment Oliver has spread it out on the sand. "So what's it today?" Already it's become a routine, this early-morning picnic.

"Cheese and crackers," Oliver replies as he sits beside me, eyes gleaming.

"Your mom must shop a ton."

"I eat a ton." He tosses a cheese cube into his mouth and washes it down with a swig of some kind of energy drink.

"That stuff is so not good for you," I say. "It's filled with chemicals and way too much salt and caffeine."

"Oh, you're the expert?" Oliver leans back on his elbows and stretches out his legs in front of him. "It's on my list from my coach, so it's okay with me."

"You have a coach?"

"Sort of — an online one anyways. He used to be my coach at St. James. When I moved back to school here, he kept in touch. He sends me a monthly diet and training plan."

"That's pretty cool."

"Yeah. He's a cool dude. He'd invested a lot of time in me at St. James. He was devastated when I told him I was leaving. I kind of feel I owe it to him to keep to the plan."

"Sounds like a lot of pressure."

"No pressure. I want to do it. Plus, I have no excuse — what with the boatshed fitted out as a gym, and this lake ten feet from my bedroom, I'd be a bit of an idiot to not at least try."

I grin. It's almost like Oliver is two people: the nut who acts like some kind of adorable Labrador puppy, and this driven, focused athlete who has his whole future mapped out. I can't help but lean over and kiss him. Oliver responds hungrily. We lie together entwined, and every part of me is singing.

Eventually, we untangle ourselves. Oliver reaches for his drink. "Hey, how are things at home?" he says. "Is it safe for me to show my face yet?"

"Mmm, maybe give it a couple more days. Mom has calmed down a bit, but that's probably because the place has been overrun with builders and painters. So she's been preoccupied. Plus, she's had three shifts in a row at the Wok and Roll." In truth, I'm enjoying keeping Oliver as my sweet secret. I love that I'm having a life that no one else in the family knows about — something other than being haunted by a stalker ghost, that is.

"The builders must be nearly finished."

"I'm not sure they are. They're working on the barn. I was hoping it was going to be a studio for Mom, but first Gran is going to move in for a bit, which is good. Mostly."

"Mostly?"

"Good that Gran is staying. But bad that Mom won't have a studio. She needs to get back to designing."

"I like your grandma. She's cool."

"Yeah. She helps keep us from killing each other."

"Every family needs a rudder."

"What?"

"Yeah, you know — like in a boat, to keep you on course, in the right direction, and all that."

"Oh, thank you, Wise One! Yes, I guess Gran's our rudder." I flip over onto my stomach and swallow the last of my cracker. "So who's the Mitchell family rudder?"

"Mom, of course."

I'm about to reply, when a strange smell wafts by, making the hairs on the back of my neck stand up.

"What's that?" I flip back over and sit up.

"What?"

"That smell. Can't you smell it?"

"Hey. It wasn't me. It was you, wasn't it, crazy eyes? Own up."

"No, I'm serious. Can't you smell it — like some kind of chemicals or something?"

"You just have chemicals on your brain."

There is a loud cracking sound, and both Oliver and I leap to our feet.

"What was *that*?"

"An animal probably." Though I can tell by the way Oliver's eyes scan through the willows surrounding us that he's not that certain. Then his shoulders relax, and he points. "It's only Grandpa."

My eyes follow to where Oliver is pointing. A small stooped man with a burlap sack slung over his shoulder is poking around the base of a willow with a stick.

"Hey, Grandpa!" yells Oliver.

The man swings around and takes a step toward us, but as soon as his eyes fall on me, he turns and takes off at a startlingly fast pace.

My head is ringing. I know that face. It's etched in my brain. That was the man — the man I saw that night by the lake.

"Silly old man," says Oliver. He sits down and reaches for another piece of cheese.

"Why did he take off like that?" I manage to ask.

"I told you before, he's a bit wacky — a recluse — you probably scared him off."

"And he doesn't speak? Right?"

"Nope, he hasn't uttered a word for about ten years. Which makes for awkward dinner conversation."

This doesn't make sense. I'm sure he's the man I saw, but that night he spoke. Definitely. *Holy mother of God! Holy mother of God!* I couldn't have imagined it, could I?

This is freaking me out and then some.

"Hey, sit down, Bails. Don't let the old guy rattle you. He's harmless. He's just collecting stuff for his collages. He does it most mornings, some evenings."

I can't sit down. I have a dreadful urge to throw up.

"No, thanks." I aim at keeping my voice steady.

Oliver takes my hands and tries to pull me to him. "Come on, Bails." His eyes twinkle at me.

But I'm nauseous and dizzy. I pull myself free. "Sorry. Gotta go — Mom had said something about getting up early and taking a walk this morning." The lie is out before I even think it through. "I don't want to be found out."

"Tomorrow, then?" Oliver's face is a question mark.

"Yeah, tomorrow. See you." And I head off almost at a sprint.

twenty-nine

That afternoon, Gran stroked my cheek, looked me deep
in the eyes, and said, "Are you okay, Bayley? Is there something troubling you, sweetheart?"

I was so touched, I nearly blurted out, *Yes! Yes, something
is wrong.* I longed to tell her everything, to say, *I have a ghost,
Gran, a freaking ghost who is telling me stories. Showing me
glimpses of her life. A ghost who is messing with my head. Tell me
what to do, Gran.*

But I caught myself and fobbed her off, pleading tiredness.

"I want you to know one thing, Bayley," she added. "I

understand what you're going through. I understand everything. Do you know what I'm saying?"

Understand? For a moment I thought Gran knew about Celina. My mouth flopped open.

"It's been tough for you all," she said. "But things will get better. They will. Your mother will find her way and be her old self again. She's just afraid and confused and . . . well, I've seen a fair bit of tragedy in my life, and it's true what they say about time . . ."

I hugged my thanks and went in search of Seth to take him down to the lake, with the sad knowledge that while Gran might have been through a lot, she has no idea about the things that are being thrown at me. And that makes me feel more alone and afraid than ever.

* * *

I light three candles on my desk. Two are in-case-of-a-blackout ones from the kitchen. The other, round and orange and sweetly scented, I stole from Amelia's room. I don't know why I'm lighting them, but it seems appropriate.

I open the peace chest and pull out the jeans and T-shirt I wore on that first night, plus the purple scarf Deb made. I slip off my tank top and pull on Celina's clothes. Next, I place Celina's creepy portrait on the bed. It's a testament to Bud's talent, because I'm seeing something very different in Celina's face now. The energy and enthusiasm has gone, replaced with something darker — bitterness perhaps? The Karinya sign and the photo album go beside the portrait, and also the notebook opened to a new page. Now I am surrounded with the things that have led me to some kind of a connection with Celina.

I know this is ridiculous, that I'm fooling myself to think that any of this is going to make any difference or that I'll be able to call Celina's spirit at will — channel her or whatever it is that's happened before. It's obvious she's the one that's been running this show. Just like in her real life. What did Deb call her? The hippie sergeant?

But the time has come. I have to know what she wants. Somehow, I have to persuade her to come clean, to stop toying with me. And I have to find out why Lakeside and Oliver's dad make me feel strange and sick.

I pick up my pencil. What to write? *Oliver.* The word is written without me even thinking it. No surprise there, I suppose. He's always in my thoughts these days.

Oliver. I write it again. I say it out loud, feel the way the syllables roll out from the back of my throat and enjoy the way the sound of his name makes me feel zingy.

Focus! I tell myself. *Concentrate on the task at hand. Be bold. Be fearless.*

I write, *Lakeside.*

Then, *Robbie.*

As soon as the word is on the page, the space around me changes, as if a damp sea fog has rolled in through the open window. My eyes scurry around the room. The yellow flames on the candles seem to grow larger. They sway and smoke, then turn from yellow to blue, and I feel Celina's presence right beside me and all around me at the same time. But it's as though something menacing has tumbled in with the fog. I'm beyond scared. What an idiot. What was I thinking calling a ghost?

My head is thrown back. Invisible icy fingers clutch my hand and force it back to the page.

I felt ripped off, if you must know, Bayley. Dying that young, when I had everything to look forward to — my whole life ahead of me. And it was going to be such a good life. I had so much passion, so much I wanted to do, to achieve.

But the worst part was knowing how everyone suffered so horribly after I was gone. It's one thing losing a loved one; it's a part of life — death. Isn't it? Death you can cope with eventually. But not knowing, that's the real killer. That's a never-ending nightmare.

And that's what drove Robbie away from the lake — away from me. I tried to call to him, to tell him to stay, not to go. But he wouldn't hear. Couldn't hear. His grief was too loud.

The not knowing is what made Mom and Dad crazy as well. That was hard to watch. I don't think you'll be surprised to hear it was no accident that their car crashed into a tree on the night of what would have been my twenty-first birthday. They planned it. Made it seem like it was some freak accident, so the family wouldn't be shamed by their suicide, so the saintly Catholic O'Malley clan could deal with this additional tragedy without getting caught up in the fires of hell and damnation nonsense. That's what kind of people they were.

But their pain, and Robbie's, was too great, Bayley. I could feel it. Deeply. That's why I'm still here. I knew one day, I'd get the chance. I just had to be patient. And then you came, like I knew you would.

When you opened the peace chest, that night, I was so excited. There you were, almost my clone. But it was more than that that made you special. Because inside you, Bayley, you were all hollowed out, like an empty shell washed up on the shore. You were perfect. There was plenty of room for me to come and go, and I knew the time had come. My time had come. My determination and patience had paid off. It took quite an effort to distract Aunty

Maree so that she left the peace chest behind. But I needed it. It kept me company through those lonely years and reminded me about what I'd lost. It was all worth it.

HE has to pay, Bayley. He has to pay for the pain he caused. And really, my sad little cousin, it's up to you. Make him pay, Bayley. Make him pay.

I'm depending on you. Now you know. Peace, sister.

Why are tears salty? Why can't they taste like chocolate or honey? Instead, they spill onto your lips and sting, leaving a bitter aftertaste to remind you of your misery.

I wipe my face on my pillow and try to pull myself together. I don't even know what I'm crying about. Am I crying for Celina? For me? For what she's asking me to do? How am I going to make him pay? And who is *he*? Is Celina ever going to tell me that part? Or do I have to figure it out myself? Was it some random stranger? I don't think so. I sense the person is still alive and still in the area.

My mind keeps coming back to Oliver's grandfather, and it sickens me to think that he might be the one. It can't be him — that's too horrible. I pray that I'm overreacting and judging him wrongly because he frightened me and he's a little odd.

"*Peace, sister,*" I mutter to the chest. "*Peace, sister.*" How can I get any peace with the burden of Celina's words pressing against my ribs?

My door flings open and I leap up, the notebook hurtling from my lap to the floor.

Amelia staggers into the doorway, the candlelight making her face appear distorted and shadowy.

"Jesus, Amelia," I hiss. "What are you doing?"

"Me?" she slurs. She sweeps her hand theatrically in front of her. "Me? What's all this? Having a freaking séance or something? Peace, sister . . ."

"You're drunk."

"And you're a freak."

I pull her inside the room, close the door, and switch on my light. "Shh. You'll wake Mom."

"Yeah right. You're so clueless. She's been knocking herself out on pills for the last week or more." Amelia laughs an ugly laugh, and in the brighter light, I can see that her lipstick is smeared across her face and her hair looks like birds have been calling it home.

"Where have you been?"

"As if I'm going to tell you." Her eyes lock on the candles. "You little thief." She blows out the orange one and swipes it from my desk.

"You're one to talk," I counter pointlessly.

She snorts, yanks open the door, and marches out, tripping over her own feet as she stumbles up the hall.

I blow out the remaining candles, turn off the light, and flop onto my bed. I only last ten seconds before the darkness starts to creep me out. I switch on my bedside lamp and stare at the wall.

My long day is going to be followed by a very long night.

thirty

My room is warm and stuffy.

I'm thinking of the beach and Loni. I can smell sunscreen and salty, seaweedy air. I hear Loni's rolling laugh and non-stop commentary. The sand is toasty beneath my feet. It's delicious.

I sit upright.

What an idiot. I've slept in.

I fling on my clothes, jam my feet into my running shoes, and dash down the stairs, nearly twisting my ankle on the holey third step — when are the builders going to fix that?

— and narrowly avoiding a collision with Mom as I sprint for the door.

"Hey, what's the hurry?" she says, spinning on the spot as I fly by.

"Going for a jog — before it gets too hot," I say and bound down the porch stairs.

Mom follows me out onto the porch. "Bails," she calls.

I turn round, jogging backward down the driveway. "What? I'm in a hurry, Mom."

"I can see that," she says. "It's just . . . it's just good to see you running again, that's all. Good for all of us."

Wow, where did that come from? I turn back round and take off across the field, emotion blurring my vision.

I'm less than a mile in and already my right side kills and my lungs are burning, and if those rotten flies don't stop buzzing around my head, I swear I'm going to scream. I'm running far too fast, but I put my head down and run through the pain.

I realize that I'm doing a fine job of wearing myself out, but after last night, the need to see Oliver, to burrow into his arms and feel their strength around me, is all consuming.

A quick scan of the lake and I see no sign of him. I suck in a couple of deep breaths and concentrate on getting there.

I finally turn the bend before our meeting spot — just

in time to see Oliver paddling off, about fifty feet from the shore. Panting, I stop, cup my hands around my mouth, and go to yell out, but something catches my eye. His name evaporates on my tongue.

Out from the cover of the willows, a bent figure scuttles across the sand. Bud. He drops his bag and strides to the shoreline, then starts brushing the sand with his boot. He works his way purposely along, his boot scraping back and forth as he goes, and it's soon apparent that he's scrubbing something out. A message from Oliver, maybe? What did it say?

Part of me wants to charge down there and demand he stop — to challenge him, strike out at him. But I don't, because I can't move. My thoughts turn to Celina, and my heart thuds so fiercely, blood bellows in my ears. I slink back behind some bushes, out of sight.

Celina, I refuse to hear you. Seriously, I don't want to know.

* * *

The night is balmy. The half-moon throws spidery shadows from the Norfolk pine across the front of the house. I steal into the soft darkness.

Once I'm clear of the driveway and into the field, I flick on my flashlight and welcome its golden beam marking the way ahead. My stomach churns with nerves. This is so not a good idea, but then again, sleeping in my room with the ghost of Celina doesn't really appeal to me either.

"Tonight. Meet me at the dock," Oliver had said this afternoon when he called. He was inexplicably broody and miffed, and he didn't seem to believe me when I told him how Bud had scrubbed out his message in the sand. I was left feeling confused and uneasy.

At the dock, Oliver is already there, waiting, and my jitters melt away. "Hey," he whispers, and the moonlight shows the shine in his eyes. "You made it."

He takes my hand and helps me into the rowboat. With a nod of his head, he indicates for me to sit, before giving the back of the boat a powerful shove that launches it off the sand. He jumps in, reaches across me, takes both oars, and rows gently, almost noiselessly, away. The boat glides across the silky water.

"Where are we going?" I ask once we are well away from the shore.

"Don't know. Where'd you like to go? The Circle?"

"Okay." I take one of the oars, and together we head toward the craggy northern side of the lake. It's exhilarating.

Neither of us speaks, and there is pleasure in this silence, neither of us feeling the need to fill it. I focus on matching Oliver's strokes, keeping the rhythm, and listening to the gentle lap of the water under the boat, the spasmodic humming of the frogs.

We're almost in the shadow of the cliffs when a distant rumbling echoes across the lake. I turn my head toward the sound, trying to make out what it is.

"Just a car." Oliver reads my mind. "Probably up on the highway."

"Really? I've never heard any noise from the highway before."

Oliver shrugs and continues rowing. My eyes sweep the ragged silhouette to the north. The noise intensifies, and then I glimpse the flicker of lights. Car lights dancing about the bush and heading toward my house.

"There," I say and point, dropping the oar. Oliver stops, and we sit in the boat and watch the car emerge from the bushes and crawl along the dirt road toward the gate.

"What the —?"

"Calm down. It's probably just Lee or Mitch."

"Lee or Mitch?"

The car stops about a hundred feet before the front gate, semihidden by the thick scrub lining the road.

"Amelia's new buddies. Picking her up."

"What are you talking about?" Someone jogs out of the gates and up to the car. It's obviously Amelia. I stand up, and the boat sways. Oliver grabs my elbow and yanks me down.

"Watch it," he says. "You'll tip us overboard."

My heart is flipping out. "What is she doing?"

"You don't know, do you? She's a sneaky one."

I shake my head, feeling like a complete idiot.

"Amelia's up in town nearly every night. Hanging out in the back of the pub or down by the river with a bunch of the locals."

"How do you know? And why didn't you tell me?"

Oliver's bangs fall across his eyes. He brushes it out of the way and shoots me a savage look. "I know because I live here," he says. "That's how. It's a small town. I've seen her. She's hard not to notice. And I didn't tell you because it's no biggie — although I didn't realize that she'd been sneaking out." Oliver laughs.

Frankly, I don't see what's so funny, and even his silly hissing laugh can't lessen my anxiety. He grabs my oar and starts to row away, just as the car turns round and heads off back down the road.

"Hey, don't worry about it. She's okay. And the guys she's hanging out with are harmless. Idiots, but harmless idiots." He reaches across and lifts my chin. "She's only having fun."

He sounds so much like Amelia that my stomach clenches. Why does stuff like this bother me so much? When did I turn into the captain of the fun police? I don't want Amelia to ruin my night, but I *am* worried about her. I can't help it. And what worries me most is what will happen when Mom finds out.

"You gonna help, or do you expect me to do all the work?" Oliver's smile is wide. "Come on." He changes direction. "Let's head for the middle. And forget about Amelia — she's no different than you, out here with me."

I sigh and pick up the oar. He's right. Mom would flip out if she knew I was here with Oliver and, perversely, it makes me grin to think of Mom peacefully asleep while both her daughters are out gallivanting. Gallivanting! That is such a Mom word, and the thought makes me laugh out loud.

"Gonna share the joke?"

"Nah," I say. "What's so cool about the middle of the lake anyway?"

Oliver stops rowing, slides off the seat onto his back, and points to the sky. "This."

I squint upward.

"Want to watch the show?"

It's a tight squeeze, the two of us lying on our backs, knees bent to fit in. Oliver threads his fingers through mine and we gaze up at the starry sky, as deep and wide as it is intense. It makes my head spin, trying to fathom the size of it. Where it starts and where it ends. We watch a satellite journey from horizon to horizon, then disappear into nowhere. We locate the Southern Cross. We hold our breath, waiting for a shooting star. It never comes, but we don't care.

I am aware of Oliver's chest rising and falling beside mine. I reach across and trace my finger along the raised blue vein that snakes across his upper arm muscles, savoring the strength in those arms, then spread my hand across the wrinkle of his T-shirt, absorbing the steady rhythm of his breathing. There is something reassuring about it. It's as if as long as those lungs continue to fill with air, and that heart continues to pump, things are going to be okay.

I am consumed with a beautiful calm.

But eventually, calmness allows my mind to drift. Infuriatingly, it drifts to Celina. Celina and Robbie watching this same sky, locating the same constellations, feeling the same reassurance that life is going to be sweet. *Together forever, sweet pea.*

A breeze tickles the ends of my hair, and I'm suddenly cold. Determined to ignore it, I grit my teeth and will the feeling away. But it won't go. My arms and legs become covered in goose bumps. I flinch and sit up.

"Hey, what's up?"

"Nothing." I fold my arms across my chest. "It's just getting cold, don't you think?"

"Uh, no. It's hot, and it could get hotter." Oliver gives me a sly grin, and beckons for me to join him.

But I can't. My senses are on overdrive. "Can't you feel it?" I say. "I think someone is watching us or something."

"Don't be dumb. Come on, Bayley." Even in the moonlight, I can see the flush in Oliver's cheeks, the look in his eyes. It excites me. But not enough to shake the feeling that someone or something is lurking nearby.

"Really, I can feel it. Someone — over there, on the shore. I feel like someone is watching us. Like someone is following us."

"Don't be crazy, Bayley. Come on, forget it."

"Maybe it's your grandpa again."

I regret it as soon as I say it.

Oliver pulls himself up and back onto the seat with a sigh. "Are you for real?"

"Well, it could be. I keep getting this feeling that he's following us." I'm trying to justify myself, but know that I'm failing.

"Can you leave the old guy alone? He's not out there, and even if he is, what does it matter?"

"It matters to me," I squeak. "It's just —"

"You don't need to explain." Oliver picks up both oars. "I get the message loud and clear. And you know what? I'm sick of it." He turns the boat and heads for shore.

I sit stiffly beside him, determined not to cry. The silence is far from easy now. And my heart is breaking because of it.

thirty-one

The last thing I do before going to bed is write in the notebook.

It's him. It was Bud, wasn't it?

I write it out of anger and frustration and, frankly, embarrassment. I have no evidence, only some bizarre kind of intuition that's probably resulted in Oliver never wanting to speak to me again.

Maybe I'm venting. Laying my stupidity onto someone else. But my anger and frustration are making me brave, and it feels right, putting it out there. It's as though I'm somehow taking control, instead of waiting for Her Supreme Ghostly Highness to decide when she is going to let me in on her big scary secret.

I wait and wait. And nothing. Not a peep — only the creak of the front door when Amelia comes in around two. I think about confronting her. I could scare her as she sneaks up the stairs, but what's the point? And anyway, I'm too exhausted to bother. I listen for her as she slips past my room, and then tunnel under my sheets, sheath myself within them, and pray for sleep to put me out of my misery. It's obvious Celina isn't going to reveal anything more until she is good and ready.

* * *

I'm jolted awake by a loud bang. The moment my eyes spring open, I sense that something is wrong. Terribly wrong. Groggy from lack of sleep, and with only predawn dimness sneaking into the room, it takes a second before I'm able to take in the scene before me.

The room is trashed. Stuff hangs out of open drawers, while other drawers rest empty on the floor. The clothes that were hanging in my closet are in a pile on the floor, as if they've been flung off the rail in one swoop. Papers and books and makeup are scattered everywhere, and the things from Celina's chest are strewn about as though hurled in a rage. Beside me, the curtain billows out from the window. It's been thrown open wide, the wire screen missing. Outside, the air is still. The branches of the Norfolk don't move even a whisper. The lacy material brushes my cheek.

I sit on my bed, gather my blanket around me, and clutch it to me. My eyes are frantic. They dash around the room, taking it all in. I slide my feet to the ground, and, with the blanket still draped around me, I step clumsily over the items littering the floor, trying to make sense of what I'm seeing.

Celina's portrait lies facedown. I reach down and pick it up, the glass falling out in jagged pieces, the blue crystals from one eye scattering onto the floor.

Have I pissed Celina off somehow?

I let go of my blanket and gather up the pile of clothes that have spilled from my closet, trying to decide what to do next. My hands tremble as I hang the clothes back up. I slip the last dress onto its hanger and onto the rail, and, as I close the closet door, I catch something written on the mirror. I barely stifle the scream that rips from my mouth.

YES BUD

BASTARD!

There's an obvious rage in the way the words are scrawled

across the mirror in what looks like red nail polish. Bile stings my throat. I trace over the words with my finger. The nail varnish, not even dry, stains my fingertip.

Bud! It *was* Bud. *Oliver's* grandfather, Robbie's father. The man who lives right across the lake and seems to be stalking me, the man who I saw by the dock that night. The man who, let's face it, I've known from almost the beginning was the one.

Oliver's grandfather!

Oliver's grandfather killed Celina.

The weight of this awful knowledge drops me to my knees.

* * *

I don't know how long I sit on the floor, unable to move, my brain clogged. I can't seem to wrestle out a single clear thought. My phone beeps, the noise coming from within the mountains of stuff covering the floor. On my hands and knees, I push aside clothes and books to find it. It beeps again, and suddenly it becomes all-important. I have to find that phone. But where is it? I become frantic, tossing stuff out of the way like a madwoman until I spy it lying under my bed.

There are two messages. One from Loni and one from Oliver.

I open the message from Oliver.

Hey, it says.

Hey? Is that all he can come up with? His grandfather is making me live a nightmare and I have no idea what to do and all he can say is, hey?

The phone beeps again, startling me so much that it jerks out of my hand.

Oliver. Again.

Sorry about last night. Want to do something later?

I toss the phone onto my bed. Oliver can wait.

I become aware that the sun is all the way up now, the bird and insect choirs in full swing. I hear someone walking by and the bathroom door closing. I look around the room. I have to clear this up before someone sees it, because, really, how would I explain it? They'd be escorting me out in a straitjacket if I even try.

I start with Celina's things. I roll up the purple scarf and put it on my bed. I've grown curiously attached to it. The rest of her things I fold and place back into the chest. I put her portrait — glass fragments, missing eye pieces, and all — on top and close the lid, wishing it was that easy to close the lid on this whole Celina horror movie.

It doesn't take long to tidy up the rest, and now I'm left with Celina's message on the mirror. I snatch my nail polish remover from the drawer beside my bed and stand staring at the words, tissues in hand. I hesitate. This is the only evidence — flimsy though it is — that I have. I grab my phone and take a photo, then get to work scrubbing off the ghastly truth.

There is only a horrible red smear left, like a bloodstain, when my door opens and Seth peers into the room. His eyes are owl-like and his face paler than normal.

I put the tissues on the floor and crouch beside him. "What's up, buddy?"

He shrugs, his chin quivering.

"Hey, you can tell me. Did you have a bad dream?"

Seth nods and nuzzles into my shoulder.

"What was it about?"

"Nothing. I don't remember. But I got really cold and really scared."

"Well, it's only a dream. Don't let it bother you."

Seth wiggles out of my hold. "It stinks in here."

He's right; it does. I close the door to keep the smell in. "Nail polish remover. I spilled some."

Seth points at the mirror.

"Yeah, I tripped and spilled the nail polish on the mirror.

Don't tell Mom. She'll be upset if she knows I've been a klutz."

Seth squints at me, tugging at his ear.

"Deal?" I say.

He nods.

"Let's go down and get some breakfast. Is Mom up?"

"No. No one is. Just me."

"Perfect," I say. "Let's cook up a feast for the two of us, okay?"

I take his hand, and we tiptoe down the hall. I'm very glad to leave my worries hidden behind my closed door, if only for a while.

thirty-two

Sitting here on the end of the dock, with the mechanical thump of nail guns from the porch reminding me I'm not alone, I stare across at Lakeside, consumed with a hideous feeling of foreboding.

What am I supposed to do? Tell someone? Mom? Gran? Deb? Confess everything to the police? To Oliver? And what would I say? *Hey, Celina O'Malley's ghost has been writing to me and told me Bud Mitchell killed her.*

Yep, that might work.

Every way I look at it, it's useless. A definite case of *be careful what you wish for.* What does Celina want me to do? Expose Bud? Seek her revenge? But how? When? Why? Then I remember her words: *Make him pay, Bayley. Make him pay.* Crap! I get goose bumps all over. How am I supposed to do that?

I wonder if Celina feels let down or anxious. Waits almost forty long years to disclose the horrid truth, only to divulge it to a coward who has no idea what to do. Not only that, but a coward who has been hanging out with the accused's grandson. A coward who, if she cares to admit it, is falling for said grandson. Am I willing to risk that? For something that happened in the distant past? For a ghost?

Is exposing Bud worth losing Oliver? Worth destroying his family? Haven't they suffered enough already? Haven't I suffered enough? Is there no end to all this? I think Celina may have chosen the wrong person to reveal this to. She can tell me whatever she likes, but she can't make me do anything about it. Can she? Scratch that. I don't want to think about the answer to that question. After the fury Celina unleashed on my room this morning, I suspect Deb could be way off in her belief that Celina wouldn't even hurt a cockroach.

The wood behind me creaks, and I turn to find Amelia walking down the dock. She is wearing nothing but her pink bikini. With a towel over her shoulder, oversized sunglasses sitting on the end of her nose, my red bangles jangling up her arm, she struts down the boards as if on a catwalk. I notice the turned heads of three of the guys working on the porch. Smirks appear on their faces as they watch her.

She slides elegantly beside me and drops my phone in my lap. "Don't say I never do anything for you," she says, pushing her sunglasses up the bridge of her nose. "It's been ringing and beeping nonstop. Must be the hillbilly boyfriend."

I stare at her. She really is a dick. I must be adopted.

"Quit staring, pinhead. And what have you been doing in your room? You've stunk up the whole house. Mom's out for blood. She says you've given her a migraine. I think it's those workmen. Wish they'd hurry up and finish and get the hell out of here."

I don't bother answering. I scroll down through the list of messages and calls. Most are from Oliver. A couple from Loni and one from Deb. I wonder what she wants. I push myself up to my feet and head off down the dock, away from my adopted sibling.

"A 'thank you, sis' wouldn't hurt," she calls.

"Thank you, sis," I say, turning and bending in an elaborate bow before marching away.

I swallow hard and call Oliver. He answers on the first ring.

"Hey. Where've you been?" The blood rushes to my head at the sound of him.

"Here."

"I've rung like a hundred times. I was about to row over."

"Sorry. I had my phone off." There's an intensity in Oliver's voice that's unsettling. "What's up?"

"I just wanted to say that I'm sorry. I was an idiot last night, crazy eyes. I . . ."

"No worries. It's cool. I was being stupid too. Forget it."

"Bails . . ."

"Yeah."

"I . . . I . . . need to tell you something."

"Okay . . ." I'm not sure if I like the sound of this. I've had enough surprises to deal with already today.

"Not now. Not on the phone. Can I come over?"

"No," I say far too quickly. "Why don't we meet . . ." I'm about to say at the bend, where we've met before, but the thought of Bud being around, spying on us, is unbearable. "In town," I say. "Let's meet in town."

* * *

It's weird being with Oliver today. I feel different. Older. Tireder. Strange.

I don't want this thing about Bud to come between us, but in a way I feel it already has. When I look into Oliver's eyes, those beautiful eyes, I can't help but wonder if deep within those greenish-blue pools, he knows something. Can you live with a murderer, know him your whole life, and not realize it? Is that possible? He must have some idea. Is that why he's so defensive about Bud? Do I really know Oliver at all?

It occurs to me that you can never really know anyone. Not without crawling inside a person's head. You only get to know what they want you to know. Like Celina. Did Deb ever *really* know Celina? Did Robbie? Or Gran?

What is real anyway? Isn't everything just bullshit? I mean, look at me right now. Oliver is holding my hand, and we are walking down Main Street, carrying paper bags filled with hamburgers and fries, chatting about nothing in particular. But I'm not the person he dropped off at the dock last night. I am the holder of a terrible secret and an even more terrible truth. And unless I tell him, he will never know this part of me. Ever.

"Hey, Bails," Oliver says. "You haven't heard a word I've said, have you?"

"Huh? Sorry." I peer up at him and smile. "Strayed off somewhere. Did you see where Amelia went?" It wasn't my idea for Amelia to come to town with us, but it was the only way I could convince Mom to let me go — which is highly ironic, given what Amelia has been up to.

"She took off to the river, I think."

"She better be back by seven, or I'll kill her."

"I want front-row seats for that one. Make sure it's bloody."

"You're such a boy."

"I try." Oliver steers me down a narrow alley between the pub and the supermarket, thankfully away from the end of town where Deb's store is. "There's a park down here. Come on, we'll eat on the swings."

I should be happy. I should be messaging Loni, telling her that I have a boyfriend. A boyfriend who has bought me a burger and wants to sit on the swings and eat with me, and who is so wonderful that I can't imagine not being with him. A boyfriend I am terrified of losing because of something that happened forty years ago.

It's so steamy hot. Storm clouds gather behind the branches of the enormous fig trees at the edge of the park. I flop onto the seat, scuff the dirt with my feet, and bite into my burger. A dozen flies hone in, and it becomes a challenge of dexterity to take a fly-free bite and shoo them away without landing on my butt in the dirt.

Oliver devours his burger in what seems like two bites, which is probably the better anti-fly tactic. But he's the one who seems distracted now. He rocks on the swing, lost in thought. Is he working up the courage to tell me what it was that he couldn't tell me on the phone?

I decide to broach the subject. Get it over with. It couldn't be worse than what Celina revealed last night.

When I ask him, he squints at me, as if struggling to find the right words. "I'm just sorry I yelled at you about Grandpa . . ." He stops and chews his bottom lip. Behind his bangs, his forehead is creased with a frown. "Bails," he continues, "there is something else, something with Grandpa, but I don't know what it is. It's freaking me out, to be honest. Mom and Dad have noticed as well. I heard them talking, arguing, which is a pretty big deal for them. Come to think of it, Dad has been weird lately too. Everything's so freakin' tense and strange at home." He smiles sheepishly. "I guess I took it out on you."

He reaches for my hand. I take my last bite, dust the crumbs from my shorts, move across to his swing, and sit on his lap. He seems so vulnerable, and it seems the natural thing to do. He wraps his arms around me, and I rest my head on his shoulder.

"What's up with your grandfather, do you think?" I choose my words carefully, concentrating on keeping my voice steady.

"It's hard to put into words. He's kind of jumpy and super active. He's been a hermit the last couple of years — keeping to himself, watching TV in his slippers, that kind of stuff. He is in his eighties after all. But now he's everywhere, buzzing around the place. He's working on some big new art thing, but it's more than that. He's pissed off all the time. Something's bothering him."

My skin goes cold. *It's me.* I'm the one who has caused the change. I know it.

"Maybe he's getting Alzheimer's or something," I try, my guts twisting.

"That's what Mom thinks. But Dad won't have it. He even accused Mom of making things up so that he'd put him in a home. And that's not like my dad — to say stuff like that to Mom."

I prop my head against Oliver's and play with the strands of hair that fall across his face. Two brains close together — and mine with the answers to Oliver's worries.

I feel tempted. So tempted to divulge everything. To tell him what is really up with Bud. I just have to open my mouth and let it out. Unburden myself.

"Oliver . . ."

"Yeah . . ."

"It'll all work out. Don't worry."

Oliver draws me closer, but his head hangs low. "There's more," he says. "When I got home last night, there was a note on my bed. From Grandpa."

"Yeah?"

"It — I shouldn't be telling you this!"

Dread tiptoes along my arms and legs. "What did it say?"

"I'm not going to do what it said, okay? Know that first. But it said to stay away from you." The last words come out in a hurry. "I don't get it. He's never been like this before. Why would he care about us seeing each other?"

Yeah. Good question.

* * *

Amelia swings a bat at the bouncing ball and misses by a mile. She tosses back her head and laughs. She sounds happy. It startles me.

"Run!" the shout goes up. The guy behind her fails to retrieve the ball, and it bumps and rolls toward the river's edge.

Amelia squeals and takes off, racing for the garbage bin wicket.

"Amelia is playing cricket?" I whisper to Oliver as we approach. "Has the planet tilted off its axis or something?"

"Don't be mean. It's what we country hillbillies do to keep ourselves entertained."

I poke my tongue out at him. A lame "Haha" is the best I can manage.

Amelia and some other girl charge from bin to bin a half dozen times before the ball is retrieved from the river — muddy and dripping.

"Six. All run!" shouts another girl, who is sitting on the grass with a bunch of others. "You're a legend, Mills!"

Mills? A legend? The world has definitely tilted. We'll be hurtling into the sun before we know it.

Amelia is leaning on her bat, puffing, when she catches sight of Oliver and me. "Did you hear that?" she calls out. "I'm a legend." Her eyes latch on to Oliver's hand in mine, and she smirks. I wait for the insult, but it doesn't come.

"Okay, Mills," the bowler says. "No Mr. Nice Guy now."

The bowler starts his run up. He is about to let the ball go when the sky is lit up by a ragged spear of lightning that's followed far too quickly by an enormous blast of thunder.

"Whoa," says Oliver. "Nasty."

Large drops of rain plop down on us, and before we even take two steps toward shelter, the clouds start chucking down rain.

There's a lot of squealing and cursing and people flapping

around grabbing their stuff. Oliver tightens his grip on my hand, and we sprint for his car parked up on the street. Amelia is beside us, already soaked, her clothes clinging to her. Mascara runs in black streaks down her face, but she's still laughing. What is she on?

The grass is slippery, especially uphill, and impossibly the rain intensifies. I couldn't get any wetter.

We dive into the car and slam the doors behind us as lightning fills the sky again. We sit, drenched to the bone, wide-eyed, waiting for the next boom. The noise of the rain on the roof is deafening. The sky lights up again a couple of times, but the rumble of thunder is far gentler and farther away. The rain stops as abruptly as it started. We look at each other, three drowned rats, and we burst out laughing, Oliver's wheezing hiss louder than ever. Amelia and I make eye contact, and we burst out all over again.

Oliver shakes his head and turns the key in the ignition. "Guess I better get you two home."

Amelia pulls out her phone and checks the time, twisting her lips. "It's only si—" There is a loud bang on the side window.

Amelia winds it down, and some guy stands there, wringing the water out of his T-shirt, water trickling off the rings piercing his nose. Amelia's eyes light up, and her mouth curls into a dazzling smile.

"You goin'?" the guy says.

"Probs. What are you going to do?"

"Dunno. Maybe go to Fitzies'. Maybe go home."

"I better get back — get dry."

"See ya later then?"

"Yeah," says Amelia sweetly, and the guy bends into the car and plants a moist kiss on Amelia's lips.

"I'll message ya," he says, running off and jumping into a car parked up the road.

"*I'll message ya,*" I repeat in a singsong voice as Oliver pulls out from the curb. "Who is *that?*"

"Lee," Amelia says, smug.

"So that's Lee," I say. "Does he go to Tallowood High?"

"No. He's left — works at the supermarket. I bet he can get me a job there too." Amelia grins at me, then adds, "Don't tell Mom."

"Sure, but I don't see why not."

"You know why. Because Mom is psycho. Because she has it in for me. Because she hates to see me happy." The bitterness in Amelia's reply is hard to miss. "Lee is nice. I like him. He's fun, and that's all there is to it. I don't need

Mom wrecking everything, like she always does." Her phone beeps. She buckles her seatbelt, turns her body toward the door, and starts typing a message. It's clear that the sisterly bonding moment we shared a moment ago has vaporized.

Oliver winks at me, takes my hand, and drags it up to rest on his leg.

And with my hand soaking up the warmth of his thigh, I am willing to pretend that life is good.

thirty-three

When Oliver says he'll pick me up at eight and to make sure I wear my running shoes, he has me wondering. So I'm perched on the top step of the porch, ears tuned in for the sound of tires on gravel and eyes trained on the bush for a glimpse of his battered Toyota through the trees, when I notice the rower heading across the lake, straight for the dock. I should have known.

I grab my backpack, and I'm feeling so golden this morning, I almost skip down to the lake's edge. It's one of those utterly gorgeous days, the sky surprising me with its blueness and the water shining like polished glass.

"Where are we going?" I ask, climbing down the dock ladder.

"It's a surprise. If I tell you —"

"You'll have to kill me, right?"

"No, if I tell you, it won't be a surprise, idiot."

I take the middle seat beside Oliver and pick up the oar.

I'm so in the moment, so damn happy to be rowing with Oliver that I don't even realize we are heading for Lakeside and almost there, until that awful sick feeling swirls into my stomach. This is the last place I want to be, and my happiness tumbles to my toes.

"Hey, what's up?" Oliver frowns at me from under his bangs.

"Nothing. Why?"

"Uh . . . you've stopped rowing?"

"Oh. I have? Sorry." I feel like a babbling-idiot moment is on its way. I suck air into my lungs, give Oliver my most beguiling smile, and sweep the oar powerfully through the water, concentrating on coaxing the yogurt and banana I had for breakfast to stay in my stomach where they belong.

By the time we have grounded the rowboat and are on dry land, I'm so churned up that I can't even look at Oliver. I'm too consumed with thoughts of Bud. *What if I see him? What should I do? How should I react? Will he know I know?* I glance up at the old farmhouse. The place is ancient and crumbly, and it's obvious that Bud hasn't spent any of his art fortune on his house. A torn lacy curtain in the front room swings down. Was that Bud?

"Come on," says Oliver. He threads his fingers through mine and strides up the bank. He takes a few steps, then stops, gathering both my hands in his, bringing them to his chest. "Bails, you're shaking. Are you okay?"

"Yeah," I croak.

Oliver brushes my hair off my face, and slides it under my scarf. "You seem kinda sick — like you did the other night when you were here. Are you sure you're all right?"

"Yep, I'm —" The curtain in the front window parts in the middle slightly. I imagine Bud in there, watching, and it terrifies me. "What about your grandpa?" I say.

"Grandpa?"

"The note — to stay away from me, remember?"

"I told you that I'm not going to listen to that. He can't tell me what to do." He pulls me up the grassy slope to the main house.

Loud music with a strong beat blares out at us as Oliver slides open the glass doors. Annie is sitting on a kitchen stool, giving a guitar some kind of violent workout, throwing her head back with a flourish. When she sees us, she stops mid-strum, and the ginger cat curled at her feet mews in disgust.

"Hi, Bayley." Her nose wrinkles as she smiles and reaches for the iPod dock on the bench and turns it off. "*El porompom-pero*. I love that piece. Get carried away with it sometimes."

Oliver slips into the kitchen area and starts filling a back-pack with bags of chips and candy, a large block of chocolate, and a couple of cans of soda. A health food feast.

"Fried chicken in the fridge, Ols," says Annie.

"Thanks," says Oliver, head in the fridge.

My eyes flit around the room, half-expecting Bud to mate-rialize through any one of the doorways. I fold my arms, tucking my hands up under my armpits, in the faint hope that I can stop them from shaking.

"Feeling okay?" Annie says to me, making me jump. "It's a long way up there."

I have no idea if she is teasing or not, but as long as "up there" is far away from "down here," I really don't care.

There's the sharp clap of a door shutting and echoey foot-steps on tiles. My fingers dig painfully into my armpits, and a tremble starts in my legs as the footsteps get closer. I study the shininess of the white tiles beneath my feet.

"Hello, Bayley." It's the gravelly voice of Bob.

"Hi," I manage. Bob's smile is friendly, but it doesn't quite mask his face full of questions.

"I haven't seen you since the hospital," he says, and I'm sure he's thinking about what I had blurted — *Together forever, sweet pea* — the words I shouldn't know. "How's Seth doing?"

"Fine. He's fine. Totally. Totally fine." There's a large photographic book about Chile on a side table in the lounge area. I direct my attention to it, not wanting to make eye contact with Bob for fear of blurting out that his father's a killer, the same person who killed his precious Celina. And, honestly, for fear of my own emotions. The thought of how I was attracted to him before — even if it was Celina who was driving it — fills me with shame. "Thanks for helping us out and everything," I mumble to the book.

"No problems. And you? Are you —"

"Fine. All good." The blood drains away from my face, and I become light-headed.

"Let's go," says Oliver, to my enormous relief. He slings the backpack over his shoulder and bundles me out of the house. Oliver points north to a gate in the far field.

We climb over the gate and then over another gate and

onto a path leading steadily uphill into the bush. Each step I take is filled with the weight of my anxiety. I imagine Bud behind every bush, every rock.

"Come on, slowpoke," says Oliver.

"Does your grandfather come up here much?" I say, cursing myself for giving voice to the thought.

"Jeez, Bayley. Forget him. I wish I hadn't told you." He forges on ahead.

This is absurd. I jog to catch up. "Where are you taking me, Mr. Mystery Man?" I attempt to sound cheerful. "Should I be worried?"

A mischievous glint lights Oliver's eyes. "Maybe." He takes my hand.

The more twists and turns in the path we put between us and Lakeside, the better I start to feel. By the time we've made it to the top of the first rise, there's a ribbon of blue sky above, and I'm feeling almost normal.

A steep ascent and then one last bend in the path, and we come into a small clearing where grasses and low shrubs chase down to a cliff edge. It looks out over the gorge and the surrounding farms and properties. Below us, the creek is a thin gray worm wiggling its way to the lake. I had no idea we'd climbed this high.

Oliver's face says it all: he loves it up here. He stands

behind me and wraps his arms around my middle, rests his chin on my shoulder. "Well, what do you think?"

"It's . . . it's . . . ." I am lost for words. "Awesome."

"Like you." It's barely more than a whisper, but those two words sizzle through me.

His chin nuzzles into my neck. "You should see it at sunset. It's even more awesome."

"What's this place called?"

"Top of the World," Oliver states.

"Original." I grin. "You Mitchells have a talent for naming places."

"What do you mean?"

"What do you call the lake?"

"Uh, the lake."

"And the circular lagoon?"

"The Circle. What's wrong with that?"

I giggle. "And what's the name of your house by the lake?"

"Lakeside."

"I rest my case!"

"Well, Miss Anderson, at least our house has a name."

"So does mine. Karinya: place of peace." I feel like a thief, as if I've stolen the name from someone else's life, and I wish I'd kept my mouth shut. I step out of Oliver's arms and gaze down into the dark depths of the gorge.

"Karinya. What kind of weirdo name is that?" Oliver says and sits himself down on a boulder.

"At least it's original," I say softly, but my insides are quivering. The wildness of the gorge, its steep plunge to the rocks below, the deep shadows lurking at the bottom — it's all making me feel strange, dizzy almost. There is something ominous about it. I step away.

Oliver leaps up. "Whoa. What's up? You've gone all white." He pulls me to him and holds me tight. I welcome the strength of his arms. "You're shaking again. What gives?"

The concern in Oliver's voice does me in. "Why do you put up with me?" I blurt tearfully.

"Bails, what are you talking about?" He scrunches his nose and shakes his head, bewildered.

Why didn't I keep my mouth shut? "I'm so flaky," I try, terrified that I am oversharing. "I'm worried you're going to think 'what the hell?' and take off."

"You're the one who takes off, remember?" He lifts my chin with two fingers. Our eyes meet. "I know you have a lot to deal with at the moment. But I'm here for you. I want to help you through it."

"I don't want to be looked after." But even as I say it, I know it's a lie. I desperately want to be looked after, especially by Oliver.

"Not like that, Bails. I just want to be with you, and I don't care if sometimes you're a little flaky. I like that you're different. I even like those stupid things you wear around your head. That you wear blankets instead of hoodies."

"Ponchos," I correct him and laugh.

"Ponchos, then."

I snuggle into his shoulder, crazy with emotion. Before I can even start to unravel my jumbled feelings or process what Oliver has said, Oliver unfurls me from his embrace, grabs my hand, and takes off at a run down the path we've only just climbed up. "Come on," he says, grinning.

"Where are we going?" I stumble behind him, confused.

"You didn't think I brought you up here to gawk at the view and eat junk food, did you?"

"Well . . . ye—" I don't get a chance to finish.

"Got to earn it first." Oliver drops my hand and runs off the trail and onto a narrow, winding path through the bush. "Keep up, slacker."

"What the —?" I follow, tearing through leaves, leaping across fallen branches, ducking under low ones, climbing steadily back up the hill until we have reached the top again.

But that's not the end of it. Oliver touches the boulder he was sitting at and takes off at a sprint all the way back down the hill again.

"What are you doing?" I say, copying his actions and tagging the boulder also.

"Cross-training!" he yells over his shoulder. "Thought you wanted to get fit."

Breath heaving, I chase him down. This is ridiculous. But ridiculously, it's also great, and we are all craziness and squeals and laughter. After about four circuits, Oliver surrenders and collapses on the ground beside our packs. He gulps down several large swigs of water, then passes the bottle to me. I am so thirsty that I devour what's left and flop beside him, my face flushed, my lungs burning. Without speaking, we dive into our cache of junk food, relishing the immediate rush of a sugar high.

I rest my head on Oliver's stomach, munching on a candy bar, and stretch my legs out and watch stringy clouds scoot across the sky then disappear behind the foliage. I acknowledge with some satisfaction the burn in my thigh muscles, savor the laughter ache in my cheeks, and for the first time in forever, I finally remember what real happiness feels like. And this is it.

"This is so great," says Oliver, putting voice to my thoughts. "It's a bummer that school will start so soon."

"Yeah," I agree.

His fingers stroke the side of my face, tracing a line from

my forehead to jaw. It's so sweet and loving. If I were the ginger cat, I'd purr. "It's going to be cool," he continues, "having you at Tallowood. We'll be able to see each other every day. Catch the bus together and stuff."

Catch the bus together — just like Celina and Robbie. My inner warmth frosts over at the thought. Bristling, I rally against it. *Go away, will you!* I'm so weary of Celina.

"Hey, what's up?"

I sit up and brush an unwanted tear from my cheek. "Nothing. Sorry. I'm okay, really."

"Is that what the thought of catching the bus with me does to you?"

"Don't be a dick." I nestle back into his arms, wrap my own arms around his chest, and cling to him like I've never clung to him before, trying to regain that beautiful sunshiny feeling of just moments ago. And as I do so, the way forward illuminates with breathtaking clarity, as if I've broken free of the pack in a cross-country meet and the finish line is shimmering before me.

My decision is made: if I have to choose between a ghost and Oliver, I choose Oliver.

Celina can go to hell.

thirty-four

Marco Moretti is Oliver's best friend in Tallowood. He's into dirt bikes, indie music, playing guitar, and he has a good singing voice, so Oliver tells me on the drive to Marco's place, as he gives me the lowdown on the "gang."

"There's Tina and Katie," he says. "You know, the horse-crazed ones — neigh when they do and you'll be fine. Ricko — we call him Thicko, though no one can remember why. He's actually very smart. Ignore Paul. He's a dickhead and a moocher. But you'll like Darsh. He's fun, kind of a joker.

And Jess Rogers-Weston — she's pretty hot — but not as hot as you," he adds quickly. And the list goes on.

I try to absorb it all somehow and commit it straight to memory. I really want to make a good impression, especially after my embarrassing bolt out of the Bowlo the other night.

Marco's place is a modern-looking, two-story brick house on a wide street on the outskirts of town.

"His parents are loaded," Oliver says as an afterthought, pulling into the driveway. "They own most of the town, plus a couple of farms around the place."

I raise my eyebrows in response, taking everything in as I steady my nerves. Tonight has a turning point feel to it — like it's the first day of the rest of my life. Not just because the "gang" that I am about to meet is Oliver's group of friends, so I need them to become my friends too, but also because next Tuesday — only four short days away — school is back in session, and these guys all go to Tallowood. And with Amelia still intent on dropping out, a few friendly faces will make all the difference to my time there.

I climb out of the car, pull down the legs of my shorts, and tighten the scarf around my head. Much like Seth's cape, Celina's scarf is becoming my security blanket. It's a bit of a risk, wearing it tonight, but Oliver assured me that it was only a get-together, and it didn't matter what I wore. But what would he know? He's a boy, for heaven's sake. What I wear tonight could seal my fate for the last few years of high school.

A large black car pulls onto the lawn and stops beside us. Two girls bound out — high-energy types — both wearing grubby jeans, T-shirts, and muddy ankle boots. Immediately I feel that I'm dressed far too city and far too beachy.

"Hey!" shouts the taller of the two.

"Katie and Tina," Oliver whispers into my ear. "Remember, just neigh."

"Neigh," I say. "Hi!" I add quickly.

"Takeout Chinese," says one of the girls. She swings two plastic bags in front of us, not appearing to have noticed my slipup. Regardless, I am dying a thousand deaths.

Oliver introduces us, and both girls give me an enthusiastic hug before almost bouncing inside.

Be cool, I tell myself. *Be yourself. No, scratch that. Channel Loni.*

Oliver and I walk up the stairs, hand in hand, through a wide doorway and into a dim entry foyer. *Channel Loni. Be sparky. Confident.* The thump of loud music and party voices waft up from a short staircase at the end of the foyer. A door opens and a couple of guys and a girl race up the stairs toward us, laughing.

They stop when they see me.

"Hey, guys," says Oliver with ease, his grip tightening. "This is Bayley. She's moved into the old O'Malley house by the lake."

There's a flurry of enthusiastic *heys*, plus a warm and welcoming hug from the girl — the oh-so-hot Jess. I do my best to respond with some Loni spark.

But as I return Jess's hug, my eyes lock on a huge artwork hanging on the wall behind her. One of Bud's. I let go of Jess and stare at the painting. It's one of his dotty ones. A striking bushland scene.

I step toward it, and the room becomes devoid of noise and people. All I can do is gawk at the painting, which now, up close, is nothing more than tiny specs of crap and stuff. But despite this, it seems so real, and I feel as if I'm being sucked into it. The trees flank either side of me. Their branches hold me tight.

Across the bottom are some kind of gritty particles that form the earth around the trees. My eyes become glued to them. They fascinate me. I run my fingers across the glass.

"Yeah," says Oliver, his voice intruding from somewhere

far away. "It's one of Grandpa's. He's pretty clever, huh?"

I don't answer. I'm hot and headachy and nauseous. My fingers dance back and forth across the glass.

I can't stop them. They're frantic and so am I; I sense Celina's involvement somehow. I just want her to leave me alone and get out of my life.

At last my fingers stop, but now I feel like I am teetering on the edge of a cliff. Horrible vertigo swamps me, and I'm overwhelmed with the need to get away. Why am I so terrified? I try to calm myself, draw in some deep breaths, but stinging bile races up my throat.

No. Not here.

I turn to bolt outside, but run straight into Jess. The jolt sends vomit shooting out of my mouth and all over Jess's oh-so-hot chest and neck.

Jess freezes. Her face contorts. She stares at the revolting yellow gunk running down her neck and across her perfect boobs. She's so shocked. She's beyond words, until she screeches at the top of her lungs. "Grr-oss!"

Mortified, I race out the door without even an apology. Oliver follows me and holds my hair back as I barf and barf onto the lawn. "Bails, what's up? Are you sure you shouldn't see a doctor?" Oliver asks, full of concern.

"I'm so sorry," I say.

"Don't be. You're sick. You can't help that. But you seem to get sick a lot."

"I don't need a doctor," I say as evenly as I can manage. A shrink maybe, but that's not what he means.

Marco appears with a towel and a glass of water. I take it from him gratefully. "Thanks. Sorry . . ."

"Hey, don't sweat it. You okay, though?"

"Yeah. Must have been something I ate, I guess." I use the towel to brush flecks of vomit off my shorts. "I feel so bad."

"No worries," says Marco. "We're used to it. Darsh is the barfing king. Hardly a Saturday night goes by without him making pizzas in the gutter."

It takes a second for me to work out what he means, but once I do, that particular visual image turns my stomach over again, and I dry retch.

Tina and Katie appear. Tina crouches beside me.

"Jess?" I manage.

"Jess is fine, but she's worried for you. She doesn't want you to feel bad, okay? She's borrowing some clothes from Marco's sister. She has the best clothes, so Jess is kinda happy about that. Come inside — there'll be something that will fit you, for sure."

I look into Oliver with panicky eyes. I don't want to go inside. I want to go home.

"Go on," he says and smiles.

Everyone is being so *nice*. It's almost too much.

Tina and Katie take an arm each and escort me back up the stairs. They both smell so horse-and-manurey that I hope it will mask the smell of my puke in the foyer. I take care to avert my eyes when I pass Bud's painting, but the wobbles come back.

"Hey, don't worry," says Tina. "Really, this is no biggie. You'll be laughing about it by morning."

"Yeah," agrees Katie. "It'll become legend. When we're old, sitting in a nursing home we'll say, 'Remember the day we met Bayley, and she barfed over Jess? Ah, those were the days.'"

They are being so kind, and I appreciate it, I really do.

But I will never laugh about it. Ever.

* * *

Oliver drops me off at about ten, and I head straight for the shower. I need to cleanse myself of the whole horrible fiasco.

I welcome the hot, steamy water as it slides over me, willing it to wash away the smell of vomit and the even stronger stench of humiliation.

What must they all think of me? What must Oliver think of me? Despite everyone being so welcoming, I clung to Oliver like a timid little mouse and hardly said a word all night, making it all so obvious that I couldn't get out of there quick enough. I'm sure everyone thinks I'm way too needy and far too strange and uptight for "their" Oliver.

But how can you relax and join in a game of pool when there's a giant-sized reminder in the foyer that a murderer is still at large, and the hairs on your neck are bristling because you sense there's a pissed-off ghost constantly looking over your shoulder? This is such a mess of a life.

I slide down the tiled wall and tilt my face up to the spray of water before dropping it into my hands and choking back a sob.

Then I get angry. *Don't let her rule you, Bayley. Don't let her. Remember your decision. She can't win.*

I push myself back up, trying to convince myself with these thoughts. Suddenly there's a click, and I'm left standing in darkness.

My scalp prickles. I turn off the water, step out of the shower, and fumble for the light switch. I flick it, and the lights blare back on.

Then I notice the mirror. Etched through the steamy fog covering the glass are the words: *MAKE HIM PAY.*

thirty-five

The days stand before me: lining up one after the other. Can I do this? Can I ignore Celina's demands? Can I keep a secret forever?

Because it is never going to go away. I know that. The awful knowledge is always going to be there, gnawing away at me like an ulcer, and it's obvious Celina is not going to let me rest.

Life is so unfair. All I want is to be with Oliver and be happy. Is that too much to ask? Especially after all I've been through. Clearly, it is if your name is Bayley Anderson.

I'm jogging back from the lake bend after my usual early morning run and picnic with Oliver. He didn't mention last night at Marco's — not even once — and I'm pretty sure that's not a good thing. It leaves me feeling uneasy.

I sigh, put down my head, and pick up speed. It's Friday, and Seth's birthday. I really want to get home before he wakes up.

Then the unthinkable happens.

Out from behind a willow steps Bud.

He stops me in my tracks, my nostrils filling with that horrible chemical smell only seconds before he is upon me.

He doesn't say anything, of course, but just thrusts a piece of paper at me.

I stand defiant, not willing to touch it, my eyes averted. My breath becomes heavy, and I start to rock on the balls of my feet. Images of the fury Celina unleashed on my bedroom fill my brain. I see the words she wrote on the closet mirror. *YES BUD. BASTARD!* The message in the steamy bathroom mirror. *MAKE HIM PAY.* I remember the sadness in her ramblings about her death. I know that what he did all those years ago now threatens my own happiness. Rage swells inside me.

I raise my head and glare at Bud. His eyes are red-rimmed and thick like soup. I think I expected to see a madman reflected in those eyes, but I see something else entirely. At first I can't put my finger on it, but then I realize what it is. Fear.

Bud is afraid. Afraid of me.

This shocks me momentarily. But then it gives me courage, or makes me foolish. It's hard to tell.

"It was you," I say. "That night." My words are strange and shaky, as if they're bouncing along a river of bubbles.

Bud takes a small step back as he processes this, then he lunges forward and shoves the paper in my face again.

"I'm not taking it." My voice is firm now, despite the fact that I'm challenging the person who has Celina's blood on his hands. "If you have something to say, tell me. Speak. I know you can."

His face is a scowl. His hand, spotted and gnarled with arthritis, waves the paper in front of me. Then he grabs my wrist. His grip is surprisingly strong for such an old guy. My fingers curl into a fist, but he tries to pry them open and stuff the paper into my unwilling hand.

Damn it, he's hurting me. I try to squirm out of his hold, push him away, and wrestle myself free of his clutch. But he won't let go. I'm so afraid that I'm sure my heart is about to burst out of my ribcage and abandon me.

"I know!" I shout, desperate to catch him off guard. "I know everything." I push at him with my free hand, and he stumbles slightly, enough to wrench myself from his grasp. I give him another shove, and he's on the ground. My rage consumes me, and I feel myself losing control.

"Bastard," I hiss. I kick him, struggling to resist the fierce temptation to kick and kick and kick him like the dog he is.

"Bails!" I swing round to see Oliver charging toward us. "What are you doing?"

Bud scrambles to his feet and scurries away, limping. "Grandpa! Wait," shouts Oliver, but Bud doesn't falter. He disappears into the grove of trees.

Oliver is torn. His eyes sweep back and forth between the disappearing Bud and me. Does he follow his grandfather or challenge me? He chooses me.

"What the hell was that about?"

"He attacked me," I say, my breath coming in gasps. "Tried to shove that note into my hand."

Oliver frowns. He picks the crumpled note out of the dirt. "Are you kidding me? Giving someone a note is hardly an attack. You pushed him over. I saw you. Then you kicked him — when he was on the ground."

"He hurt me," I say lamely.

"What the —?" Oliver shakes his head. "He's old. And, yes, he's losing it, but he wasn't going to hurt you. He wouldn't hurt a fly."

My head pounds. *Yes, he would. Yes, he has. He's a murderer.* The words peck away inside me, urging me to give them voice, to set them free.

I press my lips together, blocking their escape.

"I don't get you, Bayley. Who the hell are you anyway? How could you do something like that?" He glares at me with pure and utter disgust.

"I . . . I'm . . . sorry." I reach out to touch his arm, but he shrugs me off roughly, flings the note to the ground, and tosses my phone to me. "You left this behind." He turns sharply and walks away.

"Wait!" I shout after him. "Don't go. I can explain."

I sink to the ground, too destroyed even to cry. *Who the hell am I? Who the hell am I? I don't even know me anymore. I'm just bullshit.*

I pick up the note and straighten it out.

STAY AWAY.

I BEG OF YOU.

* * *

Seth is kneeling in his pajamas in front of the TV, his fingers working hard at his earlobes. When I burst into the living room, he looks up at me expectantly.

"Hey," I say, "you up already?"

"Your eyeballs are red."

I swipe at my eyes. "Just went running, must have gotten wind in them. Hey! Happy birthday, Mr. Seven! Is anyone else awake?"

Seth shakes his head. I can tell he's disappointed.

I summon all my strength to be cheery. "Well, Batman, how about I rustle up a birthday breakfast feast for you? What do you think?"

"With bacon?"

"With bacon," I say, hoping that Gran remembered to buy some yesterday.

"And Cocoa Puffs?"

"Mmm, that might be pushing it."

I stagger into the kitchen. Livid. I am not up to this. Where is his mother, for God's sake?

All I can think of is how I've blown it. How it's all over for Oliver and me. I have nothing now, not a thing. I swallow my anger and put together a mini feast for the birthday boy: three pieces of crispy bacon, two fried eggs, and toast with Nutella (there were no Cocoa Puffs to be found). Perfect. I arrange them on a tray, then head upstairs to get his card and present.

Mom is slinking out of the bathroom as I reach the top. She looks haggard and frowns at me.

"Seth's birthday," I state.

"Yeah," she says vaguely. "That's right. Good. Good." She heads off down the hall.

"Mom," I hiss, "what are you doing? He's downstairs. Waiting."

"Yeah, yeah. Quit hassling me, Bayley. I've got a lot to do today." She glowers at me.

"A lot to do? It's Seth's birthday!"

"Yes. But I have work and . . . and I have to go in early to . . . to pick up his present."

"Pick up? You don't have anything, do you? He's a kid, Mom. And it's the first," my words choke in my throat, "his first birthday without Dad."

"You think I don't know that?" She takes a few steps, then turns back. "I'll come and see him after my shower. This is hard for me too, you know."

Hard for you? I'm shocked. I thought she'd pull herself together for Seth.

"Don't get all pouty on me, Bayley. You'll be here and

Gran and Amelia. He'll have a great time. He doesn't need a teary mom spoiling his fun." She slips into her room and closes the door behind her.

This is too much.

* * *

We do our best, even Amelia. We put on our game faces and try to make Seth's day as birthday-ish as possible to fill the gaping holes left by our dead father and our absent mother.

Amelia blows up about a million balloons and initiates an impromptu game of pop the balloon. It's hilarious, especially when Gran's won't burst, no matter what she tries. In the end, she resorts to bouncing up and down on it until it pops with an enormous bang and sends her thudding to the floor on her behind, laughter tears streaming down her face. Once she's recovered, she heads off to the kitchen with Seth, and they decorate cupcakes. We have a sugary lunch on the dock. The rest of the afternoon we spend floating and splashing about on the inflatable plastic raft — an excellent gift from Amelia, which came as a bit of a shock. It's not often that Amelia outdoes Mom.

Then, just when I'm starting to worry whether Mom is going to get home before dinner, her car pulls into the driveway.

Seth jumps to his feet and squeals at the top of his voice, "MOM! Mom!"

Kids are so loyal. She abandons him on his birthday, scurries out the door on a hug and a promise, and here he is bursting with excitement at the sight of her. Mom waves and starts to walk down to the lake.

But the raft isn't really built for someone jumping around on it, especially when it's already overloaded with Gran, Amelia, and me. It bobs about with Seth swaying and waving and yelling.

Mom picks up her pace. "Sit down, Seth! Sit down," she shouts.

Seth doesn't sit down. Instead, the raft folds in half and chucks us all into the lake. We come up laughing, but the laughter dries quickly at the sound of Mom's screams.

"Seth! Oh my God! Someone get Seth. What were you thinking?" She is practically shrieking.

I whirl around in an absolute panic, trying to locate Seth, thinking that something has happened to him again. But he's already climbing back on the raft.

"He's fine, Kath," Gran calls. "Calm down."

"Calm down? Calm down? I can't even go to work without you guys putting Seth's life in danger. Do I have to be here every second of every day?"

We wade back to shore, Gran pulling the raft with a bewildered Seth on board. Mom has lost it again. I have no idea how to react.

We stand on the muddy sand, dripping and defeated. Mom rushes down and bundles Seth up and hugs him close. Then she lets fly.

"What is that thing anyway?"

Amelia glares at her. "That thing is my present for Seth."

"What a ludicrous present. He is only seven. It's dangerous."

Amelia opens her mouth to reply, but Gran taps her on the arm and shakes her head. She steps up to Mom. "You're overreacting here, Kath." Her voice is soothing. "Come inside and we'll get the cake. Yes?"

Mom puts Seth down. "I'm too upset for cake."

"It's Seth's birthday." Amelia rolls her eyes. "Get over yourself, Mom. I know that you're anti-fun these days, but the rest of us are doing our best to get on with our lives — move on."

It's the most sense Amelia has made in years, but Mom's not having it.

"I can't believe you'd get him something like that!"

"I can't believe you didn't get him anything." I'm sorry as soon as the words slide out of my mouth — not because of Mom, but because Seth is standing right beside her, pulling at his ears.

Mom steps toward me. "Don't you dare —"

"Stop, Kath," says Gran. Mom glowers at her, and I sense that things are about to turn ugly.

Gran takes Seth by the hand and walks toward the dock. "Come on. Grab all this stuff and take it inside for me. And then we'll get the cake ready for you in a jiffy. Okay, Seth?" Gran looks at Amelia and me. "Help him change into some dry clothes, will you, girls?"

We both nod. I don't know about Amelia, but I feel totally helpless.

As I walk away, I hear Gran speaking to Mom. Her voice is gentle and kind, like I imagine it is when she is helping her people at the Soup Van. "Come on, darling, pull yourself together — for Seth. Do it for your son."

* * *

They stay down by the dock for an hour or more. Two hunched figures sitting on the boards. I hope Gran is getting through to her. But sadly, I don't think Mom has it in her, and I wonder if our lives are ever going to mend, if any of us has what it takes to push through the pain and come out the other end still standing.

thirty-six

It's just before lunch. The house is quiet, and I sit in the shade of the front porch, encouraging even the slightest murmur of air to find me, while I nurse my laptop, chatting to Loni on Facebook.

Loni: *Got me a hottie.*

Me: *Name?*

Loni: *Sure. Just don't know it. Yet. Lol. Give me time.*

I stifle a yawn. I don't care one bit about Mr. Hottie, but I've been neglecting Loni, so I'm pretending.

Loni: *What about you and Hot Neighbor? Hooking up yet?*

Ouch. That hurt. Should I fess up? Tell her everything? That we had indeed hooked up and that he is awesome — the best thing that has ever happened to me — but now I think I've gone and ruined it big time, and I am worried that he hates me. It hurts too much to think it, let alone write it. I settle for my invented reality.

Me: *Nah. Typical country hillbilly — too busy shoveling cowshit to bother with the likes of moi.*

Loni: *Bummer.*

Gran sticks her head through the doorway. "Bails, have you seen Amelia?"

I shake my head.

"Her bed doesn't seem to have been slept in." Gran seems worried.

"Are you sure? I mean, how can you tell?"

"Because yesterday I changed her sheets and made it myself. That's how. She didn't go out last night, did she?"

How do I answer that one? "Don't know," I say, which is the truth, but not as accurate as "probably." "Maybe she's gone for a walk or something."

"Mmm. Maybe." Gran peers out across the lake, her eyes sweep to the dock and the path to the south, and then she walks back inside, but I can tell she's troubled.

Things were pretty tense last night when Gran and Mom

returned from the dock. Mom was trying too hard, and Amelia wasn't giving an inch. I'll kill her if she's run off somewhere.

Me: *Gotta go. Amelia MIA again. Need to head search party. Love you. XOXOXO*

Loni: *Okay. Good luck. Love you too. XOXOXO*

I log off and try Amelia's cell phone, even though I'm sure Gran has already tried. It rings a couple of times, then cuts out. I send her a message.

Where are you? Everyone worried. Message back. NOW.

I hear Mom and Gran thumping through the house calling out Amelia's name. Doors are opened and then slammed shut, panic rapidly building.

The only thing I can think to do is to ring Oliver, and I can't be sure if it's out of concern for Amelia or as a desperate excuse to make contact and to hear his voice again.

Flooded with nerves, I hesitate, then stab at Oliver's number, chewing on my lip.

I get his cheery recorded voice: *Hey. Not here. But I guess you worked that out already.*

I start to leave a message but tear up and it sounds like nonsense. I click out of it without finishing and send him a text.

Sorry to bother you, but Amelia is missing. Do you know if she was in town last night? Can you check with her friends? That Lee guy.

It sounds pathetic — apologetic — but I'm frazzled and I can't think of what else to write.

This is silly. Why am I so worried? It's not like this is the first time Amelia has taken off or disappeared for a day or so. But this time feels different. Where could she be?

Seth runs past me and down the steps. "Amelia!" he calls and runs around to the back. The anxiety in his voice is alarming.

"Be careful out there!" I yell. "There could be snakes." God. I sound like Mom.

I idly check my email. There's only one new email in my inbox, and it's from Deb — another person I have been avoiding. I can't cope with her going on about the wonderful Celina at the moment. I'm about to open it when my phone beeps.

A message — from Oliver.

Amelia was at Bowlo last night. Left at about eleven with Lee and others. Called Lee. He said they went to Mitch's and then he can't remember much. He's really hungover.

I message my thanks, then try Amelia's phone again. Still no answer.

But the phone beeps with another message from Oliver.

Will go into town and look for her. Probably passed out some-where. Lee is looking too.

Before I have a chance to reply, Mom and Gran both stride out onto the porch, their concern clear on their faces.

"I think we should," Gran is saying. "It's well after twelve. She must have gone somewhere last night."

"Would you put that blasted phone and computer away and help us here?" Mom says to me. I don't get a chance to deliver my defense. She continues, her tone full of accusation. "Do you know anything, Bayley? Because if you do, you should tell us now. We're about to call the police."

"She went into town last night," I blurt.

"Christ, Bayley. You just told me you didn't know." Gran's impatience is clear. "What's going on?"

"I didn't know. I messaged Oliver. He saw her. She went to the Bowlo and then to a friend's place and —"

"A friend? What friend? She doesn't have any friends in town," says Mom, confused. "How did she even get into town?"

I confess all. Tell them everything I know — which isn't that much. Neither is impressed, but they have bigger fish to fry, and I'm let off the hook.

"Tell Oliver that we'll meet him in town," says Gran, taking charge. "You stay here with Seth."

I don't argue. In fact, I'm relieved. I couldn't bear seeing Oliver look at me with disgust in his eyes again.

* * *

"They're treating her as a runaway." Gran flops onto the sofa, her exhaustion obvious. "She'll turn up once she's hungry, they said. They don't know how stubborn Amelia is, though, do they?"

Mom perches beside Gran on the very edge of the cushion. It's as if she doesn't belong, shouldn't be here in her own living room with her own family. Her head droops, and her fingers work tirelessly at a loose thread on her skirt. My heart breaks just a little.

I've railed against Mom of late, weary of her selfishness and moods, her temper, and her neediness, but the woman sitting on the sofa is like a phantom, a shadow of her former self. Where is the woman who ran a successful design studio and ruled a family? The woman who loved beauty and surrounded herself with it? Who seized the day with such vehemence that sometimes one day would turn into the next without her even making it to bed? Where has that woman gone?

Fate keeps slapping her down, and each time she picks

herself back up, she is a little less. I miss the woman she was so much, as much as I miss Dad. I lost two parents that day.

"I think they're wrong," Mom whispers, the words spoken so softly, they seem to float away. "Something terrible has happened. I can feel it. Can't you?"

She brings her hands to her face and cries.

Gran pulls her close and rubs her shoulders. Mom's head lolls onto Gran's chest. "Do us a favor, Bails?" Gran says, neck craning over Mom's head. "Do some snooping on Facebook for me. The police said that would be the best place to get some information. She may even post something if she's taken off somewhere."

I nod, grateful for a reason to escape. I leave Seth asleep on the floor where he crashed while watching a movie and pad into the kitchen to my laptop. I don't tell Gran that I've been glued to it all afternoon, looking for some kind of clue or lead.

I take another cursory glance, checking the pages of some of Amelia's friends from Cronulla, and I consider whether I should try to friend some of her new Tallowood friends.

As I ponder this, I remember the email from Deb. I flick it open — more for a distraction than anything else. I am determined to keep my distance from Deb, at least for the time being.

Hi Bayley.

I texted you a couple of times, but no reply. Maybe I have the wrong number? Saw Bud Mitchell in town last night — haven't seen him for years. He's fit for an old guy. Must be past eighty now.

Bud?

Made me think of Robbie and Celina, and you, of course. So decided to email. How's it going? Have you found out anything more? Was thinking that maybe we should see a medium . . .

I don't get much further. I can't get past the part about Bud in town. Last night. And now Amelia is missing? Could there be a connection? Please, no, there can't be. I would never forgive myself if . . . I don't even want to think it.

I read from the beginning again, trying to convince myself that it's a coincidence, nothing more, and then scan through the rest.

I think there's a reputable medium in Rosedale. Her spirit guide is a Tibetan princess. I could go with you. You don't have to do this alone. And besides I'd love to be able to contact Celina again. I have so much to tell her. I think she'd be really proud of what I've done with my life. In many ways I have kept the ethos of the Peace Sisters alive — with my yoga and meditation . . .

Deb babbles on for another couple of paragraphs. It's annoying me so much that I'm about to hit delete, when I see the word "sister" in a P.S. at the bottom of the screen.

P.S.: Almost forgot. Also saw your sister — well, I'm guessing it was your sister — at the Bowlo last night with a bunch of local kids. Her hair was tied back with Celina's purple scarf. I saw the scarf first and thought it was you. The family resemblance is strong! Think she thought I was some kind of wacko when I tapped her on the shoulder to say hi. Anyway, she seemed to be having a good time!

Celina's scarf?

Without thinking, I find myself walking up the steps and into my room. I close the door quietly behind me, my heart swelling into my throat. I remember leaving Celina's scarf on top of the peace chest. Now it's not there.

Why on earth would Amelia take the scarf of all things? She has done nothing but hassle me about wearing Celina's clothes since we arrived. I can't make any sense of it.

But it doesn't matter. Because other things are battering away inside my head.

Bud in town.

Amelia in town.

Amelia wearing Celina's scarf — looking like me. Looking like Celina.

Amelia missing.

Amelia, how could you be so stupid?

thirty-seven

I call Oliver immediately.

"Yeah?" He sounds sour.

"Have you seen Bud?"

"What?"

"Your grandpa. Have you seen him?"

"What has Grandpa got to do with this?"

I ignore the question and plow on. "Answer me. Have you seen him?"

"When? No. You're psycho. I'm hanging up."

His comment hurts, but I'm past caring. "Did you see him at the Bowlo last night?"

"No!"

"In town?"

"No! And what if I did? You can't seriously think he has something to do with Amelia."

"Where is he now? At Lakeside?"

"I have no idea. I'm still in town, with Lee — looking for *your* sister."

And he's gone.

I glance at the time. It's almost five-thirty. I don't know what to do, but then my eyes are drawn to the peace chest. As usual, the hairs on the back of my neck rise, and my veins feel as if they have been injected with ice water. Celina is with me, and her presence is terrifying.

I slump onto the floor, close my eyes, and try to settle the waves of nausea, but my mind jams with images.

Of Bud.

Bud and Amelia.

Amelia screaming.

Bud dragging her down some back alley and into his red car. The terror in my sister's eyes swirls around and around before me.

I jump to my feet and shake myself free of the nightmare images.

Bud has Amelia.

I have no choice. Celina is telling me something, and this time I can't ignore it.

I put on my running shoes and steal down the stairs, slip into the kitchen without Mom and Gran noticing, and fly out the back door. I skirt around the side of the house, and then behind the row of poplars along the southern fence line to the dock. Then I hit the path and I'm off.

I haven't run all the way round to Lakeside before, but I'm thinking it must be about five miles. In the days when I was running with Dad, and I was super fit, I could do five miles in about forty-five minutes. Now, an hour should see me there easy, which means I should be there before it's dark. For some reason, this seems important. What I'm going to do once I'm there and what I hope to find is another matter. But Bud has Amelia, and the only way to help her without everyone dismissing me as a psycho is to prove it. I only hope I get there in time. And I don't even want to consider what that means.

* * *

The boatshed provides solid cover. I lean against it, collecting my thoughts and trying to contain the queasiness that I always feel as soon as I step onto Lakeside.

My plan — rough as it may be — is to get inside Bud's studio and poke around some. I'm not sure why, but something is telling me that this is what I must do.

Intuition? Lack of other alternatives?

I don't think so. This time I am certain it's Celina.

I give myself over to her. She has my rapt attention. *Guide me, Celina. Please, show me what to do.*

A couple of hurried glances around the property don't reveal much, except that the light is fading fast. It must have taken me longer to get here than I thought it would.

Oliver's car isn't here. But there are at least two other vehicles: one, Bob's truck, and the other a red car. Bud's — like in my vision. The lights are on in the main house, but the studio and old farmhouse are both dark. The tangle of barns and sheds tucked around in the back are obscured from view. I'm aware of the faint waft of Spanish-sounding music drifting down from the main house, and I imagine Annie, pink-streaked hair gelled up in tiny peaks, glass of wine in hand, swaying to the music and preparing dinner. No sign of Bob or Bud or anyone else. Perhaps they're inside for dinner. Makes sense.

I could slip into the studio now, or wait until everyone is asleep.

But I don't have the luxury of time. Amelia's terrified eyes fill my mind, and my ears ring once more with her screams. The images of Bud dragging Amelia away are too real, too scary. They can't be ignored. Every second counts. Bending low, I scamper to a rectangular rose garden, and squat behind the thorny bushes. My senses are hyper-alert, and the perfume from the roses is sickeningly strong. I bolt up to the studio. I'm not much good at this espionage stuff, and my footfalls sound like a herd of elephants approaching and are only rivaled by the crazy thumping of my heart against my ribs.

The studio is nothing more than a glorified shed, with glass sliding doors covering the side that faces out to the lake. The doors are closed and the place looks deserted, but I decide to err on the side of caution and head for the southern side, hoping for a smaller window to peer through, just to make sure.

And I'm in luck; there are three windows along the wall. I crouch under the first window then slide up to peek inside. In the dim light, it's hard to see much, but I'm pretty sure the place is empty.

I sense Celina at my shoulder, and instead of freaking me out, it makes me more determined. I edge around to the front, checking again that no one is outside, then try the door. It slides open, and I step inside. Instantly, that awful chemical smell hits me, nearly knocks me over. It takes all my resolve not to gag.

The room is cluttered and chaotic. Several easels of various sizes are scattered about. Numerous canvases lean haphazardly against the wall. Tubes of paint, brushes, rags, large tins of solvent, and glue litter a long table. Crates filled with rocks, sticks, leaves, scrap metal and timber, and all manner of junk cover the floor. Rows and rows of jars filled with God-knows-what line the shelving on the back wall.

The rows of shelving grab my attention. While the rest of the room seems like a junkyard, the shelves are tidy. The jars are arranged neatly, each carefully labeled. I step closer to see what's inside them, reach out to touch one particular jar. It's labeled "COM" and it's filled with fine grayish-white particles.

I'm brushing off the label when a door in the back corner springs open.

I snatch my hand away and think about diving behind an easel, but there's no point. Bud is already in the room.

Obviously startled, his step falters, his face contorting from surprise to confusion to disgust. Then he takes a couple of slow deliberate steps toward me.

I back away, stumbling on a stack of canvases. But he's on

me with remarkable speed. I think he's about to grab me, but instead he reaches for a notepad and pencil from the table.

I should make a run for it, but somehow, I can't. Fear has me rooted to the spot. He scrawls something across the paper, then holds it up to me. His actions speak of anger, as do his words.

Get out of here. You have no right. He motions with his arms, dismisses me, and points to the door.

"No right? No right! Where is my sister?"

His face screws into an irritated frown.

Sister? What sister? he writes.

"I know you have her. Where is she?"

He looks at me as if I've gone berserk, then he goes to write something else, but I steal the paper out of his hands.

"Speak," I say. "I know you can. I heard you that night by the dock. *Holy mother of God. Holy mother of God.* You said it. I know you did. I heard you."

Bud backs away now. And for some reason I feel I have the upper hand.

"And I know about Celina," I say, leading with my chin like a fool. "I know everything. What you did."

Bud squints at me as he takes this in. He reaches for the paper, but I hold it away from him. "Speak," I say again, but nerves have invaded my voice box and it comes out as a squeak. I try again, more forcefully this time. "Speak, you bastard. Speak!"

His hands ball into fists. He is so close that I can smell his rotten breath, feel it puff into my face, smell years of painting chemicals oozing from his pores.

"Watch out!" he shouts, a gravelly rasping shout. "Behind you."

I'm so startled that I turn around.

Something cracks across my skull. The pain is immense. I turn back to face Bud. I catch a glimpse of the metal bar in his hand; the sick smile on his face as I feel myself falling, slowly, fluttering almost, like an autumn leaf. Then I hit the ground with a thud.

thirty-eight

I am in a haze. A nightmarish haze, entombed by an aching head and an inability to move. And God, such a dry, dry throat. What I would give for a drop of water, even a whisper of cool breeze to moisten my mouth.

But my lips are fused together. I can't pull them apart no matter how hard I try. I focus all my energy on instructing my mouth to work — groan with the effort of it — but it won't open. It just won't. And I'm sent into a suffocating panic that has me gagging until I'm flung out of the haze and into a painful reality. My eyes shoot open.

Bud. The metal bar.

The memory makes me reach for my head, but my arms won't work either. I want to scream with frustration.

And then things clunk into place and hit me right in the guts as I become conscious of rope burning my wrists and binding my ankles, of tape wound across my mouth and around my head.

Fear devours me.

Slowly, as I take stock in the murky darkness, I realize that I'm lying on my side on bare concrete, wedged into a tiny space surrounded by towers of crates and boxes.

The room is stuffy: the stinging smell of paint and glue mixing badly with the dank pungency of decay. I try to stand up, but it's useless. My hands and feet are tied to something behind me, which I can't quite turn my head enough to see.

I wiggle and twist and writhe and thrash.

I try to kick. To lash out.

But it's hopeless, so hopeless.

I keep at it, and at it and at it, determined not to give in, until finally, I'm spent.

Drenched with sweat. Chest heaving.

My head lolls back against the wall, and all that's left for me to do is sob, to cry and cry and cry.

Eventually, I don't even have the energy to cry any more.

My tears and snot dry across my cheeks, my chin, and my neck — I can't wipe them away — and beneath the tape that binds my mouth, my teeth take on a life of their own, chattering so fiercely that it's the only thing I can hear.

I'm alive, I tell myself, teeth rattling my jaw. *I'm alive.* He could have killed me, but he hasn't. That has to be a good thing, right? And if he hasn't killed me, then maybe he hasn't killed Amelia either. Maybe Amelia is in this dungeon too.

Celina! I implore. *Help me. Please. I'm here because of you — you guided me here. Please help me.*

But try as I might, I can't sense her presence. I feel utterly deserted.

How did I get myself into this? Poor Mom. No one would be able to claw themselves back after something like this. This time, fate will have landed a knockout punch, and there will be nothing left of her to pick up off the ground. It will be the end for her. The end for our whole family. Just like it was for Celina and her family.

My eyes feel droopy, and I think I'm about to drop off to sleep. But I hear a noise. I concentrate and try to work out where it's coming from. A door slides open, confirming my suspicion that I'm in the back room of Bud's studio. There are footsteps. Is it Bud returning? My entire body convulses at the thought of it.

I search frantically for some way to escape, should the chance present itself. Although the room is in darkness, a single strip of sunlight now blares across the floor to one side of me, from below a closed blind perhaps. The warble of magpies and the lonely caw of a crow suggest it must be early morning. Wind rushes through trees and rattles the window, making me start.

If I *am* in Bud's studio, then I'm still at Lakeside, and Annie or Bob or Oliver could be close by. They're my only chance, and somehow I have to use this to my advantage.

There are more noises, coming from close by now. Nothing sinister, only the sounds of someone moving about, going about his or her business, but each *clunk* or *plink* or *scrape* shoots prickles through me. Why doesn't he come and check on me? What's he playing at?

I scrunch my eyes and will someone to come to my rescue, try to conjure up a knight in shining armor. But it's futile.

* * *

I don't know how long I lie there. Waiting. Listening. Praying. My bladder is full and painful, and I'm contemplating relieving myself on the floor, when I hear the sliding door open again and then a voice.

"Morning, Bud. My, doesn't that look great. It's coming along nicely, isn't it?"

Annie! Hope balloons within me.

There is no response from Bud of course. But I presume he's writing something.

"Yeah. I think it's great," says Annie. "Are you coming up to the house for some lunch today? I'm making mango salad . . . No? Well, I'll leave you some for dinner. I'm going into town soon. That girl from the O'Malley's place has gone missing . . . the younger one . . ."

Me! That's me. They know! I cling to this tiny morsel as if it's my last meal.

Annie continues. "She disappeared yesterday afternoon. It's really bizarre. Her older sister went AWOL on Friday night — passed out somewhere. She turned up at home not long before dark yesterday, just as they realized the other sister wasn't there . . ."

Amelia! Back. I'm filled with relief. But then confusion. How can that be? I saw Bud dragging Amelia away. Heard her screams. Felt her fear. Celina showed it all to me. She led me here. I felt her.

Why would she do that if Bud never had Amelia in the first place? What is *Celina* playing at? These thoughts tornado through my brain, until I hear my name mentioned, and I tune back into what Annie is saying.

"Yes. Bayley. The one Oliver likes. He's pretty heartbroken about it . . ."

My heart pangs.

"They think she may have gone off searching for her sister. The police are combing their property. They may turn up here later. I hope she didn't head off for the gorge."

There's a pause, and I am guessing Bud is replying.

"Okay. I'll tell the police," says Annie.

What? Tell them what? What has Bud said?

"Oliver and Bob are going to join the search. Apparently, Oliver has been meeting her at the bend in the lake with the willows. He seems to think she might have been heading this way."

Another pause.

"He wouldn't say why. Just a hunch. She called him yesterday afternoon, quite upset. Irrational even. They had a fight. Poor kid, I think he's worried that she's hurt herself — blaming himself . . . God, she's a nice girl too. A little intense, but a good soul. I hope she's okay. That family has had more than its fair share of grief."

There's a quiver in Annie's voice, and tears slide down the side of my face and into my ear as I wait through another aching silence. What is Bud telling Annie?

"Not sure. We only found out after breakfast. The grandmother called, then the police. I think it flipped Bob back to that other awful time. He went as pale as the moon when he heard. I swear if I didn't know better, you'd think that that family is cursed . . . Yeah. You're right . . . He and Oliver took off straightaway, but Oliver asked me to come and see you, insisted. He thought you might have seen her — said that you've seen them out by the lake a couple of times."

Yay, Oliver.

"Okay, well, keep a lookout and expect the police later. I'll be heading off shortly."

The door slides shut, and I'm left alone with Bud. No Bob. No Annie. No Oliver. No knight in shining armor. Not even a ghost.

And I realize that I'm lying in the warm puddle of my own pee.

thirty-nine

The minutes trickle by. What is he waiting for? I'm desperately hoping that he goes away and leaves me. At the same time, I'm desperately wishing he would walk through the door, so I don't have to endure the agony of waiting any longer.

There's a creak like that of a door opening, and then the room is cast into sudden brightness as a light is switched on.

My eyes blink painfully at the glare.

And he's there.

I see his boots first. Black. Paint spattered and muddy. They clomp around the stack of crates and stop a foot or so away from me. Trembling, I keep my eyes downcast, fixated on the paint splatters and how they're like fireworks on a night sky. Striking. Vibrant bursts of color. Pretty almost.

"So you're awake." It sounds as if he is growling through a mouthful of stones, and I'm jerked away from the fireworks. But I don't look up, nor do I reply.

He kicks my leg. "Look at me."

I obey.

He seems different. Less stooped. Stronger. Dangerous. The fear I thought I saw in his eyes the other day at the lake has been replaced with a raw confidence, a maniacal glint.

"That's better. Now what are we going to do with you? Stupid girl. Why did you have to mention Celina, huh? Stupid. Stupid."

He squats before me and yanks my hair back, turning my face up to his. "Why?" he spits, his breath horrid. "What do you know, you little whore?"

I squirm, trying to wriggle free from his grip and cower away from him as best I can.

"Not so brave now, are you? Tell me! Tell me what you know!" He lets go of my hair, but lets fly with a cracking slap across my face that sends my head smacking against the floor. "Tell me, whore. Tell me." And then he's on me, and I swear he's about to strangle me, but instead he rips the tape clumsily from my mouth, the skin stripping from my lips.

"Tell me. What do you know?"

"Nothing," I whisper.

"Tell me!"

"Can I have a drink? I'm thirsty."

"Tell me . . . what . . . you know." His words are distorted by a rising anger. "Tell me."

I don't know what to say. Damned if I do; damned if I don't. "Ce-l-l-lin-a," I stutter, testing the impact of the word.

"Celina!" he roars back at me. "Always Celina. She ruined my life, that little slut. But what do *you* know about her?"

"She was my mom's cousin."

"No kidding? Well, there's a headline for you. Tell me something I don't already know. And stop staring at me like that. You're just like her. I thought she'd come back from the dead, that night on the lake. You scared the crap out of me. But it's not only in the looks that you're the same. Witches, the pair of you — wheedling your way into the family, casting your spells over the boys. Now tell me what you know."

I decide to play dumb. "What's there to know?" I say. "Please, a drink?"

"You better know something." His twisted hand grabs my hair again. "For your sake, you little Celina double, you better know something."

"I know she's dead." He pulls harder. "I know you . . ." He tugs harder still. My hair feels as though it's about to tear out of my scalp. Tears sting my eyes. "I know you did it. You killed her. You *killed* her!" I am yelling now, screaming.

He lets go of my hair and marches away agitated. He starts to pace, mumbling something to himself. His mumblings become louder and more intense. And I know I've done it. That I'm as good as dead.

I'm oddly resigned.

Sorry, Seth.

Sorry, Mom.

Sorry, Amelia. Gran.

Oliver.

My heart is breaking, not because my life is about to end, but for the pain that I am about to cause my family. Misery sinks into my skin, creeps through me.

But as my spirits sink to lie on the floor beside me, I'm filled with a strange, serene presence. An icy presence that has the hairs on the back of my neck rising. I feel altered — as if I have somehow left my own body.

"You killed my parents too, don't forget that!" I say.

But the voice is not mine.

Bud pivots slowly and glares at me. "What did you say?"

"You — it's your fault. You killed them just as surely as you pushed me off that cliff." My mouth is opening and the words are coming out, but it's not me saying them.

It's Celina. Not here to save me — here to get me freaking killed.

I will her to shut up.

Bud's anger flares. "It *is* you! I knew it. I knew it." He lunges at me and waves his fists in the air, rigid with fury. "I don't know how, but you're back. I could feel it — the moment the lights were switched on in that bloody house. Couldn't leave well enough alone. *Forget the past.* That's what Hetty said — her dying words to me. I had no idea how she knew, but she did. *Keep your mouth shut and forget the past.* But it won't go away. All these years since Hetty's passed, I've kept my word and haven't uttered a single word, but still you've come, come back to haunt me." His eyes dart all over the place. He takes a step away. "What to do? What to do?" he mutters.

"You're going to pay," Celina says through my mouth. "That's what. You are going to suffer, like I did. Like Robbie, and Mom and Dad. Like I've been making you suffer these past weeks. It's been great watching you squirm."

"Stop!" Bud hisses. "Stop!"

"Wait till Robbie finds out what an asshole of a father he has. A murderer. A liar. A sick monster. Wait till he hears what you did with me."

Bud lets out an almighty wail. He goes down on one knee, then the other, and I think that Celina's broken him.

But I'm wrong. Bud takes several long breaths and rallies himself. He raises his head and glowers at me.

"It was brilliant, wasn't it? The way I hid you. No one ever guessed — no one ever even suspected," he says, his voice that of a madman. He tilts his head and gazes into my eyes. I have a sinking feeling that I'm not going to like what I'm about to hear. "You always went on about how you were going to travel — take Robbie away from us, waste his life bumming around with you. I thought you'd appreciate it."

"You're sick. It was sick."

"It was art. And the perfect place to conceal the evidence. I couldn't risk it being found in that sinkhole. It was fine for a time, but you had to be moved. It was brilliant. Like da Vinci, Picasso. Sheer brilliance. Hiding you in plain sight for everyone to feast their eyes on."

I don't like this. I wish I could block my ears.

"Parts of me, not *me* — you sicko."

Shut up, Celina.

"Bones, hair, bits of your clothing. They are all you, my dear. I always liked symmetry, and this seemed like perfect symmetry. I was fulfilling your destiny. I thought you'd be grateful that I gave you back to your parents and your precious Robbie."

"It drove them mad. That portrait — made with my hair, you sick bastard. And only days before my birthday. It's what pushed them over the edge."

"No, I think you overestimate your power. I was simply sharing you around — like you used to like sharing yourself around. Don't think I don't know. Do you realize that there's a little piece of you in every work I've ever created? A bit of bone, a scrap of nail, a lock of hair . . ."

"Shut up! It doesn't matter now because it's over. You are going to pay, and the evidence is, as you just announced, everywhere."

Bud is thrown for a moment as he takes this in, as am I. But then he smiles. "You always thought you were so smart, didn't you? Well, you're not. It's simple. I just need to get rid of you all over again. There are plenty of sinkholes out there. I did it before. I can do it again."

"You don't have the courage. You gutless creep!" Celina yells, and as unexpectedly as it entered, Celina's presence leaves me. Vanishes.

Don't go! Don't leave me — now that you have infuriated Bud.

But she's gone.

I have never felt more betrayed in my entire life.

I have been used. Used by a vengeful ghost.

forty

My fate is sealed in seconds. My mouth is taped shut again. Bud takes out a knife, and my heart leaps into my mouth as I think he's going to cut my throat with it. But instead, he cuts me free from the pole and slices through the ropes around my ankles. He has a rifle balanced in the crook of his arm, and I'm ordered to my feet and out the door. I don't argue.

There is a fierce wind tearing through Lakeside, and the last thing I notice before I'm bundled onto the floor of the passenger side of Bud's car is a couple of small boats bouncing on the choppy lake. A tarp is thrown over me, and I'm told that he'll blow my brains out if I so much as move or make a sound. I believe him.

Rattling along as the car speeds off, the engine warming the floor beneath me, I focus on those boats. Who are they? Why are they here? Are they heading to Lakeside? Are they the police? Police divers perhaps? I hang onto them, clutch them to my heart as my last hope. It's all I've got.

We stop at what I presume is the gate. Bud hops out to open it, and I'm too scared even to peek out. Once through the gate, we turn left, which means we're heading out to the highway. The drive up and over the mountain seems to take forever, despite the fact that Bud is driving way too fast. The car bounces over the bumpy road, stones flying up and pinging the car. I find myself wishing that we'd crash.

Finally, we stop and then make a left turn — onto the highway I guess, the road smoother now, humming below me. We are heading toward Tallowood and toward my place, which surprises me, and I have the bizarre thought that he is actually taking me home, that it's all been some big gag and when I get there, there will be cameras and someone calling out "Gotcha!"

The car turns again onto what I am convinced is the road to my house. But we don't go far before Bud yanks the wheel and makes a sharp turn off the road. We bump across some rough ground, rocks hitting the floor like gunshots, until he stops abruptly.

Now that we've stopped, I feel cramped and bruised. I'm aware of wind howling through the trees, sending branches scraping against the sides of the car.

Bud shifts about on his seat and drums the dashboard with his fingers. Then the ignition is turned on again, and we bump along a bit farther, until once more the car comes to a halt. The noise of branches scraping the roof has intensified, and I have the feeling we are under a small tree or bush.

Hiding, no doubt. Out of sight.

Once more I'm filled with dread of what is about to happen.

"This should do it." Bud flicks the tarp off me. "Get up. Recognize this place?"

I unfold myself from my hideout, my legs and back stiff and aching. The first thing I see is the rifle, inches from my face, and then I see that we are in the bush somewhere.

"Like old times." Bud's laugh sends spasms down my spine. "Come on, out we go. Let's go for a little walk." He prods me with the rifle.

I climb out, the wind whipping my hair into a frenzy, flicking it into my eyes, but with my hands still bound behind me, I'm unable to do anything about it. I stagger from the car, my legs not moving properly, and try to work out where we are. On top of the gorge somewhere is my best guess.

"Hey, no games. You know the way! You remember."

I turn and plead with him with my eyes. *I'm not Celina,* I try to tell him. *I don't know where we are. And please don't hurt me.*

"Don't think you can worm your way out of this one. This is perfect. Symmetry, like I said." He comes up close, his mouth grazing my ear. "If only you listened that day. But no, you never listened to anyone. And there you were at the bus stop, early as always, waiting for Robbie. You didn't expect me, did you? But I knew. I saw your notes. You weren't going to school. You were taking off together, to be some kind of hippie bums. Soul mates — ha! Off to India. Idiots. Turning your backs on your families, your education."

Bud twists my arm as if to underline his point. And even in my pain and distress, I'm struck by the contradiction that is Celina, and how different Bud's Celina is to the Celina Deb reveres — that joyous, lovable hippie who would never run away.

"So full of plans." Bud is shouting now. "So full of yourself. Couldn't see how you were ruining things for Robbie. Selfish — that's what you were. You made me so mad, so angry. I had no intention of hurting you. I only wanted to scare you off. But you wouldn't stop going on about it. And I knew you wouldn't listen, that you couldn't listen to reason. It was India and ruining my Robbie or nothing, wasn't it?"

Bud thrusts his shoulder against me and pushes me forward, and it is then that I realize we are indeed on top of the gorge — at the very top and at the very edge. And there across from me on the other side of the gorge is the grassy clearing — Oliver's Top of the World — and my heart plummets.

But Bud hasn't finished with his story. "You kept rattling on and on, and you were so close to the edge. And I saw it, saw how simple it was. One little shove and you'd be gone. If you would just stop. Just shut up for one minute. Why wouldn't you stop and listen to me?" There is a catch in Bud's voice, but he nudges me closer and puts the rifle to my neck. I scramble, and I try to lean back and knock him off his feet, but the old bugger has the strength of close to forty years of guilt and madness behind him. I get nowhere.

"I was too smart for you then, and I still am. Never found you, did they? All those idiots never had a chance. And they won't this time either. Easy to get rid of evidence when you know how. Easy to get rid of a body when you know the gorge like I do. Lots of lovely sinkholes and caves down there — places that only I know exist."

He gives me another nudge toward the edge.

"Goodbye, Celina."

"Don't!" There's a voice, screaming above the wind. We swivel around and, in the dust and wind, a figure emerges from the bush and runs toward us. "Don't! Stop!" It's Amelia.

No! *Get out of here*, I implore with my eyes.

"Celina?" Bud says. He looks to me, then back to the wild girl running toward him, and I have never been so grateful for the family resemblance in all my life. Bud is totally confused. He lets go of me and steps toward the nearly hysterical Amelia, and I'm sure he is going to take aim and cut her down.

No! He can't. I slam my hip into his side. It's enough to make him unbalanced, and he stumbles slightly. He regains his footing and swings back to me, and there is such anguish in his eyes. I grit my teeth and shove into him again, just as something barrels in from the side and knocks both Bud and me off our feet. Oliver! The gun flies into the air and goes off with a cracking bang as it hits the ground.

I scramble away to Amelia. She wraps her arms around me and pulls my shaking body behind a large rock as we watch Oliver try to restrain Bud.

"Grandpa! What the hell? Stop!"

Bud scurries on hands and knees for the gun.

"Grandpa. It's me. Oliver. Stop, for fuck's sake."

Oliver and Bud lunge for the rifle at the same time. There's a scuffle. They tumble and scrabble in the dirt, and I'm terrified that someone is going to get shot. Bud somehow frees himself, rifle in hand, and teeters up to stand. Oliver dives and knocks him back down, but the force of his tackle is too strong, and the pair of them roll away. The gun is once again free of Bud's grip.

Thoughts of Mom losing Dad and Bob losing Celina flash through my head. I can't lose Oliver. I can't let Bud or Celina destroy us. I have to get that gun.

I wrench myself from Amelia and run clumsily toward the gun. A wrinkled hand is reaching for it. And at that moment, the world shrinks to that hand and the wooden butt of the rifle. That's all there is, all that matters. My arms are still bound, so I kick at the rifle with every inch of my strength. It clatters away, but the hand clutches my ankle, and I'm pulled to the ground. Bud wrestles with me, pinning me down, until I am jolted painfully sideways as Oliver tackles Bud yet again. The two tumble away in a dust cloud.

Then there's a hideous scream. And there's only dust and the wind ripping through the trees left in its wake.

I wait for the dust to settle, my heart in my throat.

And when it finally does, a single person is sitting bent over at the edge of the cliff.

Oliver.

Oliver with his head in his hands. His whole body convulsing.

Bud has gone over.

Amelia runs to me and frees me from my bonds, rips the tape from my mouth. I hug my thanks — take hold of her fiercely. Then race to Oliver, kneel beside him.

Together, we stand and step to the edge. I take his hand, and we peer over. It takes us a moment or two, but then we see it. Bud's broken body wedged between two boulders about two thirds of the way down. Oliver turns and walks away, but his legs go from under him. He collapses onto the dirt. I rush to him and help him sit up, and we lean on each other's shoulders like a pair of bookends.

I don't know how I feel. Relieved? Guilty? Stunned? Numb?

Amelia pulls out her phone. "Should I call the police?"

Oliver nods.

I don't know what to say. Thanks? Sorry? I say both.

He doesn't reply.

"He was going to throw me over," I say, trying to explain, but feeling horribly guilty, as if everything is my fault.

Oliver nods again. "I know," he whispers, but the words hurt him, I can tell.

"You saved me."

"I guess."

"He killed Celina," I say, hoping that this will help him cope with what's happened. "Pushed her over."

"Celina?"

"My mom's cousin, who disappeared years ago."

He stares out at the horizon, his eyes vacant.

"How did you know where to come?" I ask.

"The note." Amelia crouches beside me.

I turn to Amelia, puzzled. "What note?"

"The one you left in that notebook where you were writing that creepy story."

I am more confused than ever. "I haven't written in there for ages. What did it say?"

"That Bud was the one or something like that and that he had you at the top of the gorge near the bus stop. And we had to hurry." Amelia sits in the dirt beside me. "We didn't know what it meant, but Mom and Gran and Seth were in town at the police station. Oliver was supposed to get me and drive me out to be with them, and we thought we'd stop here first, seeing as we were going past it."

"How did you even find it — this note?"

"I was in your room. I had to bring some of your stuff for the search dogs and find a recent photo. It was on the top of that wooden chest."

I look Amelia in the eyes. "I hid that book under my mattress, and I didn't write that note."

"Oh my God," is Amelia's reply, and we don't have time to go into it any further because the air has come alive with sirens.

forty-one

Celina saved me. She didn't desert me. She saved me.

For reasons I can't even begin to explain, I am enormously relieved. But only momentarily as it hits me that the sirens are closing in and once the police arrive, I'm going to have to explain everything. Including Celina.

"Don't mention the note," I say, out of impulse. First to Amelia and then to Oliver, as the blaring becomes louder and closer.

Oliver doesn't seem to register that I've even spoken, but Amelia grips my arm. "What? What do you mean?"

"When the police get here, don't mention the note. Trust me. Okay?"

"Trust?" Amelia's voice is a blend of alarm and confusion.

"I'll explain later. I promise. Just don't mention that note. Please!"

Amelia looks at me, bewildered. "Sure," she says finally. "But what will we tell them?"

Good question.

My mind is in overdrive; I can't think straight. A siren is upon us, and I can hear tires on the gravel. "Say that you saw a flash of red, or movement or something, and you told Oliver to pull in. You'll think of something."

Oliver is on the ground beside us, his head bent. I crouch beside him. "Okay, Oliver? No note. Amelia said 'What's that?' and you drove in to check it out. Okay?" He doesn't respond. "Okay, Oliver? Please. For me. There was *no* note."

A police car screeches to a halt, sending curling clouds of reddish brown dirt into the air, and two uniformed officers hurry over to us.

The sight of them brings all that has happened over the last twenty-four hours back into my head and it hits me with a mighty blow. My chest starts to heave. I can barely breathe.

"Bayley Anderson?"

I must have nodded, because one officer bundles me up,

and tries to whisk me away. But I clutch Amelia fiercely. I demand that she comes too. And then before I know what's happened, I'm in the backseat of a car next to my sister.

I sense kindness, a calm efficiency. A blanket is draped over us. It's soft and woolly, but it does nothing to stop my body from shaking. I don't know where Oliver is. I want him to be here too. I want to hold him close, take away his pain, but I can't seem to move or speak.

Stuff is happening around me. More sirens. More lights. More cars. More people. I feel detached from it all: in the middle of everything, but also on the edges, looking in. Then I glimpse Oliver, bent over like an old man, a blanket hanging from his shoulders. Someone in blue has him by the elbow. Others approach him. They are pointing to the cliff and talking to him. He nods. Is he telling them about Bud? My heart aches for him. This is all too terrible. And all my fault. I shift in my seat, trying to get up, but I can't. I just can't.

"Hey," says Amelia, rubbing my back. "It's okay. You're okay. It's over now."

Is it? I wonder. All I can see ahead of me now is despair. With no way through it.

"Bayley," says a voice nearby. Female. "My name is Officer Phelan. You can call me Joanne, if you like. An ambulance is on its way and so is your mom. Are you hurt? Any injuries?"

I want to answer, but my brain has turned to mush.

"I think she's okay," says Amelia. "She just needs to get home."

"And she will, but she will have to go to the hospital for a checkup first. And we'll have to ask you both a few questions. Work out what's happened here. Okay, Bayley? Will you be able to answer some questions for us? Amelia, you too?"

Amelia tightens her hold around me. "Are you kidding me? She was nearly thrown off a freaking cliff!" Her tone is full of enough Amelia fierceness to scare off even a police officer. I love her for it. "Leave us alone, will you?"

I hear the officer slide across the seat and out of the car. I lean into Amelia. The only way I have to say thanks.

"You are okay, aren't you, Bails?"

I honestly don't know.

Out the corner of one eye, I watch as Oliver is escorted toward another police car, and I wonder if I'll ever see him again, if there will ever be an "us" again. I don't know what he's going to tell the police, have no idea if he even heard me before, but it's out of my hands now.

Suddenly, I hear running, scurrying. A voice shouting. Shouting my name. And Mom is there, clutching Oliver. Looking around her. Shouting.

Then she's beside me, scooping me up in her arms.

Hugging. Sobbing. She pulls Amelia to her also, and we are one big hug. A family hug of tears and dirt and snot and heartache and joy all mixing together. Then Mom pulls away from us, sits cross-legged on the dirt beside the car, holds her head in her hands, and sobs. Deep and mournful and long.

"Mrs. Anderson," Joanne's voice intrudes. "Are you okay? Can I help you up?"

Mom ignores her, as if she hasn't heard. The police officer sits beside her and places her arm across Mom's shoulders. Mom pushes her off and curls onto her side, bringing her knees into her chest. And my worst fears are being acted out before me, as I watch my mother retreating into herself once more. Perhaps for the last time.

Somehow, someone coaxes Mom off the ground and helps her to the waiting ambulance. Amelia and I cling onto each other as we climb from the police car and into the ambulance behind her.

As the door is pulled shut, I take one last look out over the gorge, to the place where almost forty years ago Celina O'Malley's life was cut tragically short, where my life nearly ended as well. I take in the blue cloudless sky and the wind-swept trees. I try to be thankful that I'm still here to see them, hopeful that Mom will recover and confident that

Oliver will forgive me. But it's a struggle, and I realize that I'm not ready to leave yet.

I shrug out of the blanket, push open the doors, and step out onto the dirt.

"Bails?" says Amelia. "Where are you going?"

I ignore her and walk toward the cliff. People move out of my way, but their eyes follow me. I have some unfinished business to take care of, though I'm not sure what. Perhaps I need to somehow rid myself of Celina, once and for all, or to make sense of all that has happened.

I'm at the cliff edge now, the wind dancing in my hair. I imagine Celina's spirit out there somewhere. I feel her strange energy, sense her freedom and her joy at finally getting her revenge. Will she be able to rest now? Will she leave me be? Am I free of her?

Someone holds my arm firmly. I pull out of it.

"Bayley." It's Amelia. "Come on. Let's go back now."

"Hold on." I step closer to the edge. Something is gnawing at me, something I need to figure out. I just need some time.

"Bails?" I feel Amelia's arms around my middle, urging me back.

I turn and see her fearful face close to mine and feel the strength of her hold. Behind her I see Mom, confused and disoriented, and Oliver, tormented and broken, never to be mine again.

I turn away.

Then Oliver's warm breath is in my ear. "Bayley, step away." His lips brush my neck. "Please. For me."

I gaze down at Bud's lifeless body, now covered by a dirty white canvas and flanked by two police officers hanging from ropes. I didn't want any of this. I only wanted some happiness. Is that too much to ask?

Bud's final scenes play over in my mind. I try to take it all in. Work it all out. How did it go so wrong? I stand teetering on the edge, and I'm sent back to the other time I felt as though I was teetering on the edge — at Marco's, looking at Bud's artwork — and I understand now what Celina was showing me. I shudder.

"Bayley. Come away." Mom's voice this time. And there is a steel in it that surprises me — shocks me — into swinging around. "It does you no good to look," she continues, her eyes holding mine. "It's in the hands of the police, and soon everything will come out. Everyone will know the truth."

Yes, they will. Just like Celina wanted. I guess that was something about Celina Deb did get right — Celina certainly got me to do her bidding.

Make him pay. It's up to you, Bayley. Make him pay. Peace, sister. Celina's words come back to me. They pound away relentlessly in my head. *Make him pay. Make him pay. It's up to you, Bayley. Make him pay.*

I made him pay all right. Well, Oliver did. And now Oliver is left to explain to the world how his own grandfather came to end up dead in the gorge. How did that happen?

Something twists inside me.

I am so gullible. *Celina didn't save me.* She didn't care about me, or Oliver, or anyone but herself. She needed to make sure history didn't repeat itself. She had to be certain that Bud was exposed, that he didn't get away with it this time. That he paid, one way or another. If I had gone over the cliff, it would have all been for nothing. That's why she wrote that note.

And right this minute the *real* Celina is laid bare before me. And she is nothing like the sweet, loving girl that Deb remembers, or Gran's favorite niece, or Robbie's sweet pea. Perhaps, like one of Bud's paintings, they were all too close to see the real picture. The Celina I know is bitter and callous and manipulative. She stops at nothing to get what she wants — no matter who she destroys along the way.

I go weak at the knees at the betrayal and stumble backward.

"That's the way, honey." Mom's voice is soft against my

face. "Come on. Away from the edge."

"For me, Bails." Oliver again. "Please."

I give in to them — gladly. I am done here. I am done with Celina.

Oliver drapes his arm across one shoulder. Mom drapes hers across the other. Together they guide me away from the cliff and back toward the ambulance. I'm shaking with the knowledge of how close I had been to becoming Celina's ghostly playmate.

I stop suddenly then and swirl around.

Bud is dead. So is Celina.

Together forever. They deserve each other.

And despite all the grief and anguish of the day, my mouth twists into a sly smile.

Careful what you wish for, cousin.

epilogue

The day I turned seventeen we buried Celina.

Not her body, of course. But her peace chest, with all its memories and secrets, her purple scarf, and a single jar from Bud's shelf labeled COM.

It was my idea, and everyone thought that I was more than a little crazy when I suggested it, but to me it felt right. Besides, I wanted to put Celina to rest — for good.

Oliver has never mentioned anything about the note. It's as if he's wiped it from his memory. And I'm glad, mostly, though it kills me to keep from him all that happened with

Celina. Maybe in time I will be able to share the freaky truth, but for now it stays locked inside.

Apart from Deb and Amelia, no one knows about my stalker ghost. It wasn't an easy thing for Amelia to believe. Nor was it easy to deny. But between us we concocted an almost-true, ghost-free story to tell the police and the rest of the family. We told them how I had gone looking for Amelia and ended up at Bud's studio. How Bud thought I was Celina and how he cracked me over the skull and then confessed everything to me in his dank little back room. How when Amelia and Oliver drove past, Amelia glimpsed a flash of red in the bushes and persuaded Oliver to investigate. It made sense. In fact, I prefer this version of events.

Of course, it was Bud's sick little fetish that clinched it — and a wonderful thing called DNA. The police are still collecting his body of work for examination and evidence — much to the repulsion and disgust of the owners. It could take quite a while before it's all sorted out, though it's his portrait of Celina that's the key piece of evidence.

The day of the "funeral" was gloriously sunshiny, the sky and lake competing in the most dazzling blue contest. Oliver and Bob dug a pit under the Norfolk pine and lowered the chest into it. We gathered around, a semicircle of new friends and old: Oliver holding my hand in his; Mom and Amelia, standing together; Gran in the wicker garden chair with Seth (minus his cape) on her knee; Annie and Bob, side by side. Loni was there too — Gran had brought her up for the weekend for my birthday (though she was pretty shocked when I told her we were going to have a funeral to celebrate it). Even Deb drove in for the occasion. I haven't had the heart to tell her the truth about Celina. I can't see the point.

Bob said a few words. He spoke about love and loss, about mistakes and the healing nature of time, and the powerful poison of dark secrets long held. And, with Annie's arm around his waist, he announced that he was starting up a charity with Bud's money to support the families of the hundreds of people who go missing every year.

Afterward, we sat at a long table under the poplars and enjoyed a feast, with a calorific birthday cake supplied by Deb. We toasted Dad and Celina, and even Bud. We toasted my birthday, Amelia getting into a tech college to study hospitality, Mom's new design studio, the future.

I looked across at Oliver at this point and our eyes met. For a second or two, we held each other's gaze. What would the future hold for the two of us? I wished I knew. A lot had happened since the day we lay on the bank of the creek and his finger stroked the bridge of my nose.

What I was sure of though, sitting there among those

people, laughing and eating and sharing stories, was that the Andersons/O'Malleys had turned a corner. And despite being convinced that Celina was so intent on exacting her revenge that she was willing to destroy our whole family in the process, I believe she actually helped save us. Somehow, the horror of that awful day shook us enough to push us through our pain and out to the other side. We were still on wobbly legs, and had a way to go yet, but it seemed that the troubles of the past had strangely brought us a little closer together, and that maybe, just maybe, we had even started to heal.